THE CASE OF THE

CHRYSANTHEMUM MURDERS

THE CASE OF THE

CHRYSANTHEMUM
MURDERS

an Augusta McKee mystery

Susan Moore Jordan

ISBN: 978-1-950625-09-3

Published by Shaggy Dog Productions, LLC

Library of Congress Control Number: 2020908654

Cover design and art by Taylor Van Kooten

Books by Susan Moore Jordan

The *Carousel* Trilogy:
How I Grew Up
Eli's Heart
You Are My Song

Jamie's Children

The Cameron Saga:
Memories of Jake
Man with No Yesterdays

"More Fog, Please"
(non-fiction)

Augusta McKee Mysteries:
The Case of the Slain Soprano
The Case of the Disappearing Director
The Case of the Toxic Tenor
The Case of the Purloined Professor
The Case of the Chrysanthemum Murders

Table of Contents

*with heartfelt thanks to two
people who have helped bring
Augusta and Malcolm to life:
friend and editor Ashleigh Evans,
and Det. Lt. Stephen Kramer (ret.), CPD,
friend and police procedural consultant.*

Prologue
After-Opera Party Gone Wrong

Thursday, June 10, 1965
11:30 p.m.

Mecklenburg's Bier Garten held its own special magic for the large, enthusiastic, after-opera crowd. Augusta glanced around the outdoor garden, sparkling in the overhead lanterns hung from intertwined grapevines. A slight breeze stirred the air and carried snatches of conversation: "Jamie Logan was incredible." "What a beautiful performance!" "The orchestra absolutely outdid themselves. I've never heard them play better."

As always, Augusta relished being in one of her favorite places. Europe had certainly been magical, but it was definitely nice to be home and with some of her favorite people.

If Mal were here, this would be absolutely perfect. She sipped her beer. *Well, he'll be back tonight. He may be waiting for me when I get home.* She smiled at the thought.

Her close friend and honorary escort for the evening, Father Dennis Halloran, glanced in her direction. "So, when does your groom get back?"

"Tonight, actually. I was just thinking about him."

Dennis laughed. "I thought so. I saw that smile."

Jamie Logan, star of the production of Puccini's opera *Manon Lescaut*, sat on Augusta's right. "Tell me again why the good detective allowed his bride to fly back from the honeymoon by herself?"

"Well, I'm sure you read about poor Saul Kronenberg being found dead in a room in our hotel in Paris. They ruled out foul play, but Mal wasn't so sure, and he had a chance to learn something about French police work while he did some snooping around. Mainly because he met a French detective—a fellow veteran of World War II—who was interested in learning about how the Yanks do it." Augusta took a small bite of her schnitzel. "I would have stayed with him, but I had to get back since the summer session was about to begin and I have responsibilities at the Conservatory and at Cliffside College."

Jamie's attention was called away by fans who stopped at their table to ask for autographs, and Dennis leaned closer. "Hell of a thing to happen two days before you were scheduled to return. What was the guy's name again?"

"Saul Kronenberg. A violinist with the Cincinnati Symphony Orchestra and a member of a new string quartet that had engagements scheduled for later this summer." Augusta took another sip of beer from her stein. "He was in Paris attending a seminar at the Sorbonne. Being informed he had died in that hotel room was definitely a shock. The hotel management spoke to Malcolm because they knew we were from Cincinnati. And they also knew that Mal is in law enforcement."

Dennis nodded. "The Chrysanthemum Quartet. I heard their debut recital last fall at the Art Museum. Most impressive."

"I don't know what Manny will do now. It's most likely too late to find a replacement for the European tour in August, but I hope he'll manage to keep the quartet going."

Father Halloran signaled their waiter and indicated Augusta's stein. She shook her head *no* but commented, "I would like water. I need to leave in a bit. Malcolm should be home soon."

"There's that smile again," Dennis teased. He spoke to the waiter briefly, then turned back to Augusta. "Why'd Immanuel Levine name his group 'The Chrysanthemum Quartet,' anyway?"

"Interesting you should ask. Puccini wrote a beautiful piece for string quartet, *I Crisantemi* – 'The Chrysanthemums.' It was the first piece the quartet prepared for performance when they came together last year. It immediately became their signature piece, and they adopted it as their name. I had that on my mind during the opera tonight, because Puccini used the music again a few years later, incorporating it into *Manon Lescaut*."

"No kidding. Where exactly did he include it?"

"It's some of Puccini's most haunting, elegiac music. In acts three and four, where it becomes obvious Manon is probably going to come to a bad end."

Dennis laughed heartily. "Another Puccini heroine bites the dust."

"And always to music that simply rips your heart out." Augusta took a final bite of schnitzel and dabbed her mouth with her napkin.

Dennis stood with her and they said their goodbyes to the group at their table, old friends of Augusta's: Jamie and his wife Meredith, Sam Varnay, the baritone who portrayed the role of Manon's brother, and his partner, pianist Josh Fleischer. All professionals now living in the New York area who thought of Cincinnati as home and were delighted to spend part of their summers in the city they loved.

A strange sound reached Augusta's and Dennis' ears as they moved onto the sidewalk: a sustained car horn. The sound grew louder as they continued to move away from Mecklenburg's toward their cars.

"It's this car," Dennis said. He glanced in the front seat and saw the driver, who seemed to be asleep.

"Hey, friend," Dennis rapped sharply on the window.

The street lights didn't provide much illumination, but Augusta could make out the driver slumped against the steering wheel, immobile. She felt a flutter in her chest. "Dennis, something's very wrong. He's not moving at all."

Dennis banged more urgently, then tried to open the car door. He stared at Augusta in dismay.

"Locked."

The horn continued to blare as Augusta ran to the other side of the car and tried both doors. Dennis yanked repeatedly at both doors on the driver's side.

Her voice shook as she said, "I'm going back to Meck's and have them call the police." Augusta darted inside the restaurant and hastily told the host what had happened. Sam Varnay hurried to join her as she returned to the street. She filled him in on the situation.

"Maybe I can help. I've had some emergency training."

"Oh, Sam, we can't get the doors open." Augusta felt her heart racing. "The driver is in real trouble. I'm not sure he's breathing."

Sam nodded and ran back into the restaurant, re-joining Dennis at the car in what seemed mere seconds. He swung the meat mallet he had grabbed from the kitchen against the passenger side front door, breaking the window after three strikes. Reaching inside, he released the lock and jerked the door open. With considerable effort, Sam shoved the driver back against the seat, reached across him and unlocked the other door. The sudden silence was jarring.

Sirens sounded as Dennis and Sam pulled the driver from behind the wheel and stretched him out on the sidewalk. Sam knelt beside him and began chest compressions. Dennis took the man's head in his hands and prepared to perform mouth-to-mouth resuscitation.

Augusta stood by helplessly, clenching her hands as she watched the men valiantly trying to save the driver.

She stared into the man's face for the first time and gasped. "Oh, dear God. It's Michael Robinson."

She heard patrol cars screeching up to the curb. The Cincinnati Police Department officers moved quickly, some keeping spectators back so others could attend to the victim. Augusta watched as two patrolmen pulled a stretcher from the back of the scout vehicle, designed and equipped for medical emergencies, and deftly lifted Robinson onto it, covering his nose and mouth with a portable oxygen device. They loaded the stretcher into the back and slammed the doors shut, preparing to race to nearby General Hospital as quickly as possible.

As the scout car sped away, siren blaring, a hand pressed Augusta's shoulder and she turned to see Malcolm's partner, Detective Jim Edmonds, standing beside her.

"Oh, I'm so glad to see you." Trembling, she leaned against him briefly.

"What happened, exactly?" He flipped open a small note pad, clicked his pen and stood ready to take notes.

"Augusta and I had just left Mecklenburg's and we heard this constant car horn sounding. As we came this way to get to our cars, we realized it was coming from this one." Dennis ruffled his blond hair, leaving a smear of blood across his forehead.

Startled, Augusta cried out. "Dennis! Did you cut yourself?"

"No. Why?"

Jim said calmly, "There's blood on your hand. It must have been on the driver's head somewhere."

Dennis stared at his hand. "I didn't even notice."

"How about you?" Jim turned to Sam Varnay, who spread his hands out to examine them.

"I might have cut them when I smashed the window open and unlocked the door." They all watched as he studied his hands. "No. Nothing."

Jim spoke to the patrolmen on the scene, who began unrolling crime scene tape and giving directions to onlookers who had spilled from the restaurant. "This is a crime scene at the moment. We don't yet know what happened here." He turned toward Augusta. "Do you know who the victim is?"

"Yes, Michael Robinson. He's on the faculty at the Conservatory, and he plays with the Summer Opera orchestra." She clasped her hands together to keep them from trembling. "The viola."

Another car pulled up quickly, and out stepped Homicide Detective Malcolm Mitchell, fresh off the plane from Paris. He moved to Augusta's side, protectively wrapping a strong arm around her waist.

"Well, Augusta, this is some welcome home."

Chapter 1
The Wedding

(two months earlier)

April, 1965

"I had a surprise visitor this morning."

Professor Augusta McKee paused before entering the bridal shop in Hyde Park Square. "Carla Henderson came to see me."

Her closest friend, fellow music teacher Mildred Devereaux, stopped short. "Mal's first wife? Less than four weeks before your wedding?"

"I know. She asked me to invite her parents to our wedding. 'Because of Mal's sons, you know. After all, they're the only grandparents they have.'" Augusta laughed and shook her head.

Augusta and Milly had an appointment with the shop's owner, Diana Miller, to look at dresses for Augusta's wedding to Homicide Detective Malcolm Mitchell. Augusta and Malcolm had met two years

19

earlier while he was on a case—the murder of one of Augusta's voice students, Linnea Murphy. A first confrontational meeting became a friendship as Augusta uncovered evidence which helped Malcolm arrest Linnea's killer.

The friendship became a romance, and in less than a year Malcolm and Augusta were engaged. She had given him assistance in several subsequent cases and six months earlier they had set their wedding date for May.

Diana Miller ushered the two women into a private room where she had several gowns hanging on a rack. "I'll leave you ladies to look these over for a few minutes."

"Thank you, Diana." Augusta and Milly turned their attention to the dresses. "Oh, these are lovely." Augusta surveyed a gown in a soft lilac color with a flowing skirt. "I knew she'd come up with perfect suggestions."

"Back to Carla. What did you tell her?" Milly frowned at the gown Augusta was holding. "Purple? For a wedding dress?"

"It's not purple, it's lilac. I agreed to Carla's request. Mal wasn't too thrilled when I told him, but we have room for a couple more people. It just wasn't worth arguing over. And I like Carla's parents. They've always been pleasant." She laughed. "I wouldn't be surprised to learn they like me better than Carla."

"Carla's not an easy person to like. I wonder sometimes why Mal ever married her. Don't answer that. He was twenty, and she's still a looker. But I have to say that I'm surprised you even let her inside your house, after what she pulled at Martha's and Danny's engagement party." Milly smoothed the skirt of the dress she was examining. "And I'll bet you never told Malcolm about that."

"What was the point? Carla is who she is, Milly."

Augusta took the dress she'd been examining and held it in front of her, frowning into the full-length mirror. "Mal didn't need to hear it. She'd probably had one glass of champagne too many and didn't even think about what she said."

Carla had found Augusta alone in the powder room of the Hyde Park Country Club. She'd reminded Augusta in no uncertain terms that Ryan and Danny were her children—hers and Malcolm's—and to not ever forget that. Augusta had been taken aback, but let it pass. She refused to be drawn into an altercation with Carla.

"You're probably right. It just irks me how she acts sometimes." Milly lifted the gown she'd been admiring from the rack. "Take a look at this one, Augusta. I love the color. This is perfect with your hair and eyes, too."

"Champagne." Augusta smoothed the soft luster of the peau de soie fabric as she examined the dress. "Simple but elegant. Love the cowl neckline in the back."

She frowned. "I'm not sure about the sheath skirt, though. You know I prefer a skirt that swings."

"Look, there's a slit to the knee. I think this is perfect for your model's figure. You'd look stunning in it, Augusta. You have to try it on."

Milly beamed and clapped her hands when Augusta stepped through the curtains. "Good Lord, Augusta. You look about ... well, not even forty. Nobody would believe you're fifty-four." She chuckled and added, "And it's not just because Jason keeps your hair that shade of chestnut you like. Keep up the ballet exercises."

Augusta turned slowly in front of the mirror, taking in the dress from every angle. She had to agree with Milly, the color complemented her hair and her hazel eyes. "I love it. The drape is elegant."

She giggled as she extended a slender leg through the slit. "I feel positively giddy."

Next an attendant dress for Milly, a deep purple beaded chiffon gown with a cascade jacket, soft neckline, and flowing sleeves. Milly stared at herself in the mirror. "Wow. Not bad for an old broad. It almost makes me look tall and skinny."

"I like how it complements your hair," Augusta said. Despite her best efforts to persuade Milly to visit her hairdresser, Milly claimed she liked her bouncy dark curls peppered with silver.

The two women chatted happily as they left the boutique. "Well, now I have an idea for the flowers. I wanted to wait until we chose our dresses. Lots of options." Augusta commented.

"Let's check with the caterer to be sure she's on track. D-Day—or should I say 'W-Day?'—is in less than four weeks."

***

Friday, May 14, 1965

"We should get going soon." Augusta took one last sip of her wine. "Big day tomorrow."

"Yes, and tomorrow starts in about an hour and a half." Malcolm pushed his chair back as he gazed at his bride-to-be.

"Correct. Which means we don't see each other from midnight until the ceremony tomorrow."

Malcolm laughed and shook his head. "Are you serious? I thought you were kidding about 'no seeing the bride' on the wedding day. Anyway, the day starts when the sun rises."

"Nope. Not kidding. I meant that. It's one tradition I intend to keep."

Ryan, Malcolm's elder son, turned to his father. "Want to come home with me? That's probably the best way to avoid an altercation with your bride. We can run by your house and pick up your stuff quick."

"Nonsense," Augusta said. "Our house is certainly big enough for us to avoid running into each other for a few hours in the morning. The bed in the guest room is quite comfortable."

The small group, having enjoyed a repast at the Hyde Park Country Club, filtered out into the parking lot and shared embraces and goodnights. Ryan, his brother Dan—both so apparently Malcolm's sons, though Ryan had his mother's auburn hair. Dan's fiancée, Martha Van Camp—an attractive young woman with blond hair and a womanly figure—a recent Conservatory graduate and Augusta's student. Milly and her Garrett, a dynamic defense attorney with a shock of white hair. Augusta and Malcolm wanted this opportunity to focus on these, their nearest and dearest, the evening before their wedding.

Augusta took a moment to gaze at this man who was everything to her, the most amazing man she'd ever known. She well recalled that first meeting, stepping from her car to face this ruggedly handsome, dark-haired detective with intense blue eyes, who at six feet one topped her by only an inch in her stilettos. He had ordered her off the campus at Cliffside, and she defied him, re-entering the grounds through a back way which meant she had to climb a four-foot rock wall. Malcolm was dumbfounded when she reappeared, but allowed her to stay. Later that day he even enlisted her assistance, and something sparked between them.

As they grew to know each other Augusta found him to be brilliant, witty, tender, strong, dedicated to his calling as a law enforcement officer. It had been a surprise to learn of his love for opera, and even more to learn the first opera he had ever seen was *Carmen* at the Cincinnati Summer Opera, in which Augusta had appeared as Frasquita. At that time, she had just joined the voice faculty of her alma mater, the Conservatory of Music.

In the intervening years Malcolm, who was seven years her junior, had married, had children, served with the Marines in the South Pacific, attended the University of Cincinnati, and joined the police force. Crossing paths over twenty-five years later when he was investigating the murder at Cliffside College, where Augusta was also teaching, proved to be momentous. Now here they were, mere hours from becoming man and wife.

***

One last kiss before Augusta went into her—*their* bedroom—and closed the door.

It does feel a little strange. We've been together for two years almost to the day, and haven't slept in separate beds.

A light tap on her door woke her. "Gus, I forgot my new tie when I took my clothes out last night. I'll just slip in and get it. Pull the covers over your head and I promise I won't even glance in your direction."

She bolted out of bed. "*No!* Turn your back. I'll hang the tie over the doorknob in the hall. Don't you *dare* look until I give you the all-clear."

"Okay, if you insist," he laughed.

Augusta glanced at her clock. Seven a.m. "Why are you getting dressed so early, anyway?"

"I'm not. I was just checking my clothes and realized I didn't have the tie. I'll go down and fix breakfast."

She opened the door just enough to slip her hand through and drape his tie over the hall doorknob, closing it firmly. "Okay, there's your tie. How am I going to get my tea and toast, anyway? I can't come downstairs."

"You mean you *won't* come downstairs. Milly's supposed to be here at seven-thirty. I'll ask her to bring it up. Augusta McKee, you're tenacious—you know that, don't you?"

With Milly playing the role of the dragon guarding the gate, the morning passed without incident as Augusta remained in the master bedroom suite.

Malcolm's sons Ryan and Danny greeted the guests, seating them in the spacious living room of Augusta's Tudor home. French doors opened into the dining room and the doors to the alcove were also open, giving a spacious, airy feeling to the entire first floor of the house.

Martha arrived early to help Augusta and Milly dress. She put the finishing touches on Augusta's French twist, topping it with a gold clip inset with seed pearls and small crystals, a gift from the groom.

"You look absolutely gorgeous," Martha said, wide-eyed.

Milly handed Augusta the nosegay Malcolm had ordered. White roses and ivory satin ribbons surrounded a white chrysanthemum with a few sprigs of white wisteria dripping over one side. "Perfect. The man has good taste," Milly commented.

"Of course, he does." Augusta smiled.

"Don't you dare say something corny like 'look who he's marrying,'" Milly admonished.

Martha gave them each a hug. "I'll see you after the ceremony."

***

With his sons at his side, Malcolm stood to Judge Edgar Demarest's left as he waited for his bride to descend the staircase and join him. *Why am I nervous? I've wanted this for a long time. Maybe since the first time I ever laid eyes on Augusta, all those years ago.*

The guests were quiet, enjoying the music. Augusta had requested the "Raindrop" Prelude by Chopin as her processional music. Since Milly, a virtuoso pianist, was her attendant, a graduate of the Conservatory, Dan Cunningham, was at the piano for the wedding.

Milly entered and crossed the room to stand at the judge's right. There was a murmur among the guests when Augusta stepped into the room.

Malcolm breathed in sharply. *My God, she's ... stunning.*

Augusta gazed at him with shining eyes as she glided across the floor and took her place beside him. *My beautiful Malcolm.* The look in his eyes nearly brought her to tears. *This is so right, what we're doing today.*

Chopin's music drew to a quiet close. Augusta handed Milly her nosegay and nodded to Dan Cunningham to begin. She had prepared the Schumann song "Er, der Herrlichste von allen" to sing for the man she adored.

The piano part depicted a rapidly beating heart, the woman deeply in love with a man she doesn't think she deserves.

He, the most glorious of all,
so gentle, so good!
Strong mouth, clear eyes,
a bright mind and steadfast courage.

In my heavens, he is a star,
brilliant and far off ...
I only need to observe him.
My prayer is to be consecrated to your happiness.

Only the worthiest should be your choice.
I will bless her, whoever she is.
I will rejoice, even if it means
my heart will break.

She moved closer to him as she ended the song with a repeat of the words of the first stanza. Malcolm responded with the brilliant smile she so loved as she sang again:

He, the most glorious of all,
so gentle, so good!
Strong mouth, clear eyes,
a bright mind and steadfast courage.

Judge Demarest spoke the opening words of the traditional ceremony, ending with "if anyone can show just cause why this couple cannot lawfully be joined together in matrimony, let them speak now or forever hold their peace."

To Augusta's relief, Carla didn't make a sound, and the judge continued, "Malcolm and Augusta have chosen to write their own wedding vows." He gestured to Malcolm to begin.

"Augusta. The first time I ever saw you was on stage at the Summer Opera, singing the role of Frasquita in *Carmen*. It was my first opera ever. The second time I saw you was on the campus of Cliffside College, and though I tried my best, I was unable to intimidate you."

Augusta chuckled and there was quiet laughter among the wedding guests.

"We've had some pretty interesting adventures over the past two years, and I've learned that the fiery gypsy Frasquita is alive and well in my Gus. I know you just sang about 'a bright mind and steadfast courage.' Those are certainly a big part of who you are, and I've seen it many times. You are without a doubt the most remarkable woman I've ever known, and I feel incredibly blessed that we are together."

He paused and saw the tears gathering in the corners of her eyes. "You're also a woman who personifies kindness and goodness, and who has a heart full of music. You've brought music into my life in ways I never anticipated." He gently wiped the tears from her face.

"I know you hate when your tear ducts overflow, so I'll wind this up by saying it means the world to me that you respect and honor what I do. You'd be a good cop, Gus. Along with your other wonderful qualities, you have initiative, integrity, respect for and knowledge of the law. You have compassion and you care. As a cop, I have a highly elevated appreciation of what a *partner* is. I'm humbled and honored that you're about to become my partner for life."

He took a deep breath, concerned his voice might shake. "I love you with all I am and all I have. And I'll always have your back."

Augusta leaned forward and kissed him softly as the guests applauded.

"Detective Mitchell. The second time I met you, you foolishly tried to intimidate me." Laughter from the guests. "Sorry, I couldn't resist that." A soft laugh.

Taking both his hands in hers, she began again. "Malcolm. The Schumann song truly expresses my feelings for you. How am I so fortunate that you've chosen me? You're my hero."

She put a hand to his face. "And you are my world, my love. You are tender, strong, witty, compassionate, brave, brilliant. That we are together and taking this step is the highest point of my life."

She pressed both his hands against her heart. "You've taught me so much about your world, and even allowed me to share in it from time to time. That is such an expression of trust. You make me feel honored, cherished, and loved more than I knew was possible. It means more than you know that you share my love of music. I love you with every atom of my being."

She paused for a moment. Her eyes shone as she added, "And as best as I am able, my beloved partner for life, I will always have your back."

***

More applause from their guests. Rings were exchanged and they were pronounced husband and wife. Milly handed Augusta her nosegay. Judge Demarest, grinning broadly, proclaimed, "Detective Mitchell, you may kiss your bride."

For the reception, several tables and chairs had been set up in the garden, in the front yard, and on the porch, so guests could sit wherever they wanted and move about if they chose.

Hot and cold hors d'oeuvres and a variety of vegetable and fruit salads were placed on a long table in the garden. A server sliced roast beef and ham. Two kinds of punch, alcoholic and non-alcoholic, were on another table, along with several bottles of red and white wine. Chilled champagne waited in the kitchen for the toast. A variety of desserts stood on a third table.

Milly's caterer had plenty of servers on hand who strolled among the tables with trays of all the items that were being offered. The weather was perfect, and the wedding guests happily chatted with friends and family.

Augusta and Malcolm circulated among their guests, sitting briefly at some tables to take a bite or two of the delicious offerings the caterer had provided.

They found the three nuns Augusta worked closely with at Cliffside College sharing a table with Claudia Prince, Augusta's fellow faculty member from the Conservatory. Sister Mary Norbert giggled as she said, "This is my second glass of punch."

Sister Mary Vincent, the dean of the school, commented, "Sister Norbert decided to try the one that has a kick to it."

"Congratulations, Detective Mitchell." Sister Mary Patrick, president of the college, lifted her glass. "It's good to have you as part of the Cliffside family."

Augusta caught the slight smirk on Mal's face and gently dug him in the ribs. "Thank you, Sister. I should tell you that while I'm now officially Mrs. Mitchell, I will continue to use Augusta McKee as my professional name."

31

Malcolm held her hand as they moved down the steps. "I wasn't going to say anything, Gus. Honest."

Augusta kissed his hand. "Maybe. But I saw the look on your face."

"But do you suppose it's just a coincidence that the first time she got my name right was after I made an honest woman of you?" They both chuckled.

Father Dennis Halloran, a young priest on the faculty of Cliffside, found the newlyweds and led them to the garden, where the other guests had gathered, to offer his toast. Augusta and Malcolm had asked Dennis to make the first toast because they believed he had helped bring them to this point, the realization of how much they wanted—and needed—to become man and wife.

Danny Mitchell tapped his fork against his champagne flute to get everyone's attention, and Dennis turned to the bride and groom.

"Augusta and Malcolm, I've been privileged to watch your friendship grow into a romance. And last fall, I was on hand when circumstances took you from each other for a time. While that was difficult for both of you, I believe it convinced you how much you needed to join your lives by taking this step, and today we've all been part of this celebration of your union."

He raised his glass. "My dear friends, I wish you every happiness and a long and blessed life. To Augusta and Malcolm."

Glasses were raised all around. "To Augusta and Malcolm."

Ryan stood next. "Danny and I were both Dad's best men, but I claim precedence as firstborn to make the second toast." Ryan turned to his new stepmother and gave her a smile that rivaled his father's. "Augusta, it's my privilege to officially welcome you to the family. Danny and I love you already. Thank you for making our dad so happy." He raised his glass. "The bride and groom."

Again, glasses were raised and the toast was echoed.

Milly stood. "As Augusta's oldest friend and the closest thing she has to a sister, I get to make the final toast." She lifted her glass. "Malcolm, God love you for taking her on. It's undoubtedly one of the bravest things you've ever done." Laughter all around.

"Seriously, though, my friend. You've already given her more happiness than you realize, and I foresee much more in the future. To the groom and bride." She added, "Bottoms up," as she drained her champagne glass.

Some of the guests followed them inside, others preferred to return to their tables and enjoy desserts and coffee. Daniel Cunningham played the opening chords of Franz Lehar's "Yours Is My Heart Alone" from *The Land of Smiles.* In the operetta, it was sung brilliantly by the tenor. Augusta had asked the pianist to reinterpret it as a quiet, gentle love song.

She sang softly to Malcolm as they danced.

You are my heart's delight,
and where you are, I long to be.

You make my darkness bright,
when like a star you shine on me.
Shine, then, my whole life through,
your life divine bids me hope anew,
that dreams of mine may, at last, come true,
and I shall hear you whisper,
"I love you."

They held each other close and swayed in time to the music.

Chapter 2
The Not-So-Perfect End to the Honeymoon

Thursday, June 3, 1965

Augusta gazed at her husband as he stood on their balcony, taking in the sights of Paris once again. The Hotel Le Colbert in the Latin Quarter had been their place of residence when they first arrived, and after visiting other places dear to Augusta's heart—Vienna, Salzburg, Munich, and Innsbruck—they had returned to Le Colbert the previous evening.

During their first visit, Detective and Mrs. Mitchell had become great favorites of the hotel staff, and the manager, M. Henri Duplessis, was pleased to provide the same room on their return, with its spectacular view of Notre Dame de Paris which stood only a short distance from the hotel.

"Duplessis," Augusta had commented when they first saw the manager's name. "The same as Dumas' courtesan."

"You're losing me." Malcolm gazed at her with raised eyebrows.

"*La Traviata.* Verdi drew his material from a book by Alexandre Dumas *fils*—the son—called *The Lady of the Camellias*. The character of Violetta in the opera is based on Dumas' heroine Marguerite Gautier. And that character was based on an actual historical figure, Marie Duplessis."

"And her claim to fame was—?"

"Dumas apparently was madly in love with her. She was a courtesan—I guess the closest thing these days would be a high-class call girl—and the mistress of several powerful, wealthy men. When she died, Dumas was completely devastated."

"Does this have anything at all to do with what we want to see while we're here?"

Augusta laughed and sank onto the bed. "Not a thing. It's just fun to be back in Paris and remember the great times Milly and I had when we were here, decades ago. And to share it with the man I adore."

Recalling that conversation, she smiled and went to her husband, wrapping her arms around him from behind and pressing her face against the back of his neck.

He rested his hands on hers and they stood quietly, savoring the moment and the view. The sound of a traditional French waltz played on an accordion wafted up from the street below.

"This has been—I'm not even sure what word to use. An incredible trip. More than I dreamed it would be." He turned and kissed her softly. "Do you have any idea how happy you make me?"

"Oh, I think I might. Hopefully, as happy as you make me." She returned the kiss. "I think magical is how I would describe this time we've had together. Unforgettable."

"That, for sure."

A brisk rap on the door surprised them.

"Did you order room service?" Augusta reached for her dressing gown as Malcolm grabbed a shirt.

"No, I didn't." He went to the door. "*Qui est-ce?*"

"Show-off," Augusta teased. Mal had picked up several useful French phrases.

"Henri Duplessis."

Mal checked to be sure Augusta was covered before opening the door.

"*Pardon*, Detective Mitchell, Madame Mitchell," M. Duplessis ran a chubby hand over the back of his head, his dark eyes darting from one of them to the other. "I regret the intrusion, but I require your assistance."

Malcolm had registered them as "Mr. and Mrs.," but the staff soon learned of his position with the Cincinnati Police Department. They had also become aware of Augusta's profession and thought the American *l'inspecteur* and his diva a fascinating couple.

"Come in, Monsieur Duplessis." Malcolm opened the door wide.

"It is most distressing. Most regrettable." Duplessis squeezed his hands together as the Mitchells waited to hear what in the world he was talking about.

"We have a guest from your city, Cincinnati. A musician. A Mr. Saul Kronenberg."

Augusta replied, "Saul is a guest in this hotel? What's happened?"

"It is beyond belief. When the maid went to wake him as requested about an hour ago, he did not respond. She unlocked the door." He hesitated, once again swiping his hand over the back of his head.

My word, he does have a knack for building suspense, thought Augusta.

"She found him dead," Malcolm pronounced flatly.

Augusta gasped, hugging herself tightly, her heart pounding. Malcolm wrapped a strong arm around her waist, steadying her.

"*Mais oui. C'est terrible.*" Duplessis sank into a chair, mopping his face with a handkerchief.

"I'm sure the police have arrived and are investigating," Malcolm said.

"*Certainement.* There is a doctor with him as well." He turned to Augusta. "You know him, this Monsieur Kronenberg?"

"I'm acquainted with him. He's a violinist. We both teach at the Conservatory of Music. What a shock."

"What can we do to help?" Malcolm asked the hotel manager.

"Madame Mitchell ... since you are colleagues ... it would be helpful to contact his next of kin. He is ... was ... traveling alone."

"Yes, I can certainly do that." She gazed at Malcolm. "I'll call Manny Levine. He knows Saul much better than I do. I don't know about family. Saul wasn't married. I know he moved to Cincinnati from Hartford, Connecticut."

Monsieur Duplessis struggled to his feet. "Please allow me to have breakfast delivered here for you," he told them. "I regret disrupting your day in this manner."

***

"I don't like this." Malcolm pressed a hand against his forehead, frowning.

Duplessis had returned about an hour later to inform them the police had completed a preliminary investigation and saw no indication of foul play. The death had been attributed to natural causes, most likely a massive coronary event, by the doctor.

"You think this is too hasty a conclusion?" Augusta asked, stepping into her dress.

"A relatively young man dying suddenly? How old did Manny tell you Kronenberg was?"

"He said he just turned fifty-one. So, yes, definitely a relatively young man, and Manny wasn't aware he had any health problems." She quickly pulled up the zipper.

"It's too pat, Gus. Too slick. The hotel wants it this way, it's less of a problem to them." He slipped into his shoes. "Bad enough to have an American tourist die in their hotel. They sure don't want any hint of foul play.

"The other thing is … it's possible there wasn't a thorough examination of the room." He ran a hand over his hair. "Or an interrogation of the staff members Kronenberg came into contact with. While the Paris police have their own detectives, it's my understanding that the best detectives are part of the National Police. There's a special criminal investigation department."

Mal stood and began pacing the room. "This is an American citizen, suddenly found dead in a hotel room. A complete and thorough investigation has to take place."

"And you're trying to figure out how to make that happen."

He stopped and stared at her. "I think I need to make a visit to the American Embassy and present that request. But before I do that, I want to know my boss will back me up."

Cincinnati Police Chief Stanley Schrotel had a wide reputation as one of the best police chiefs in the world, heading up one of the best police departments. Augusta knew Stan Schrotel was a past president of the International Association of Chiefs of Police, and it was widely acknowledged that FBI Director J. Edgar Hoover was an admirer of Chief Schrotel, and sometimes sought his advice.

"That makes sense, Mal. Are you comfortable calling on the hotel phone?"

His set jaw and narrowed eyes told her that her husband had gone into what she thought of as "full detective mode."

"I think I'll use a pay phone, Gus. Excuse me for a bit, will you?"

Augusta nodded. She understood why he'd prefer to not take the chance of putting such a call through the hotel switchboard. While it was highly unlikely anyone might listen in on his call, it wasn't impossible.

What a way to end a perfect honeymoon, she thought. *Poor Saul. What an awful shock for his family in Hartford.* Manny had told her while Saul had never married, he had siblings, nieces and nephews, and an uncle and aunt in Connecticut. Manny wasn't aware of Saul having any history of heart disease, but he promised to ask the family when he contacted them with the sad news.

Saul was the second violinist for the Chrysanthemum Quartet, a new organization based in Cincinnati which Immanuel Levine had established about a year earlier. They had a successful debut recital at the Cincinnati Art Museum in the fall, followed by a series of performances in Northern Kentucky, Lexington, and Louisville. They were set for a short European tour at the end of the summer.

What will Manny do now? It's probably too late to replace Saul for that tour. All of the other quartet members are playing in the Summer Opera orchestra, so rehearsal time would be limited.

Malcolm returned, a look of determination on his face. "The boss gave me his blessing. He doesn't like this any better than I do. Saul Kronenberg may have died in Paris, but he's a resident of our town. We need to know more about this."

The phone rang, and Malcolm picked it up. "Mitchell." His customary way of answering when he was on a case. *Well, and it seems he is on a case.*

She saw him frown slightly as he listened. "Thanks, Manny. That's helpful to know." He hung up and commented, "He says Saul had problems with his heart as a kid, but as far as the family was aware, nothing recently. Not for years."

"What kind of problems? Did they have any idea?"

"No, but they promised Manny they'd see what they could find out." He stared off into the distance. "Look, I'm going to head for the embassy and see how far I can get trying to connect with the ambassador."

"You're aiming high, Mal. Why not ask to see one of his assistants?"

"Good suggestion." He opened the door but paused and turned to her.

"I don't have any idea how long I'll be. Do you want to come with me?"

"I do not. I don't want to be a tag-along. I'll walk over to Notre Dame and do some shopping, that's what I wanted to do today anyway." She picked up her bag and the hotel key.

"That's right." He grinned at her. "Gifts for the good Sisters at Cliffside."

"Just some small items. Things I can easily tuck in my luggage."

They left the room together. "Are you getting something for every blessed nun at that college?"

Augusta laughed. "Prayer cards for most of them. Something special for the three I work closely with. Rosaries, maybe."

Malcolm glanced at his watch. "Want to set up a time and place to meet? Or shall we just both come back to our room as soon as we can?"

"That makes more sense," Augusta remarked. "You have no idea how long you'll be. I may poke around in some of the shops near the hotel, so I don't either."

***

"You were right about asking to speak with an assistant to the ambassador. A terrific young guy showed up pretty quickly, and he turned out to be exactly the right man for me to talk to. He'd heard of Chief Schrotel, he's been to Cincinnati, and he agreed the detectives on the Paris police force might not have done as thorough a job as they should have. Unfortunately, they have that reputation."

Augusta nibbled on a croissant spread with brie and poured each of them a second glass of wine. She glanced around at their picturesque surroundings, glowing in the slanting rays of the late afternoon sun.

"I've been trying to think what kind of heart problems Saul might have had as a child, which he could have outgrown." Augusta shaded her eyes as she gazed at Malcolm.

"And?"

"Well, he could have had a heart murmur as a child which corrected itself when he was a teenager. I believe that can happen. I guess his uncle and aunt might have remembered it."

"Yes, but would it have resurfaced all these decades later? That doesn't make any sense to me."

"Well … one other thing … it could have been an aneurysm. It's a weakness in an artery and sometimes people can have them all their life and they never cause trouble."

"Yes, I know. And if they rupture, it can be fatal." Malcolm frowned as he pulled pieces from his croissant, slowly destroying it.

"The doctor didn't give a definitive diagnosis," he continued. "He didn't perform an autopsy. He just ruled it a death due to natural causes since there was no indication of foul play. It's common knowledge that kind of death is most often caused by a myocardial infarction. And while Saul was only fifty, he wouldn't be considered young."

"Who was the ambassador's assistant you talked with?"

"His name is Garth Willis. He invited me to sit in on his meeting with the lead investigator who has been assigned to this case. A member of the *Police Judiciaire*." Malcolm finished his wine in one final gulp.

"It's not your case, Mal," Augusta said softly, resting a hand on his wrist.

"I know that." He frowned. "I'm there as a guest and have no official authority. I appreciate that I was included. We're meeting at nine a.m. tomorrow."

Augusta again glanced around the plaza where they were enjoying wine and cheese at a sidewalk café. "I know you'd love to be working this case, but it's not your town. Not even your country."

A crooked grin. "Are you suggesting I take off my detective hat and go back to being a newlywed on his honeymoon?"

"Something like that. Regardless, you can't do any sleuthing for the present. We only have two nights left in Paris, Mal. Let's enjoy ourselves."

He gave her the smile that melted her insides. "You're right, as usual, Mrs. Mitchell. What tickles your fancy?"

"Why not find a bistro and have dinner, and then maybe just stroll along the Seine for a while? Watch the sun set. Watch the moon rise."

"And then walk back to our hotel?"

She batted her eyelashes at him. "Exactly. It's a lovely suite."

Malcolm laughed. "I like your plan, Mrs. Mitchell." He leaned toward her, softly kissing her on the cheek.

"So, no more detective talk for the present." She caressed his face. "Agreed?"

"Agreed." He took her hand and kissed the rings he had given her.

Augusta smiled as she gazed into his eyes.

He may be the consummate cop, but he's also pretty darned romantic.

Chapter 3
Memories

Friday, June 4, 1965

Augusta stretched out on the chaise lounge in their suite, smiling as she thought back over the past three weeks. *It was all I hoped for, and more.*

She had planned their itinerary for the honeymoon, retracing her time in Europe when she was young, wanting to share that part of her life with Malcolm.

"When Meyer died, I felt my world had ended. Milly insisted we go to Paris, but for the first six months I did almost nothing," she explained while seated in the alcove of their Hyde Park home, drinking coffee and looking over the trip.

"You were grieving for Meyer," Mal responded, nodding. She had told him about her first love, a gifted, charismatic young cellist named Meyer Abrams who died when only twenty, during Augusta's senior year at the Conservatory.

"Milly realized that. She figured I needed something more, and we closed up our apartment and headed for Vienna. It was a good move. The first thing we did was go to a performance of the Brahms Requiem at the Staatsoper. I sobbed non-stop."

"Gus." Malcolm placed a sympathetic hand on her arm.

"No, it was a good thing. I needed to let myself cry like that, and I felt so much better. We stayed for six months, making side trips to Salzburg and Munich. We went to every musical event we could get tickets for."

"When did you start singing again?"

"There, in Vienna. Then I was ready to go back to Paris. Milly had begun study at the Sorbonne when we were there the first time. I found a teacher, and began to study in earnest."

"Why did you include Innsbruck on this trip?"

"Oh, you'll see. I think that completed my healing … being in the Alps. Going back to Paris was wonderful. We were there for almost two years. We did everything the city had to offer. I felt like a real *Parisienne* for a time."

"You are excited about going back, aren't you?" He reached across the table and covered her hand with his.

"I'm excited about sharing my Europe with you. I hope you love it."

She leaned toward him, eager to say more. "There's this about Paris—the best way to experience the city is to take time to be a Parisian." Augusta tipped her head to one side, trying to think how best to explain her comment. "What's your favorite thing about living in Cincinnati?"

"I'm not sure what you mean."

"Well, don't you sometimes just like to walk around different parts of town, appreciating that they are there? Eden Park, for example. Or Fountain Square. It's great to wander around and marvel that those places even exist. Parisians are the same way. They love their city."

Mal hadn't been too thrilled about leaving his gun—and his detective persona—in Cincinnati. Augusta never commented when she saw him check all the exits every time they entered a building. *It's part of who he is*, she thought, happy to watch him gradually relax and begin to enjoy himself.

They had arrived in Paris in the late hours of Sunday, May 16, and spent a week before flying on to Vienna. Salzburg was next, a pleasant two-hour train ride. A few days in Innsbruck, where they made time to relax, and then a quick side trip to explore Old Town in Munich on their way back to Paris.

Oh, we've made some wonderful memories. Malcolm's awe at viewing the antiquities in the Louvre. His delight at standing at the top of the Arc de Triomphe, gazing at the sweeping view of all of Paris, the Eiffel Tower in the distance.

"Let's do the steps when we visit the Eiffel Tower," he suggested, eager for a new adventure.

"Not on your life. I did the first level once. I could barely walk for two days. Three hundred steps?"

"I guess that was in your pre-stiletto days," he laughed.

"It just takes way too long. The lifts are better, even though they make a lot of noise."

The thrill they both experienced at the Paris Opera, hearing the great Maria Callas perform the title role in *Norma.* Augusta congratulated herself on thinking ahead when she ordered those tickets. They held hands as they strolled through the Champs d'Elysées, the Tuileries, along the Seine.

Vienna was a dream. Mal seemed to truly relax, enjoying the music that was everywhere in the city. Two opera performances, *Tosca* and *Don Giovanni.* Augusta was thrilled to hear the young German tenor, Fritz Wunderlich, as Don Ottavio in *Don Giovanni.* She told Malcolm she believed it the finest tenor voice she'd ever heard. "He's headed for stardom. Maybe the next Caruso."

"Better than Jamie Logan?"

"Well, it's hard to say. Wunderlich is a few years older. But he has something special."

Another lovely memory: Mal enjoying a cruise on the Danube, making her laugh helplessly as he speculated about the people who had lived in the castles and fortresses high up on the hills along the bank while he dreamed up outlandish crimes for them.

Best of all—Innsbruck, seeing in Mal's face the same overwhelming awe she had felt when she first stood and looked up at the majestic peaks of the Alps rising above them. And then taking the funicular up to the Hungerburg, enraptured by the silence and the astonishing connection to the universe.

As they surveyed the magnificent vista spread out before them, Malcolm pulled her close and murmured in her ear, "Thank you for sharing all this with me, my Gus. It means more than you know."

Malcolm interrupted her reverie as he returned from his meeting at the American Embassy.

"I ordered lunch." He leaned over and kissed her. "Let's eat on the balcony. It's a beautiful day."

This was a productive meeting, she guessed. Room service arrived quickly and set up the table for them. Paris was at its best, presenting them with a pleasant spring day with high, puffy clouds and a gentle breeze.

"The lead investigator, Inspector Marchand, is terrific. I feel much better about this. I'm sure he'll do as thorough an investigation as … well, as I would."

"What is Inspector Marchand doing that you approve of so highly, Mal?" Augusta took a forkful of quiche and held it in her mouth for a moment, marveling at the flavor. *How do the French do this? So good.*

"For one thing, he has a forensics team going through the room again. Yesterday while I was at the Embassy, Garth phoned the manager and instructed him not to clean the room, but to seal it. The Paris police came back and did that. For another, Marchand and one of his team are interviewing the entire hotel staff. He spent some time at the Sorbonne as well. Kronenberg was here for well over a week. He came in contact with quite a few people."

"What about employees of shops and bistros near the hotel? He must have spent time at some of those."

Augusta leaned forward, intrigued. She had helped Malcolm with more than one case.

"Yes, those people need to be spoken with. Marchand is working with the local police on that, and they have photos of Kronenberg to circulate."

"So, they can ask if anyone had any interaction with him, but also if they saw him talking with anyone. Saw anything the least bit unusual or odd."

"Exactly. This won't be rushed, but there is some urgency. Kronenberg's relatives want his body returned as soon as possible. They've agreed to an autopsy, though." He paused to take a bite of quiche. "This is delicious."

"Isn't it?" They concentrated on their lunch for a few minutes, appreciating the cuisine.

Mal put down his fork and wiped his mouth with his napkin. "Gus ... Ambassador Bohlen phoned Chief Schrotel this morning during our meeting. He asked if we would consider remaining in Paris for a few days longer, until the investigation and autopsy officially confirm this was a death by natural causes, and then accompany Saul Kronenberg's body back to the United States."

Augusta gazed at him. "You're due back at work on Monday."

"The chief gave me permission to extend my time since this would be an official assignment."

"What was your response?"

"I told them I was honored to be asked. I also told them my wife has responsibilities beginning on Monday back in Cincinnati. Summer session is beginning on both campuses where she teaches."

Augusta sipped from her water glass. "Yes, I have to leave tomorrow. But Malcolm … you should stay. Accept the ambassador's request."

"I'm not comfortable with you traveling back alone. It's our honeymoon, Augusta. Someone from the Embassy can fulfill that duty, don't you think?"

"I don't know that I agree with you." She leaned back and gazed at him. "You were concerned enough about Saul's death to ask for a more complete investigation. You and Stan Schrotel both said you wanted to do everything you could for a fellow Cincinnatian."

Augusta rested a hand on Mal's arm as she watched conflicting emotions cross his face. "If you don't stay and find out what Inspector Marchand comes up with during his investigation, it will probably drive you a little berserk."

He grinned at her. "You know me far too well, Gus."

"It's difficult enough that you can't be on this case, except as an observer. Stay, and escort Saul Kronenberg home." Her voice shook slightly. "I really want you to do this."

He gazed at her thoughtfully without commenting.

"And here's the other thing," she added. "You seem to have hit it off with Inspector Marchand. Why not see where that leads? You may have an international friendship developing here."

Malcolm pushed his chair back. "Would you be okay with me asking him to join us for drinks later? He's a fellow veteran—he served in Indochina and later was part of the western invasion of Germany. We've traded war stories. You'd like him, Gus. He's a charming guy with a great sense of humor."

"I'm sure I'll enjoy meeting him. Do you want to invite him to have dinner with us?"

"No, it's our last night together before you leave. Hopefully, it will be only three or four days before I get home. I have his phone number." He reached into his pocket and pulled out a slip of paper. "We can meet downstairs in the lounge. Say, four o'clock?"

***

Augusta glanced at the man striding across the room toward them. She did a double-take, scarcely believing her eyes. She gripped the arms of her chair, barely able to breathe, fearful she might slide straight out of it. *Oh, good Lord. It's Jean-Luc.*

It had been over a quarter of a century since she had last seen him, but he had changed very little. He was tall and lithe and moved as she remembered, with an air of confidence. The touch of silver in his dark hair enhanced his good looks. His eyes widened, and she was sure he had recognized her.

Mal stood to make the introductions. "Augusta, this is Inspector Jean-Luc Marchand. Jean-Luc, my wife, Augusta."

Okay, Augusta, how do you play this? Pretend you're meeting for the first time? No, I can't do that. I'll have to tell Mal the whole story, may as well dive in.

54

Augusta tipped up her chin and willed her voice not to shake. "Hello, Jean-Luc. Mal, Inspector Marchand and I knew each other years ago when Milly and I were living in Paris."

Jean-Luc lightly grasped the hand that Augusta extended.

"What a surprise to see you again, after all this time. You have not changed, Augusta."

Malcolm glanced from one to the other.

"Jean-Luc was an aspiring pianist at the time," Augusta commented, as the two men seated themselves. "And an excellent one to boot." She turned to the Frenchman. "How did you end up as a detective?"

"I served in the military during the war. The opportunity presented itself to me to assist with a few cases while in Indochina."

Augusta noted Jean-Luc's excellent English was only lightly accented. *He must use English often,* she thought.

"As you no doubt know, crimes can happen on a military base. I found it fascinating and decided that was my calling. Being a detective is an exciting vocation, Augusta." He smiled at both of them. "As you may have discovered. Congratulations, I understand you are on your honeymoon."

Augusta laid a hand on Mal's. "We are indeed. And I will attest to that excitement being very real. Never a dull moment."

"Augusta planned our trip in order to share some memories with me," Mal commented.

She pressed her lips together as she kicked his ankle. *Don't you dare go there.*

Mal grinned and added, "I suppose you knew Milly Devereaux."

"*Oui, certainement.* How is Milly?"

Augusta decided that was a safe subject. "She hasn't changed one bit. Still irrepressible. Still a brilliant pianist. She's now on the faculty of the Conservatory of Music, where I teach as well. Oh, and she's still single, though she has a beau who asks her daily to marry him. A defense attorney."

"Jean-Luc tells me he has a family. He and his wife have two sons, the same ages as mine." Malcolm chimed in.

Oh, didn't you two get chummy in a hurry?

"How nice." She smiled.

What else did he tell you? Or did you tell him? Did he know he'd be seeing Augusta McKee today?

Augusta took a long drink from her wine glass. She listened and said little as the two men discussed U.S. police procedure versus French police procedure.

***

"Malcolm Mitchell, you set me up." Back in their suite, Augusta crossed her arms over her chest and glowered at her husband, too annoyed to even think about dinner.

"Guilty as charged." He chuckled, attempting to take her in his arms.

"It's not funny." Augusta shook free and pushed him away. "I never told you about Jean-Luc. How did you make the connection?" She punched him in the chest.

"Milly told me. She said after the two of you got back to Paris, there was still something missing in you. Something important."

"Did you tell him about me?"

"Not really. I told him I was here on my honeymoon with my beautiful bride. I never mentioned your name. Wasn't it apparent he was surprised to see you?"

Slightly mollified, Augusta sat down on the bed. "Yes, he did seem a bit taken aback."

Malcolm joined her, wrapping an arm around her waist. "According to Milly, Jean-Luc was the final step in healing your broken heart. She said it was a good thing."

"Milly talks too much." Augusta leaned against Malcolm. "Yes, Jean-Luc and I were close for a time. He was … considerate. Neither of us had any expectations for anything permanent."

"Milly told me that as well. She never told me his last name, just referred to him as Jean-Luc. But when he and I were talking earlier today, he mentioned he had every intention of pursuing a career as a pianist until he found out how great detective work is. I figured right age, right nationality, good-looking guy. So I thought, I wonder if this could be Gus's 'Jean-Luc.' It seems I deduced correctly."

"Who'd have ever thought he'd end up as a French detective and we'd run into him in Paris?" Augusta gently patted Mal's chest. "Sorry I punched you." She pulled back. "No, I'm not. You need to apologize for not warning me."

"I could very well have been wrong. Anyway, circumstances make strange bedfellows, to misquote Shakespeare."

"Ha ha. Very funny," Augusta half-laughed. "Please don't put it that way. Oh, and one thing."

"What's that?"

She took him by the shoulders and stared into his face. "Promise me that you will never ... never *ever* ... talk about me with him."

"Why wouldn't I talk about you?" Malcolm grinned. "You're the center of my world."

"You know what I mean. This is beyond strange. Awkward, to say the least."

"Why do you say that? Because I just met a man you had a relationship with many years ago? You know Carla. You see her probably more often than you'd like."

"Well, that's different. I knew about Carla before you and I became involved. Anyway, I was never in love with Jean-Luc."

Malcolm gathered Augusta in his arms. "I promise I won't swap Augusta stories with Jean-Luc. Ours is the only story that matters to me, and I know I'm the luckiest guy in the world. I love you."

"Good." She buried her face in his shoulder.

He tipped up her chin and kissed her. "What should we do about dinner?"

"Room service. Later." She murmured. "Much later."

Chapter 4
Manon Lescaut and *I Crisantemi*

Saturday, June 5

"I'm still not sure about this." Malcolm gazed at his bride, frowning slightly.

"I'm fine. I'll be fine. We made the right decision." She rested a gloved hand lightly on his cheek and brushed her lips across his.

"You're okay with driving the car home from the airport? Chief Schrotel said he'll arrange to have me picked up once I return."

She smiled at him. "I'm a big girl, Detective. I can handle this."

Her flight was called for the final time, and Malcolm held Augusta for a long moment before she turned to leave.

He pressed something into her hand. "I know you don't like take-offs and landings," he said, quietly.

"Here's something for you to hang onto since I won't be sitting next to you."

She closed her fingers around a small box. "What is it?"

"You'll see. Wait till you're headed down the runway." He smiled and kissed her. "I should be home no later than Friday. Hopefully sooner. The investigation is wrapping up, nothing suspicious found, and Garth is working to expedite all the reams of paperwork."

Augusta moved to the jet bridge to board her flight. She turned back to wave just before she exited the terminal.

Once in her first-class seat, she opened Malcolm's gift. A small silver charm of a mountain chalet, attached to a bracelet with tiny silver links. A memory of the closeness they had experienced in Innsbruck. Augusta leaned back, gazing at her gift, wondering when on earth he'd managed to make the purchase without her knowing about it.

Before she even realized it, they were airborne. She removed her gloves and worked the bracelet onto her wrist. *I may never take it off.*

Driving home by herself from her honeymoon did seem strange, and entering the quiet Tudor on Vista Circle seemed even stranger. Since they had begun their relationship some two years earlier, she and Malcolm had seldom been apart. The last time, some months earlier, had been under extremely difficult circumstances, and Augusta had a fleeting moment of *déjà vu.*

She shivered slightly. *It would be wonderful to come home to Caruso the Wonder Dog*, she thought. But the Golden Shepherd she and Malcolm had taken care of the previous summer for a few months had been happily reunited with his owner, Trevor Davidson, another member of the Cincinnati Police Department.

A tap at her door and she guessed correctly it was Milly.

"Welcome home, Augusta. You do have a protective husband."

"Don't tell me Mal called you." She hugged her friend.

"Oh, he timed your flight, your drive home, and gave me an approximate E.T.A. which was pretty darned accurate." Milly picked up one of Augusta's bags and the women went upstairs.

"He's being ridiculously overprotective, but I'm glad to see you."

"Do you want to get unpacked?" Milly placed the bag on Augusta's bed.

"No, I'd rather talk. I can unpack later. Let's have coffee."

Downstairs in the kitchen, Milly put the coffee on. "What a way to end your honeymoon."

"I had that exact thought when the hotel manager told us about poor Saul." Augusta pulled coffee mugs from a cabinet. "What's happened here since the news crossed the pond?"

"There was an obituary in the paper today. Manny is making arrangements for a memorial concert in a few weeks." She eyed Augusta. "Not a lot of fun, coming home without your groom."

"He was needed in Paris. I think he's secretly enjoying being in on this, even if he's not working the case." She gave Milly a sideways glance. "You won't guess in a million years who the lead investigator is."

"I don't believe I know any French police officers." Mystified, Milly sipped her coffee. "Who?"

"Our old friend, Jean-Luc Marchand."

Milly spit out her coffee. "You're kidding."

"Nope. He served in the military during the Second World War, did some investigative work for something that happened on the base where he was stationed, and that was it. Now he's what the French call an 'O.J.P.'– Officer of the Judicial Police."

"I take it you've seen him." Milly blotted her chin with her napkin.

"Malcolm actually invited him to have drinks with us."

"Well, that must have been interesting." Milly lifted both eyebrows as she stared at her friend.

Augusta laughed. "Oh, indeed it was. I almost fell out of my chair when he came into the lounge. He's hardly changed at all. Still the suave, handsome Frenchman. Maybe even more so."

Milly, her coffee cup halfway to her mouth, set it down abruptly. "Any more surprise remarks before I try drinking my coffee again?"

"No, not really," Augusta chuckled. "Mal and Jean-Luc really hit it off, though." She waved a hand. "I'll tell you all about our fabulous trip later. How is Manny handling this? I would think it will be upsetting if he has to cancel the tour he's been so excited about. What a shame."

"He hasn't made a decision yet, but he told me finding a second violinist for his quartet and getting in the rehearsal time they would need won't be easy. He and the violist and cellist are all three playing with the Summer Opera orchestra."

Augusta nodded. "Michael Robinson, and that sweet kid Ariel Rosen. Ari played cello for our *Pirates of Penzance* orchestra two years ago at Cliffside, and he reminded me so much of Meyer."

"Yes, I remember that. A talented young man with a future ahead of him, I believe." Milly stood. "I should probably get going and let you unpack in peace. Unless ..." She hesitated. "Would you like me to stay?"

"It's not necessary, and I don't want to annoy Garrett. As I told Mal when I got on the plane, I'm a big girl." Augusta took a final sip of her coffee.

"He's remembering last fall, Augusta. We all went through an ordeal. I'm happy to hang out here." Milly rinsed out their cups and placed them in the dishwasher.

"If I know Malcolm, he's going to have a patrol car come by here about every hour. I'll keep the doors and windows locked, and the phone is right by my bed. But there is no way I will let that incident turn me into a shrinking violet."

"Yes, and the man who intended you harm is safely tucked away in a federal prison. Did you actually say 'incident'?"

"Cop talk, my dear." Augusta laughed again and walked Milly to the door. "Go home and be good to Garrett. I'll see you Monday at the Conservatory. Unless you expect to be there tomorrow. I want to go through my student list and do some planning."

"I'll probably stop in my studio for an hour or so. Well, if you're sure you don't want company, I'll take off."

Malcolm phoned early the next morning.

"I'm fine, but I do miss you," She said. "You don't need to call every day. Just when you have some news."

"I need to hear your voice. I miss you like crazy."

"Mal—I love your gift. What a beautiful bracelet. I have no idea when you bought it."

"You were busy yakking it up with that couple from Philadelphia, remember?" He chuckled. "The nice woman in the gift shop had a great time conspiring with me to make the purchase behind your back."

Long-distance calls are hard. But at least we have a great connection, Augusta thought. "Well, it's perfect. Thank you again."

"Do you have anything on for today?"

"I'm headed for the school to do some lesson plans. Milly stopped by last night, but of course, you knew that." She smiled into the telephone.

"I don't like that you're there alone. Not after last fall."

"I don't feel alone. I noticed this patrol car late last night and again early this morning. Slowly driving around Vista Circle. Probably freaking my neighbors out. I can't imagine how that happened, can you?"

"Guilty as charged," he laughed. "Indulge me in this, will you, Gus? I feel better knowing they're on duty since I can't be. Too bad Caruso isn't around to keep watch."

"How funny you should say that. I thought about Caruso last night when I got home. Any idea where Jean-Luc is with his investigation?"

"Nothing suspicious has turned up as yet. Nothing on the autopsy, either. And Garth is moving forward with all the certificates that are necessary to release Saul's remains."

***

Before she headed home from the Conservatory Monday afternoon, Augusta stopped by Immanuel Levine's studio to express her condolences and concern.

"I'm so, so sorry this happened, Manny. Your quartet was off to such a great start. Any thoughts about what your next step might be?"

He leaned back in his desk chair and locked his fingers behind his head. "I think we're going to have to cancel the tour. It's a shame. And you know, we just had a nice offer for some financial assistance. Barry Whittier—you know, the artist and writer—has been to every concert, and he offered to be a patron."

"What a nice offer. Perhaps he'll still be willing to do that."

Manny sat forward. "Possibly. We'll regroup and figure out our next step. It's worth keeping this organization going, Augusta."

Mal called every morning, and finally on Wednesday he told Augusta, "Good news. We're leaving tomorrow, so I should be back in Cincinnati sometime late in the evening."

"Dennis and I have tickets for *Manon Lescaut* tomorrow night. Do you want me to cancel? Maybe give mine to Milly?"

"No, don't do that. It may be after midnight before I get in. Go to the opera, I know you'll have a good time with Dennis. And don't rush home."

"If you're sure. I *am* looking forward to being there. A special night."

***

Thursday, June 10
8:00 p.m.

"Were you here the night Jamie Logan became the darling of the Summer Opera crowd?" Dennis flipped through his program.

"I certainly was. He sang the last three acts of this opera exceptionally well, especially considering he'd only ever performed the second act. It was quite a feat."

It had been three years earlier when Jamie, then a graduate student at the Conservatory, agreed to finish the performance. The tenor singing the leading role of Renato Des Grieux had struggled through the first act, obviously ill, and requested to be replaced. His understudy couldn't be located. Marco Angelico, the stage director, knew Jamie had the role memorized and had performed scenes while a senior in college.

Jamie had performed a supporting role in the first act of the opera and changed into street clothes to be part of the audience. He agreed to sing the final three acts in the leading role with no rehearsal. He had the full support of the audience after they heard the announcement that a tenor graduate student at the Conservatory would be stepping onstage under extraordinary circumstances.

Now considered Cincinnati's operatic 'golden boy,' Jamie had made an impressive Metropolitan Opera debut only a few months earlier which resulted in numerous invitations from opera houses worldwide. A prolonged ovation greeted his first entrance and Maestro Aaron Rubin had to hold the performance for a few minutes to let this crowd greet their tenor.

The audience settled and the performance continued. *Manon Lescaut*, an intense and emotional opera written by a master of theater, Giacomo Puccini, has many powerful moments. Augusta was thrilled by the performances of this fine cast, and when Jamie cried out Manon's name at the end of Act Two as she is arrested for prostitution, Augusta was one of the first people on her feet.

"Oh, this is almost too much," she sighed to Dennis. "I always forget how much I love this opera until I see it again."

"I'm not sure that makes a lot of sense, Augusta," Dennis remarked, grinning.

"Oh, you know what I mean. We get so swept up in what Puccini does. And Jamie—I know he's singing better than he did then because his voice is more mature. His technique is stronger. But honestly, Dennis, he gave a wonderful performance then as well. Because I think he's always done what I hope I teach my students to do—put the music first. Always. We serve the music, and it's our great privilege to share it."

Near the end of Act Three during the duet between Manon and Des Grieux, Augusta heard strains of the music which Puccini first used in the string quartet piece he composed prior to the opera. He wrote it as an elegy to a friend who had died, and hearing it reminded Augusta of poor Saul Kronenberg, who so loved playing it.

In the Fourth Act, Augusta heard even more of the mournful, heart-wrenching music from Puccini's *I Crisantemi*—"The Chrysanthemums"—expanded and embellished, with the voices of soprano and tenor soaring above the orchestra.

Prolonged applause from the crowd at the end of the opera, numerous curtain calls for all, especially Jamie Logan. While the opera is titled for the leading female character, it was definitely his night.

"Want to go to Meck's?" Dennis asked her, as the audience, obviously elated by what they had just experienced, slowly filed from the pavilion in the Zoological Gardens.

"Are you kidding? After that? I wouldn't miss it. And Mal won't be home from Paris until after midnight. Jamie and Meredith invited us to sit with them. I'll meet you there."

Chapter 5
Who Would Murder a Violist?

Friday, June 11

"Steady, Gus."

Malcolm's strong arm around her shoulders did steady Augusta. She still could scarcely believe he had arrived at Mecklenburg's at the moment he was most needed.

He spotted her car parked nearby, guided her to it and opened the front passenger door. Malcolm motioned for Augusta to sit inside as he beckoned to Jim Edmonds.

In a few words, Jim brought Malcolm up to speed on the events of the evening. "I'll head for General Hospital to see where we are with Michael Robinson."

Malcolm nodded and turned his attention to the situation at the restaurant, stepping into the role of lead investigator without a pause. Augusta marveled at how her husband and his partner seemed to almost read each other's minds. Events unfolded quickly as she watched.

So strange. In the past few hours, I've experienced a splendid performance of Manon Lescaut, enjoyed being with great friends in one of my favorite places in Cincinnati, and now I'm sitting here right in the middle of what most likely is another murder investigation.

To someone driving past, the busy activity around Mecklenburg's Bier Garten might have appeared chaotic, but Augusta knew each of the members of the Cincinnati Police Department worked efficiently to fulfill his responsibility. A team diligently examined Michael Robinson's car, inside and out. Crime scene tape surrounded the entire block, and other patrolmen directed traffic away from Highland Avenue.

Anyone who had been at the after party at the restaurant had been moved back inside for questioning. Once inside they had been separated, and some of the cops were taking names and phone numbers from those who weren't in Michael Robinson's party, collecting any small bit of information that might be helpful.

Augusta left the passenger door open. She shivered occasionally, not because of the air being uncomfortably cool, but because of the ongoing trauma of being part of these distressing events. She glanced around at the officers on scene, recognizing several of them. She had met them during various cases Mal had been part of, where she had somehow ended up in the midst of the action.

She nodded at Matt Winters and Harry Johnson, two patrolmen who had been her security detail for a few days during a John Doe murder Mal investigated. Also on the scene, she saw Trevor Davidson, the young cop originally from Philadelphia who was Caruso's owner. They'd cared for the dog when Trevor had been wounded nearly a year earlier in a shootout while he worked on a drug case with Malcolm. Augusta had never owned a pet in her life, and at first, found it challenging. Now she could look back and laugh at the affectionate, goofy, smart, amazing animal who loved to gnaw on her stilettos.

Off to one side barking orders stood Sergeant Jake O'Malley, running the show for this current operation. She'd met him the previous fall during the most frightening experience of her life.

Augusta admired all of them, part of a well-coordinated team of dedicated law enforcement officers. Oh, she knew they weren't supermen, but they had chosen what she considered one of the toughest jobs in the world. Daily they strapped on a gun, clipped on a shield, and walked out of their homes, sworn to protect and serve the citizens of this city.

Sometimes they didn't make it back. *Like poor Patrolman Martin. Don and his wife expecting a child...he survives three campaigns in Korea and comes home to be killed on Reading Road.* Augusta knew it could happen to Malcolm as well, and breathed a prayer every time he left the house: *Lord, keep him safe.*

Before Malcolm had gone inside the restaurant to oversee the witness interviews, he loaded his luggage into the trunk of her car.

"Do you have any idea how glad I am to see you?" she had asked, gazing at him. "How in the world did you manage to show up at the exact moment I was most wishing you were here?"

"I told you the chief had arranged for a patrol car to pick me up at the airport." Malcolm gave her what she thought of as his thousand-watt smile as he eased the trunk closed. "We'd just driven across the bridge when we received the call from Mecklenburg's, so I asked the patrolmen to bring me directly here. You'd told me you had tickets for the opera tonight so I figured you might still be around."

Mal glimpsed around quickly to be sure no one was watching and kissed her softly. "I'm glad to see you, too, Gus. I sure missed you."

A glance at her watch showed the time as nearly two-thirty. She knew Malcolm had been interviewing the people who sat with Michael during the evening. *It's surreal. It might be a movie.* She was sure Michael was dead, despite Dennis' and Sam's best efforts. *Not just dead. Murdered.*

Patrol cars blocked each end of Highland Avenue where the restaurant was located. Another pulled up, and Jim Edmonds, who had been at General Hospital, jumped out at the same moment Malcolm emerged from Mecklenburg's. The men met next to Augusta's car.

"Robinson was sitting with five other men from the orchestra," Malcolm said. "I'm told he had dinner and a couple of beers. One of his friends offered to drive him home, but he insisted he'd be okay. They all agreed he left just after one a.m. and he didn't seem impaired."

"What did the patrolmen learn from the other witnesses? Anything?" Jim ran a hand over his dark crew cut.

Mal shook his head. "Not really. Since it was a private post-opera event, the crowd in the restaurant consisted of musicians, their friends, and some family members. Everybody appeared to be having a good time, and nobody saw anything out of the ordinary. Just your typical post-opera celebration, a lot of talking and some singing. Food and drink in abundance. We're going to let them go as soon as we have names, addresses, and phone numbers for everybody."

"The doc in the ER who examined Robinson pronounced him dead as soon as he arrived at the hospital. The body is on its way to the morgue, but it was pretty apparent what happened," Jim said. "The doctor showed me. Two puncture wounds in the inner carotid artery."

"Any idea what he was injected with?"

"Whatever it was, it was a massive amount, enough to stop his heart within minutes."

"Sounds like the murderer knew what he was doing, injecting into the carotid artery. And had some pharmaceutical knowledge as well. A person with a medical background, maybe?"

"Any thoughts from the witnesses about a possible perp?" Jim asked.

"They're all in shock. Michael Robinson was as nice a guy as you'd ever want to meet. Happily married, nice wife—also a musician. Two teenage kids. Went out of his way to be helpful. Very popular with the orchestra members."

Jim leaned against the car. "Well, somebody had it in for him. Whoever killed him may not have even been at the beer garden, but knew he would be here. Here's one theory: the perp waited for him to come out and then somehow got into the car with him and killed him, then locked all the doors and took off. He may have even deliberately pushed the body against the steering wheel so he'd be found pretty quickly."

"*Dear God.*" Augusta gasped involuntarily and both men glanced over at her. She stepped out of the car and stood next to them, hugging herself. "That's horrible. Why would anyone do that? Call attention to a murder they had just committed?"

"Some kind of warning?" Mal speculated. "Who kills a violist? And why?"

The witnesses were permitted to leave. Some scurried away quickly; others lingered, talking to friends, their faces troubled. A tow truck arrived to take the car to the Crime Lab for additional tests. Two patrolmen would stand duty at the restaurant for the night as others scoured the restaurant interior and grounds for anything suspicious.

"One thing's for sure … the musical community in this town has never seen anything like this." Malcolm turned to Jim. "I have the address. I'll take this one."

Augusta shivered again. Someone—most often a detective—had to notify the next of kin. What had Malcolm said? *A wife, two teenage kids.* She had met them: Alicia, Mike Junior, and Jake, who had just turned thirteen. Three lives changed forever.

"No, I'll handle it," Jim offered. "I was first on scene, anyway. Besides, you have to be exhausted. An eight-hour flight from Paris, two hours with Saul Kronenberg's family at JFK, and then flying home? How long have you been up?"

"Feels like forever," agreed Malcolm, nodding. "Are you sure? This is going to be a tough one."

"Go home and get some sleep. We won't know anything more until the coroner has completed his examination of the body and run toxicology tests, and that's going to take a while."

Mal glanced down the street. "*Damn.*"

Jim turned to see what caused the outburst and spotted Arnold Richter, a reporter for *The Cincinnati Morning Call*, striding toward them.

"Ah. One of your favorite people," Jim grinned. "I'm out of here. You're on your own with this guy." Jim stepped into his car and quickly pulled away.

"Detective Mitchell." Richter gazed at Augusta. "Mrs. Mitchell."

"Fancy meeting you here, Arnold." Mal did sarcasm well.

Richter, a slight, scholarly-looking man with thinning light hair, whipped out his notebook, pen at the ready. "We had a tip that one of the Summer Opera orchestra members was found dead in his car outside the restaurant. Can you provide any additional information? Name of the deceased?"

"The victim was transported to General Hospital, so your information about him being found dead is incorrect. We have no further comment at this time."

"Was there foul play involved, Detective?" Richter scribbled as he talked.

"Again, Mr. Richter, no comment. I'm sure a statement will be issued by the department when appropriate."

Richter slapped his notebook shut. "May I congratulate you on your marriage?"

Augusta fielded that one. "Of course. Thank you, Mr. Richter."

Malcolm glared at the reporter's back as he wandered away.

"Mal … he's just doing his job." A hand on his arm.

"I know that. The guy gets under my skin. I can't forget how he tried to pump you for information when I had that John Doe murder case."

"He was just doing his job then, too." She smoothed a lapel, studying his face. "You really dislike him, don't you?"

"What I dislike most was that he brought up Meyer Abrams and lied to you about the paper doing a feature on him." A frown. "Playing on your sympathy."

Augusta waved a hand. "It's ancient history. Let's go home so you can take Jim's excellent advice and get a few hours' sleep. Want me to drive?"

"No, I'll drive. I'm fine." He moved to the opposite side of the car and Augusta returned to her seat.

I'm not so sure you're fine, my love. She saw the lines of exhaustion etching his face but didn't comment.

Mal adjusted the mirror and turned on the engine, driving down Burnet Avenue to Oak, as he worked his way toward Madison Road.

"What you said when you first arrived at Meck's ... about this being some welcome home." Augusta stared out of the window.

"Nothing like jumping right back into the fray," Mal remarked. "Did we have that great honeymoon, or was it a dream?"

"Oh, it was real. And it was definitely wonderful ... until the last couple of days."

"Kronenberg's relatives are nice folks." He worked to stifle a yawn. "I offered to accompany them to Connecticut once we arrived at JFK. They wouldn't hear of it, so I grabbed the first flight to Cincinnati. Obviously, a good choice."

Malcolm rubbed the back of his neck as they drove in silence for a few moments. *Another sign of how tired you are*, thought Augusta. *Well, we're almost home. And you're going to bed the minute we walk through the door.*

"Premeditated murder. A musician who was well-liked, respected, apparently no enemies. It makes no sense." He shook his head.

"Yes, he was well-liked. A fine performer." Augusta sighed. "Poor Manny. Now I think all his dreams of resurrecting the Chrysanthemum Quartet may never come to fruition."

Malcolm sharply whipped the car to the right, pulled up against the curb, and stopped so abruptly Augusta had to grab the dashboard.

"What did you say?" He stared at her.

"He was well-liked? A fine performer?"

"No. That last part. About the quartet."

"Michael played viola for the quartet. So now they've lost two members."

"The quartet's second violinist suddenly died in Paris. And now the violist was apparently murdered." Mal smacked his palm on the steering wheel. "Obviously, Saul didn't perform with the Summer Opera orchestra, or he wouldn't have been in Paris, he'd have been in Cincinnati rehearsing. Was he a member of the Cincinnati Symphony ... or were he and Michael only associated through the quartet?"

"He used to be in the symphony, but he left about three years ago. So, at present, he and Michael only performed together in the quartet."

Oh, Lord. She returned his stare as the implications of what had just been discussed dawned on her. "You mean maybe Saul's death wasn't from natural causes after all. Two string players who were closely associated, both dead within a few days of each other." She clenched her suddenly icy hands together. "It's hard to believe it could have been a coincidence."

"One in Europe, one here. If those two deaths are connected ... that took a lot of careful plotting. For one thing, the killer must have been someone who knew Kronenberg well."

"Why do you say that?"

"How else would he have known Kronenberg would be in Paris?"

"You know—when his body was found in our hotel, that shocked me. But it didn't surprise me to learn he was in Paris. I knew he was attending an event at the Sorbonne. How did I know that?"

"Well, you worked in the same building. Maybe someone told you about his plans."

"Maybe, but I don't think so." She thought for a moment. "Oh, I remember. An article appeared in the *Cincinnati Morning Call* not long before our wedding. All about the Chrysanthemum Quartet's plans for their upcoming European tour. One paragraph discussed what they'd be doing over the summer, and Saul was quoted that he'd be spending time in Paris, attending a seminar at the Sorbonne at the end of May."

Mal nodded. "So, anyone who followed the quartet's activities would likely have read that article."

"I would think so."

His eyes narrowed. "Tell me this—why would anybody want to kill off a string quartet?"

Ignoring the question, Augusta gripped Malcolm's arm, alarm bells sounding in her head. "Mal—what about the two remaining members? Immanuel Levine and Ariel Rosen?"

"If someone *is* targeting the quartet—either of them could be next."

Susan Moore Jordan

Chapter 6
Coincidence or No?

As soon as they walked into the house, Malcolm headed for the alcove and picked up the phone.

"Get me Hartford, Connecticut. Office of the coroner," he barked at the operator. Covering the mouthpiece with his hand, he said to Augusta, "Can you put some coffee on?"

"Saul's body won't be there, will it? I would imagine the family had it taken to a funeral home." *No way am I fixing coffee for you, my love. You're about to pass out on your feet.*

"Yes, but the coroner can find where it is and have it brought to the morgue. Provided the family agrees."

Augusta pointed at the clock. "Well, you can hardly call them now. Won't this wait for a few hours?"

Malcolm reluctantly replaced the handset. "Yes, you're right. I'd probably only get an answering machine at the coroner's office at this time of night anyway."

Augusta put her arms around her husband. "Let's go to bed, Mal. You're exhausted. You can get four hours sleep between now and seven."

Her weary detective fell asleep almost instantly, but Augusta found her mind churning. *What about Manny and Ari? They have to be made aware of this. They could be in danger.* The question Malcolm had asked in the car stayed foremost in her thoughts. *Who would want to destroy a string quartet by killing off its members? What kind of twisted person would do this?*

While she had been acquainted with Saul and Michael, Augusta considered Manny a friend and she had a special fondness for Ari Rosen, who reminded her so much of another young, vibrant cellist from her past. She recalled her first meeting all those years ago with Meyer, an encounter in the school dining room which resulted in an immediate connection. She was a junior, he a freshman, but Meyer's passion for music had awakened in Augusta a deeper understanding of her art. She had been technically proficient, but Meyer showed her how music could inspire and uplift as nothing else could.

She saw that same passion in Ari. Augusta felt Ari's youthful enthusiasm spilled over to the other, older members of the group, adding excitement and fire to their performances. Augusta had wondered how long Ari would be content to be part of a quartet, because she also saw ambition, and thought he'd eventually embark on a solo career. Just as she was sure Meyer would have if he hadn't died so young.

The aroma of coffee woke her a few minutes after seven, and she drew on a robe and ran downstairs to find Malcolm, showered, shaved, dressed, and ready for the day, just hanging up the phone.

"That was the Hartford coroner. He's going to try to locate Saul Kronenberg's body and ask the funeral director to hold off on any plans until I've had a chance to contact the family." He poured a cup of coffee for her.

"That isn't going to be an easy call to make." She added sugar and cream and stirred.

"No, it sure isn't. How do you tell a man that his brother might have been murdered, and it would be helpful to have a second autopsy performed?" He pulled a strip of paper from his wallet and she watched him transfer information to his note pad.

"That's the number you have? Saul's brother?"

"Yes, Roger. Very nice guy. We exchanged numbers at JFK yesterday ... just in case." He sighed. "I had a bad feeling about this from the beginning."

"Yes, I know you did. I also know your instincts are seldom wrong." She stood and started into the kitchen. "What can I get you? Cereal? Eggs?"

"Toast is fine. I'll get something later. I need to get to Headquarters."

Augusta put bread in the toaster. "How about some fruit? I picked up grapefruit and some fresh apricots and plums."

"That sounds good." Mal stared at the phone number on his notepad.

"Mal—Saul's body was embalmed. They can't do another toxicology test, can they? After blood is removed for embalming?"

"Actually, they can. It won't be complete, but there could be traces of drugs or poison in the tissue samples. And the coroner can certainly examine the body for a puncture wound. My bet is the perp injected him in a place he figured nobody would find."

"How would he do that?" Augusta put a plate with buttered toast and fruit in front of Malcolm.

"Probably drugged him before he was injected. Slipped a Mickey into a drink would be my guess. It most likely was somebody Saul knew, or had met in Paris."

"And then the killer injected him, carefully cleaned up after himself, and left the room, locking the door. So that it wouldn't appear anyone else had been there."

"You got it." Mal ate quickly, then picked up the phone, clearing his throat. "Roger Kronenberg, please." A pause. "Mr. Kronenberg, this is Detective Malcolm Mitchell with the Cincinnati Police Department. We met at JFK yesterday."

Another pause. "Yes, I appreciated the chance to speak with you as well, Roger." A deep breath. "This will be difficult for you to hear. When I returned to Cincinnati last night, I learned a colleague of your brother's had died. There may have been foul play involved."

Augusta realized she was holding her breath as she listened.

"The death is still under investigation, but yes, it's possible he was murdered."

There it is. That awful word. She shuddered slightly.

"Because of this, I need to make a request of you. I need to ask if you would allow the Hartford coroner to perform a second autopsy before Saul is interred."

A longer pause, and while she couldn't make out the words, Augusta could hear the anguish in Roger Kronenberg's raised voice.

"Yes, it would be helpful, and I'm sure if Saul did not die of natural causes, you and his other family members would want to know that."

Mal glanced at Augusta as he listened to the response. "Thank you, Roger. I'll ask the coroner to be in touch with you to make the necessary arrangements. You'll hear from one of us after we have the results. I can only imagine how hard this is for you, and I regret it's necessary."

Mal blew out a breath as he hung up the phone. "Poor guy. That was tough."

"On the detective as well, I think." Augusta laid a sympathetic hand on Malcolm's arm.

He drained his coffee mug. "I'll call the Hartford coroner from Headquarters. I need to let Jim Edmonds and the chief know what's going on."

She stood, wrapped her arms around him, and kissed him. "Please keep me posted. When will you have results from the coroner about how Michael died?"

"I don't think there's any doubt he was murdered by means of a lethal injection. We just need to find out what."

"How will they do that?"

"It's very possible testing his blood will show what it was. That could be done pretty quickly. They may want to run a full tox screen, and test tissue and other bodily fluids as well, just to be sure. That can take weeks."

Augusta gazed at him. "If somebody is gunning for string quartet members, I doubt we have weeks."

Mal held her by the shoulders and stared into her face. "Did you just say 'we'?"

"Well … yes, I did. I'm very concerned about Manny and Ariel. Can the CPD provide protective details for them?"

"You're getting way ahead of yourself, Gus. At the moment all we know is that Michael Robinson died last night under suspicious circumstances. Coincidentally, a fellow Chrysanthemum Quartet member died a few days earlier in a Paris hotel room." Malcolm headed for the front door, ready to leave.

Augusta ran ahead of him. "Call me and let me know if the coroner has finished his exam, will you? Especially if he confirms that Michael was poisoned by injection."

She positioned herself between him and the front door. "The next thing you'll need to do is find out everything you can about these four men, correct? Saul, Michael, Manny, Ari? I know—knew—all of them. I can help you with this."

He shook his head and grinned at her. "Don't you have lessons to teach today?"

"That's the point. I'll already be at the Conservatory. You know I have access to the school records. I can get some preliminary information for you, at least."

"I don't suppose there's any point in me telling you not to start sleuthing, is there?"

"Not a bit. Call me when you get a chance." She embraced him warmly and kissed him again.

***

Augusta looked over her notes about the quartet members. The three established, mature string players all had earned two degrees, performed in various musical organizations, and were well regarded by their fellow musicians in Cincinnati. Their files all showed several newspaper articles of each man receiving recognition for some accomplishment. Saul had been part of a group of musicians who established workshops for high school students. Michael and his wife had organized a children's orchestra in the charming village of Wyoming, just outside Cincinnati. Manny was known as a mentor and coach for aspiring violinists and had provided funds for more than one to enter competitions. Exemplary human beings, exceptional musicians. Young Ariel Rosen had a bright future. He'd been a stellar student as an undergraduate at the Conservatory, and had won a prestigious competition himself last year.

She sighed. *I know Malcolm and Jim will investigate each of them thoroughly, just to see if there are any potential enemies in their backgrounds.* Certainly, at first glance, there was nothing in the school records.

When Malcolm called and told her the coroner had found the drug digoxin in Michael's blood, the confirmation of the murder saddened but did not shock her. *What a senseless act, taking the life of a kind person who had a family and tried to do good by sharing his music with kids.*

"Ironically," Malcolm had explained, "digoxin is a drug used to treat patients with atrial fibrillation, to slow their heart rate, so it saves lives. But an overdose is deadly."

"So the Hartford coroner will be looking for digoxin in Saul's body, too?"

"They may or may not find it. The drug disappears within a number of days. But a puncture wound could still be there."

A tap at her door roused her from her reverie, and Manny Levine opened it and stuck his head into her studio. "I didn't hear any singing. Do you have a minute?"

Augusta casually moved a music book on top of the papers on her desk. "I'm finished for the day, Manny. Please, come in."

The slender, dark-haired, bespectacled musician eased into a chair across from her desk. "What do you know about Michael Robinson's sudden death?"

"What have you heard?"

Manny gripped the arms of the chair. "You may know I didn't go to Meck's last night after the opera performance. Linda was with me, and she wasn't feeling well, so we went straight home." He leaned forward, taking off his glasses and wiping them with his handkerchief. "Ari was there, at Michael's table. He tells me you and your priest friend found Michael in his car."

He replaced the glasses, shoving them far up on his nose with an index finger. "Then the police showed up, and they rushed Michael to the hospital. Some other cops asked questions and kept everybody there until they'd finished. It was obvious something bad had happened. And now we get word from Alicia that he died last night."

"Yes, I'm sorry to confirm all of that. How sad for Alicia and the boys."

Manny nervously repeated the eyeglass-wiping routine. "Augusta, I need to know how Michael died. There was some speculation about a heart attack. Saul died of a heart attack in Paris, about a week ago. What the hell is going on?"

"The police are investigating Michael's death, Manny. That's really all I know," Augusta lied.

He stared at her piercingly. "I have a hard time believing that, Mrs. Mitchell. Ari said your husband showed up and he was the one who questioned the people who were sitting with Michael at Mecklenburg's."

"Honestly, Manny, Michael's death is still under investigation."

"Yes, I get that. I also have to think the police found it a—what do they say? —a 'suspicious death.' Otherwise, why would they be asking all the questions and detaining people?"

"I understand your concern."

Manny leaned back and heaved a sigh. "I have to tell you. I'm very uneasy about this."

And I believe you have every right to be, thought Augusta. "What are you thinking, Manny?" she said aloud.

"Saul dies in Paris, and we're told he had a heart attack. Well, that's not impossible. Saul just turned fifty-one, but he was a bachelor who had never been great about taking care of himself. His diet was terrible and he never exercised, that kind of thing. His family told me they thought he had some problems with his heart when he was young. So, it's terribly sad, but everybody accepts that's what happened. You were there, so I guess you knew about all this."

Augusta nodded. "Yes. The police in Paris did a thorough investigation."

"Then only a week later, Michael has a heart attack, or that's the story we're getting at the moment. Michael wasn't even forty, and he was in excellent health. You're damn right his death was 'suspicious'." Manny drummed his fingers on the arm of his chair.

"Well, as I said, the police are still investigating."

"You were right there, Augusta. You and Father Halloran found him, right? How did he look to you?"

Augusta hesitated. *I have to be honest with Manny, but I don't want to say too much.* "Dennis and Sam Varnay tried to perform CPR on Michael. The cops got there very fast, and rushed him to General Hospital. They had a bag over his nose and mouth."

"Did you think he had a heart attack?"

"I'm not sure what you're asking."

"I mean, did you see any wounds? I know this sounds gruesome, but maybe you can imagine what's been going on in my head. Did he look like somebody may have attacked him in some way?"

"Why would anyone have done that? Michael was a great guy, a real asset to the music community in this city. A great husband and father, from everything I know about him."

Manny stared off into the distance. "I'm probably letting my imagination run away with me, Augusta. I just don't believe Michael died of a heart attack." He sighed. "But I sure can't imagine anybody wanting to murder him, either."

Careful, Augusta. Leave that question to your detective. Don't say it. "Do you know if he had any enemies?"

"Certainly not. You just said yourself Michael is— was—one of the best people we know." He stared hard at her again. "You realize this pretty much means the end of the Chrysanthemum Quartet. The only people left now are Ari and myself."

"That's so sad. Please don't give up on your dream, Manny. Why not wait until after opera season ends and then hold auditions? I'm sure you'll find people who would love to be part of your quartet."

He stood. "Really? Would you want to be part of a quartet that's seen half its members die within a week? And the second under suspicious circumstances?"

Manny walked to the door and opened it, but turned back to Augusta. "Whether deliberate or not, I think it's the final curtain for the quartet."

Augusta stood. "Wait, Manny. Do you think there could be any reason—any reason at all—someone might want that to happen?"

He stood quietly for a moment, then slowly closed the door. "I can think of one person." A pause.

"But he died nearly a year ago."

Chapter 7
Anton

Friday, June 11
6:00 p.m.

"Anton Portnov."

Malcolm served himself another generous piece of lasagna. "Did you know him?"

It pleased Augusta to see Malcolm thoroughly enjoying her cooking. Until he came into her life, she had avoided learning to cook, but she liked preparing meals for the two of them. While not the gourmet cook her friend Milly was, she had come a long way, and lasagna was her specialty.

"I met him briefly one evening. Young—I'd guess mid-twenties—very good-looking. He and Manny were headed to Manny's studio for a quartet rehearsal. Over a year ago, I think, maybe in early March. They needed a cellist, and Anton had answered the notice Manny posted."

"What else do you know about him?"

"Not a lot. He had an opportunity to audition for the Cincinnati Symphony Orchestra because they were looking for a cellist to replace a musician whose bad health forced him to resign. The orchestra hired Anton, and he moved here I think in January."

Mal wiped his mouth and hands and pushed the plate back, resting his elbows on the table. "You said he didn't work out with the quartet. Does that mean he wasn't very good?"

"Not at all." Augusta sipped her wine. "In fact, he was brilliant. Manny said he was technically one of the finest cellists he'd ever heard. And that could have been the problem."

"Why is that?"

"Well, a string quartet is a unique organization," Augusta remarked. "I don't care what your musical genre is, you need to be technically proficient. That's true for a singer—have you ever tried to listen to someone who can't sing in tune or keep a beat? Painful. It's even more true for instrumentalists. The other thing you need is the ability to connect with the listener. To express the composer's emotional intentions as well as your own."

"He couldn't do that?"

"No, he did it well. But with a quartet, there's an added complication. Four musicians who have to perform as if they are one person. They have to be sensitive to each other, to be willing to sometimes compromise their own ideas for the sake of unity of performance."

Mal lifted an eyebrow. "That can't be easy."

"It isn't. But when a great quartet comes together and can do that, the music is magical. It's fascinating to watch and hear such a group. It was sad, but apparently, Anton had too much ego to make his participation possible. And after six weeks of rehearsal—nearly daily—they decided to replace him. Apparently, Anton didn't take it well."

She pushed her chair back. "Anyway, you need to hear all this from Manny. There may be more he can tell you."

"Yes, I need to see him. You said Manny was uneasy about the two deaths following so closely, especially since Michael's death was already under investigation."

"One of the last things he said to me was he planned to call Bell Telephone and make arrangements to have a burglar alarm installed in his house. I think he's scared, Mal."

"With good cause, I'm afraid. The Hartford coroner got back to me. Of course, any toxicology report is going to take some time, and will probably be incomplete. But his examination of Saul's body did show a possible, if unusual, injection site. A bruise under one arm, and even all this time later some redness that might indicate a possible puncture."

"How did they miss that?"

"The medical examiner in France didn't remove the hair."

Augusta shivered. "You're saying it's entirely possible Saul was murdered as well."

"I'm saying I think it could be what happened. It's still inconclusive." He stared at her piercingly. "I know I don't have to tell you to keep that under your hat."

"Of course not. Cause of death is never revealed unless or until necessary."

"And since Anton Portnov has been dead for months—we've lost our number one suspect." Mal pushed his chair back. "Well, fortunately Aaron Rubin was cooperative and agreed to cancel the opera performance. We can go over to the Levins' tonight. I called him earlier and they're expecting us around eight."

Augusta carried the lasagna dish into the kitchen. "You know, I wonder if that's ever happened before— the Summer Opera canceling a performance. You must have been very persuasive, Detective."

Malcolm helped Augusta in the kitchen, cleaning dishes and cutlery, and wrapping the lasagna for another meal. "By the way, Gus, Jim Edmonds thinks we should investigate you," he smirked.

"*What?!*"

"Well, you were present when Saul died. At least, you were in the hotel. And you were on hand when Michael's body was found. At the moment, you're the only person we can place at both scenes."

Augusta stared at her husband, open-mouthed, and he burst out laughing. She punched him on the arm.

"That's not funny, Mal." But her twitching lips gave her away, and she joined in the laugh.

"Gotcha. Jim dared me to do it. It's his fault."

"Cops can have the strangest sense of humor. I guess you sometimes have to find humor somewhere in the midst of all the—I don't even know what to call it. The constant bad stuff you have to deal with."

"It's one way to keep from being overwhelmed by what we face daily. You should be complimented. I'd never say something like that to another civilian."

"Does this mean I'm an honorary member of the CPD?"

"Hardly. Don't get carried away, Gus." He frowned. "And you know exactly what I'm referring to."

Augusta lowered her eyes contritely. "I'll be good, Detective. I promise."

***

"I love this house," Manny Levine said. They were seated in the study in his stately Victorian house in North Avondale, only a few blocks from historic Rockdale Temple, where Manny and his family frequently attended services, and where Augusta had on occasion been part of a special choir for the Jewish High Holy Days.

Linda, Manny's pretty blond wife, placed a tray of tea and cookies on the coffee table and served them. Linda was popular with Manny's colleagues, some of whom remembered her as a graduate piano student some twenty-five years earlier who performed with a fellow grad student, an outstanding violinist named Immanuel.

97

Linda eventually converted to Judaism and married the man she adored.

Manny smiled thanks at Linda as he continued, "Some of my neighbors are moving to the suburbs, but I grew up here. My family is comfortable here, and I'm reluctant to leave."

Augusta glanced around the room. Floor to ceiling bookshelves, crammed with books, lined three of the walls. A Baldwin Acrosonic spinet piano stood against the fourth wall, bracketed by tall windows draped in green damask.

"Just the idea of moving all our books is daunting," Linda laughed.

Augusta picked up a book from the coffee table. "Have you read this yet? I see it's by Barry Whittier." She glanced at the title, *The Death of a Prince.*

"I'm reading it. I bought it at a book signing he did recently at Pogue's. You know, he's quite a supporter of the Chrysanthemum Quartet. In fact, he made a lovely offer to Manny to be a sponsor."

"Yes, I'd heard that."

"He wanted to take us to dinner to discuss his ideas. I was looking forward to it but I guess that can't happen now." Linda sighed.

"We can still go out for a nice dinner, Linda. Just maybe not quite so fancy. We're not rich like Barry Whittier," Manny commented. "Maintaining this old house is becoming increasingly expensive. But our kids are happy here. The schools have been wonderful," Manny remarked.

Augusta sipped her tea. "Walnut Hills is a great high school. They certainly have an outstanding music program."

Manny set his cup and saucer on the coffee table. "But you're here to find out more about Anton Portnov."

Malcolm nodded. "Yes. Augusta explained he moved to Cincinnati in the winter of 1964 and died in an auto accident only a few months later. How well did you know him?"

"Anton wasn't social at all. Nobody really knew him; he lived in a one-bedroom apartment in Clifton. I only saw him at quartet rehearsals. I have no idea who his friends were—or even if he had any."

"Augusta told me you replaced him as cellist for the quartet. Something about ego? She gave me an idea of how a string quartet works."

Manny glanced at Augusta and nodded. "When you spend as much time rehearsing as we do, it's important to have four people who have similar goals. Who are comfortable with a lot of give-and-take. Anton didn't seem to get that. He wanted to be the dominant musician in the group, and for us to accede to his ideas about the music we played. It just doesn't work that way, and he was never able to understand that. He left rehearsals angry more often than not."

Linda nibbled on a cookie. "It was more than that, though, Manny." She glanced at Malcolm. "The other members of the quartet gave him every chance. It perturbed Saul that he could tell Anton sometimes drank before a rehearsal. Michael was concerned about his mood swings. But the final straw was when he showed up obviously high on something."

"When I told him we regrettably needed to find another cellist, he was positively livid. He accused us of ruining his life. We tried to reason with him and pointed out he was doing that all on his own, and he needed to get himself straightened out."

Malcolm leaned forward. "Did he threaten you?"

"Well ... yes, in a way. He told us we'd be sorry for firing the greatest cellist of the modern era. We didn't take the threat seriously." Manny shook his head sadly. "Anton was a talented young man, despite his failings, and we were sad to hear about the accident in which he was killed."

Malcolm sat back, elbows on the arms of his chair, and steepled his fingertips. "After I spoke with Augusta earlier, I looked into the accident. Just north of the airport. He veered off the road to avoid a collision and hit a tree head-on."

Manny rubbed the back of his neck. "We weren't aware he'd been killed until we saw it in the news. I remember hearing something about his apartment being searched, trying to find a name for next of kin. But that was odd, apparently there were no family names or addresses. No indication as to where he lived before he came here. It almost seemed as if there was no Anton Portnov before January of 1964, you know?"

"You may know that more than a week after his death, a couple showed up at the coroner's office in Boone County and identified themselves as his parents," Malcolm said. "They arranged transport for the body.

For some reason, there's no record as to where it was taken. My partner, Detective Edmonds, is attempting to locate the family."

Manny leaned forward. "How do you even know where to start looking?" He grimaced. "It's almost as if Anton might have been an alien." He whistled the theme of *The Twilight Zone* television program, making them all laugh.

"There's been some change in staff since the accident, but one of the old staff members believes the people were from somewhere in the D.C. area." Mal reached for a second cookie. "Since Portnov was so non-communicative—I suppose he never mentioned any associates of any kind? Did anyone ever show up to meet him after a rehearsal?"

"No, no one. I wish I could be of more help, Malcolm."

Malcolm stood and extended a hand to Augusta, helping her to her feet. "Thanks for seeing us, Manny, Linda." He glanced around as they left the study and moved into the spacious entrance hall. "This is a beautiful old mansion. Something I love about my city, these great houses built in the nineteenth century."

Augusta linked her arm into Linda's. "I can't leave without viewing the photo gallery that lines the staircase," she said, and the women started up the steps, chatting.

"Five sons, Linda. My goodness. And all such handsome young men." Augusta looked carefully at each photo as Linda proudly described the occasion at which it was taken.

"I have two sons," Malcolm told Manny. "One's an attorney, and the other I'm afraid is following in his old man's footsteps."

Manny chuckled. "Do you believe, not one serious musician in our lot? Oh, they love music, and all of them were—or are—involved in music in high school. Aaron's the oldest, he's in med school now. The next two are in college, and the two youngest are still at Walnut Hills. Since Aaron's at General Hospital and Barry and Seth are at U.C., all five of them still live at home."

"About that burglar alarm," Malcolm began.

Manny lifted a hand. "It's being installed tomorrow. It seemed like a good idea." He ran a hand across the back of his neck again. "Maybe Saul's death was a coincidence. But I'm having a tough time processing why anyone would want to kill Michael."

"It could have been a robbery attempt gone wrong," Malcolm offered.

Augusta glanced at her husband, thinking, *that might ease Manny's mind a little. Not a bad idea, at least for now.*

They drove past more beautiful mansions as they left the neighborhood, Rockdale Temple a majestic sentinel standing proudly in the moonlight. "I love these grand old neighborhoods, Gus. The thing about a city is, though … you wonder how long they'll be here."

"Beautiful young men. Five sons. And Linda says they all still live at home, even though the older three are in college."

"Yes, Manny's fortunate to have a houseful of strong young men around him. I believe he made a wise

102

choice about that burglar alarm, though, and I'll make sure a patrol car comes around this neighborhood frequently."

Augusta rested her head on the back of the seat and gazed at her detective. "What did you learn from your background checks of the quartet members?"

He glanced at her. "So far, not a thing. No defaulted debts, no arrest records—oh, Saul had some unpaid parking tickets—no unsavory family members. At least not that we've uncovered at this point."

"It sure seems as if Anton Portnov would have been the most likely suspect. He sounds like a real piece of work. Alcohol, drugs, maybe a mood disorder? And a threat the last time Manny saw him."

"It was strange that no trace of his past showed up in his apartment. I need to know who the people were who claimed his remains from the accident in Northern Kentucky. I sure hope whoever handled that transfer didn't totally screw up the records."

"You're thinking Anton's death is somehow connected to Saul's and Michael's?"

"We can't ignore that possibility ... or any possibility for that matter. The other thing, we need to talk to other residents in that apartment building, and neighboring buildings as well. See if we can learn where Portnov shopped. Bars and restaurants in Clifton he may have frequented. Maybe someone knew Anton better than his fellow musicians did."

"What about the person who manages the building he lived in?"

"Yes, we'll need to talk to that person as well." He gave a sharp laugh. "This situation may give a whole new meaning to the words 'cold case.'"

Augusta sat up and turned toward him. "I'm concerned about Ariel Rosen. I think he's more vulnerable than Manny. He lives in an apartment in Mt. Auburn, close to the Conservatory."

Mal pulled up into the driveway of their Tudor home. "What else do you know about him?"

"Unlike Anton, he has a lot of friends. He's quite gregarious. I've told you he reminds me of Meyer."

Malcolm locked the car and they went up the steps to the front door.

"Yes, you have. More than once." He sounded slightly annoyed.

Oh, dear. I have to fix this. She wrapped her arms around his waist and pulled herself close to him.

"Are you still on Paris time? I know how tired you were last night," she breathed in his ear.

Malcolm unlocked the front door and abruptly swept his bride off her feet, lifting her into his arms. Augusta's gasp of surprise turned into a giggle.

"Isn't this a wedding tradition?" He grinned at her rakishly. "The groom carrying the bride across the threshold?"

"I've heard that." She caressed his face. "What comes next, groom?"

"Oh, you're about to find out, bride."

Chapter 8
Ariel

Saturday, June 12
2:00 a.m.

They were standing someplace high up—on a hilltop? She couldn't really tell. Strange lights illuminated the darkened sky. Augusta heard sounds but couldn't sort out what they were. She was frightened but didn't know why. Ariel Rosen stood nearby. She could barely make him out, the lights were a problem. Augusta shaded her eyes to see him better. He gazed at her and started to speak.

Her eyes flew open and a chill ran through her entire body. Heart racing, she fought to orient herself. She pressed her face against her husband's back, pulling the covers tight to her body.

I heard Ari's voice. No, I couldn't have. I'm lying in bed next to Malcolm. But it seemed so real.

Malcolm reached over to the bedside table and turned the lamp on. "Bad dream?"

Augusta nodded. "The worst. Something was very wrong. I would swear I actually heard Ari's voice. But I can't remember what he said." She shivered.

"I know you're concerned about him, Gus." Malcolm put his arms around her and pulled her close. "And I understand. It's more than concern for Ari. It's the thought that another bright young cellist could have his light extinguished too soon, like Meyer." He stroked her hair back from her face.

Augusta sighed and relaxed into Malcolm's warm, strong embrace. "What did I ever do in my life to deserve you? I'm the luckiest woman in the world."

"Maybe because you climbed over a rock wall in a dress, disobeying police orders—my orders. That was kind of amazing." He chuckled. "I think I'm the lucky one."

They lay quietly for a moment, basking in the strong connection they shared.

"Where did you say Ari's living?" Malcolm kissed her forehead.

"In an apartment near the Conservatory. I don't think he has a roommate, and everybody in that building is either a student or a teacher at the school. So, he's surrounded by friends, all of whom would do whatever they could to protect him."

"I need to see Ariel." He leaned up on one elbow. "Michael's murder will have to be made public today. That's going to be tough for everybody. We won't say anything about Saul at this point; we suspect it was murder but we won't know how strong our case is until we get the tox screen back."

"Despite what you said to Manny last night, I think he's pretty sure Michael was murdered, don't you?"

"Yes, I do." He glanced at the clock. "We need to try to get back to sleep, Gus. I think this is going to be a pretty draining day."

Malcolm switched off the light and again held Augusta in a close embrace. "Good night, my beautiful bride."

She smiled in the darkness. "Good night, my dearest love."

***

Malcolm lifted an eyebrow in surprise at Augusta when he walked into Manny's spacious studio at the Conservatory. It was one of the choice rooms, on the second floor of Main Hall, the building which had originally been a Victorian mansion. Large enough to accommodate a string quartet for rehearsals, with a grand piano, shelves for music, bookcases, comfortable chairs, an oriental rug and heavy damask draperies on the two windows in the room.

"I think you spoke with Ariel Rosen at Mecklenburg's Thursday night," Augusta remarked. She could see Malcolm sizing him up as they shook hands and could guess what he was thinking: *about six feet, 165-170 pounds, curly dark hair, gray eyes.*

Firm handshake, she added to herself when Mal commented, "Do you play tennis?"

107

Ari grinned. "Raquetball. How'd you know?"

"Just a guess," Malcolm commented, returning the smile. "I shake a lot of hands. I'm not sure that grip comes from playing cello."

Laughter all around.

"I'll get going. I know you have some serious business to discuss with these gentlemen." Augusta started for the door.

"No, stay, Augusta. You might as well hear this, most of it will be made public when Chief Schrotel gives a press conference at noon."

She nodded, and all of them found seats.

"I regret having to tell you that our investigation into Michael Robinson's death has proved that he was murdered," Malcolm told them. "At the moment, we are looking for a motive, and of course for the killer."

Manny nodded, a grim look spreading over his features, while Ari appeared completely stunned, even though he had been at Mecklenburg's two nights earlier.

"This information is not to be shared. Since Michael's death comes so closely after that of Saul Kronenberg's in Paris, there is some concern that Chrysanthemum Quartet members are possibly being targeted. Therefore, Chief Schrotel has approved protective details for each of you for the present. In order to avoid speculation, they will not be in uniform. They'll be on duty from midnight until eight a.m., and will need access to your home, Manny, and your apartment, Ari."

"Why would anybody do this?" Ariel's clenched fists rested on his knees. "Does Alicia know? I mean, know that Michael was … was murdered?" His voice shook slightly on the last word.

"My partner is with her now. It's a terrible shock, not just for his family, but for the music community in our city."

"What you said about Saul," Ari stared at Malcolm. "We were told he died of a heart attack, Detective Mitchell. Are you saying that might not be the case?"

"No, that's not what we're saying, not without further investigation. We can't rule out the possibility that the two deaths are somehow linked, however. Don't be surprised if you see some speculation in the press."

Manny leaned forward. "Thank you, Detective Mitchell. I appreciate the protection. Are we to continue our regular activities? Ari and I both are playing with the Summer Opera orchestra, as you probably know. And I have violin students several days a week."

"Yes, of course. I suggest you take precautions. When you come and go at the opera, it would be good to be with other people. Avoid going places by yourself if at all possible. And I know you will let the patrolmen know if you see or hear anything unusual." He gazed at Manny. "You might consider locking your studio door during each lesson. That may seem overly cautious, and I hope we find the perpetrator quickly so that you can get back to your normal lives."

Ari stared at Malcolm. "I live by myself."

"Yes, I'm aware of that. The patrolmen will be right outside your door and can be in the apartment if you'd feel safer. I know it's summer, but keep your windows closed and locked."

He stood. "I regret all of this, gentlemen. But our primary objective is to keep both of you safe." Malcolm handed each of them his card, first writing on them hastily. "Here's my personal phone number, and please, don't hesitate to call me if you need anything, or just would like to talk."

Ari studied Malcolm's card and glanced up at him. "Detective Mitchell?"

"Yes, Ari?"

"Do you really think—I'm having trouble wrapping my mind around this." A deep breath. "Do you really believe someone might want us dead?"

"We're thinking it's a possibility, I'm sure that's unsettling, to say the least. I sincerely hope we're wrong, but as I said, we want to keep you safe."

Augusta accompanied Malcolm down the steps and to the entrance of the building. "Only from midnight until eight? You can't have protection assigned to them round the clock?"

"Unfortunately, we can't. And frankly, without evidence of imminent danger, I don't know how long the chief will allow us to provide even that. They haven't been directly threatened. It obviously was a shock to Ari to learn Michael had been murdered."

Augusta sighed. "Yes, this is pretty unnerving for Ari. And I'd sure feel better if there were some way they could have twenty-four hour protection, but I understand. The CPD doesn't have unlimited funds." She put a hand on his arm. "What about your search for the Portnov family? How's that going?"

"No luck at all. No Portnovs anywhere in the greater D.C. area." He grimaced. "Maybe Manny was right. Maybe Anton Portnov materialized out of thin air in January of last year."

"You're still interviewing neighbors, though. And the building landlord? Did you have any luck with him— or her—or whoever?"

"The building is run by a real estate company and several different people have overseen that particular apartment building. Jim's still following up on that. I can't believe Portnov didn't make friends, or become acquainted, with at least one of his neighbors."

"And no identification of any kind for Anton showed up in his apartment."

"None. No mail. No checkbook. No credit cards. All he had was his driver's license, and that was issued in January." Mal kissed her briefly. "I have to join Jim in the neighborhood where Portnov lived. It's fortunate Manny asked Anton to have a headshot taken when he started working with the quartet. At least we don't have to show people the one from the Boone County coroner's office."

***

Augusta guided her beloved 1963 sapphire blue Chrysler Imperial onto the John Roebling Suspension Bridge and glanced ahead to see the town of Covington, Kentucky, spreading out before her. She sensed Malcolm's frustration with this case and wanted to help in some way, and this might be something she could do.

Since Augusta had no voice students on Saturday, a little drive to Florence and the Boone County coroner's office might give her a chance to come up with some information.

Her attempt to reach Malcolm by phone to let him know her plans proved fruitless, as she had suspected it might. *It can't hurt for me to try to help. He's a little overwhelmed with this case. Anyway, I doubt anything will come of it.*

As always when she traveled the Roebling Bridge, she felt a strong connection to the history of her beloved city. John A. Roebling was still working on the Brooklyn Bridge—undoubtedly his most famous—when his bridge spanning the Ohio River was completed in 1866. Pedestrian walkways had been popular from the time the bridge first opened, and Augusta had walked the bridge several times, beginning in her days as a Conservatory student. *My bridge is about to celebrate its centennial,* Augusta mused. *Malcolm and I need to make that walk together.*

Even after the Brent Spence Bridge on Interstate 75 opened, she preferred to use this means to cross into Kentucky unless she was headed for the airport or Lexington. In most cases, if the river is the dividing line between two states, the state line is considered the center of the river. It intrigued Augusta that Kentucky claimed ownership of all the Ohio River, so as soon as she began her crossing—whether in a car or on foot—technically she was already in Kentucky.

Northern Kentucky is a beautiful area, with rolling hills, charming towns, and Augusta enjoyed her drive to

Florence. On the seat next to her, she had a portfolio with music and a couple of newspaper clippings about the Chrysanthemum Quartet. She had put this together after the meeting that morning with Malcolm.

Maybe a charming lady friend of Anton Portnov's who wants his family to have some of his belongings will get further with the staff at the coroner's office.

She decided to put on her best "charming lady friend" face and use a hint of a Southern accent. *When in Rome ... but don't overdo it, Augusta.*

"Good afternoon, ma'am. How may I help you?" A pleasant young man greeted her from behind the desk just inside the door.

"Lovely day, isn't it? Yes, I surely hope you can help me." She hugged the portfolio to her breast. "I'm here about that poor young man who was killed in an auto accident last year. I think maybe last June? About a year ago?"

"May I have the name of the victim?"

"Anton Portnov. He was a very fine musician. He played the cello, you know."

The clerk flipped through a Rolodex as he glanced at her. "Um, no. I don't believe I knew that."

He pulled a card from the Rolodex. "Yes, here it is. Anton Portnov. June 3, 1964. Auto accident."

"Oh, dear. Yes, that's the one. It was so sad." She dabbed at her eyes.

"So, what can I do for you?"

"Oh, yes. Sorry. Well, I'm manager of the quartet he played with." It never ceased to surprise Augusta how easily she lied when she had her detective hat on.

113

"We were going through a cabinet last week and found some things that belonged to Anton, and thought his family would appreciate having them. But we don't have an address for him down in Washington. I mean, D.C."

"Let me check for you," he offered, and moved to a filing cabinet.

"Such a talented boy," she murmured. "It really was *such* a shame that he died like that. So suddenly."

The clerk removed a file and brought it to the desk, where he rifled through it. "This is kind of odd," he commented.

"What is?"

"There's no address for his family. Only the last name."

"Oh—you know we couldn't notify his family about the accident because we didn't know where they lived. Do you know how they found out about it? Maybe a mutual friend contacted them?"

"Sorry, I don't know that. There was a delay in them coming forward and claiming his remains. I know we circulated an artists' sketch in major newspapers. I'm sure D.C. would have been included."

"Maybe that's how they learned he'd died. What a terrible way to find out you've lost a loved one. That is just such a shame." *Don't say that again, Augusta. You've said it twice now.*

"Yes, it certainly is. I'm sorry I can't help you with this. I need to speak to my supervisor and find out why this is an incomplete file."

"Well, why don't I just leave this here with you? If you do find the address, would you be so kind as to mail this to poor Anton's family?" She extended the portfolio in his direction.

"Yes, you can leave it, and I certainly will send it on as soon as I can."

"Thank you so much. You've been most helpful."

"Sorry you drove all the way down here for nothing." He smiled at her again.

I probably remind him of his favorite aunt. "Oh, it wasn't for nothing at all. It's a beautiful day and driving to Florence is always lovely."

She waggled her fingers at him. "Thank you again. Have a nice day."

Well, that was an exercise in futility. But at least I tried.

Chapter 9
The Show Goes On

Saturday, June 12
6:30 p.m.

Augusta headed down the steps, purse in hand, to find Malcolm standing in the entrance hall, his arms folded across his chest, looking none too pleased.

"That phone call was from Jim Edmonds. He just had a discussion with the Boone County coroner's office about a visitor they had this afternoon."

He took a step toward her, fists at his waist. "It seems a very attractive older woman was there asking a lot of questions about Anton Portnov's death. Would you know anything about that, Augusta?"

"He called me an older woman?"

"A very attractive older woman. Good Lord, Gus. What the hell were you doing over there? You promised me you wouldn't do anything like that."

"Do you think of me as an older woman? I'm not that much older than you, Malcolm Mitchell."

"*Augusta!*" He took her firmly by the shoulders and stared directly into her eyes. "This isn't about you. You just interfered in an ongoing homicide investigation; do you realize that?"

Augusta stepped back and smoothed her dress, a favorite: an apricot A-line with a flared skirt and matching short jacket. "I tried to call you before I drove over there. I couldn't imagine what harm it would do if I presented myself as an … interested party … not there officially."

"Let's see." Malcolm crossed his arms over his chest again and leaned against the door frame. "This woman told the clerk she was manager of the string quartet Portnov had been part of at one time."

"Well, I just thought maybe I could play on their sympathy and they might let something slip. I'm sorry, Mal. I promise it won't happen again." *Oh, dear. The last thing I wanted was to annoy him.*

"What did you do, bat your eyelashes at that guy?"

"I decided against doing that. I tried to present myself as a sympathetic friend of the quartet and of Anton's. I honestly thought it might be helpful."

She saw the twitch at the corner of his mouth and relaxed.

"You'd do better to stick with fiery gypsies like Frasquita in *Carmen*." He laughed and shook his head. "Come on, I want to get to the pavilion early for this performance so I can keep an eye on things when the orchestra members are coming in."

118

He extended an arm. "By the way, for a 'not that much older woman' you look great to this not that much younger guy. Love that dress."

"Mal, I am sorry about driving over to the coroner's office." She slipped an arm through his. "I won't do anything again without talking to you about it first."

"Very well, Mrs. Mitchell." He kissed her cheek. "I'll let you off this time with a warning. I'm too busy to visit you on Sundays anyway. You know that's a punishable offense, though."

"Let's blame it on the Frasquita part of me. She tends to be impulsive."

"She's also irresistible." He grinned again as they headed for Augusta's car.

***

"Are there extra police on duty this evening?" Augusta stared out of the window as Malcolm maneuvered her Chrysler Imperial into a reserved spot at the end of the Zoo's parking lot.

"Full house tonight, remember? *Carmen*'s a popular opera and Jamie Logan's singing. But yes, I think there are a few extra cops helping with traffic control. Doesn't hurt to send a message to any potential bad guys hanging around."

The lot at the moment held cars primarily of Zoo and Summer Opera employees and performers. Most singers were called for an hour before curtain time, and some preferred to get there even sooner. As they stepped out of the car a cacophony of sounds assailed them, singers

119

vocalizing and animals adding their own melodies, lions and peacocks chief among them.

Another unique offering of her city, opera on the grounds of the Cincinnati Zoo. Music was such a strong part of the city's past it didn't seem at all unusual when concerts were offered on the spacious grounds. Constructing a bandstand also seemed logical to the city fathers. During her days of performing at the Summer Opera, Augusta had learned one reason for the concerts was to extend employment for the Cincinnati Symphony Orchestra members.

That bandstand had been expanded to a roofed, open-air pavilion. While walls at one end of the building protected the performers from the elements, hastily lowered tarps on the other three sides of the pavilion occasionally weren't up to keeping the audience members dry. Augusta recalled more than once sitting in the audience during a storm and being drenched to the skin by blowing rain. Opera goers knew this could happen, but she'd never heard many complaints.

They moved toward the pavilion as Augusta slipped a hand through Malcolm's arm. "Let's stop here for a minute. My favorite animals." They had reached an exhibit where river otters cavorted, clambering up a steep, rocky hill and sliding down the banks into a pond. Augusta had always been enchanted by them.

Malcolm stood beside her for a moment. "I'll leave you here while I find Jim. I need to speak with him."

"Where is he? I didn't see him."

"Probably talking to Aaron Rubin." He headed through the tall wooden fence to the backstage area.

Since the stage wings inside the pavilion were severely limited, a group of buildings had been constructed where the performers dressed and relaxed when not on stage. During the performance that evening, Jim would spend his time back here, keeping an eye on this part of the facility. He could also spot any suspicious latecomers as they walked up from the parking lot.

Augusta turned her attention to the otters, fascinated by the scampering, happy little creatures who seemed to be laughing all the time. Meredith Logan, Jamie's wife, joined her.

"Aren't they just the best? I had Laura over here earlier this week when Jamie had his sitzprobe orchestra rehearsal for *Carmen*. We must have spent an hour here, and Laura wants to come back to see them again."

"She must be about a year and a half, isn't she? I'd love to see her."

"We'll have to make plans. Yes, she'll be two in October." The two women watched the otters for a few moments. "So sad about Michael," Meredith said. "And definitely frightening. Yet here we stand, taking some comfort in these sweet creatures."

Malcolm joined the two women and greeted Meredith. "I need to be over by the orchestra gate," he said to Augusta. "Here's your ticket. We're in the front row, over on the right. Excuse me, ladies."

"Augusta, Malcolm can't be here just as a member of the audience." Meredith's eyes widened. "I know enough about law enforcement officers to be aware they never sit in the front row in a public place unless they're working."

"I'm sure it's just a precaution, Meredith," Augusta responded. "Why don't we get a glass of champagne?" Meredith's comment made her aware of a difference in the audience; they were definitely more subdued than usual. *The cast has their work cut out for them tonight.*

Malcolm joined her in their front row seats which were close to the orchestra gate, an entrance for the instrumentalists which were near the steps that led down into the orchestra pit. Augusta was very much aware the front row was the last place Mal would ordinarily sit, but having two uniformed patrolmen assigned to positions behind the audience during the performance eased his mind.

"Ariel seems fine," he said. "Manny was a little nervous and said he was relieved to see me here."

They both spotted Michael's chair in the orchestra pit, draped in black fabric with a small wreath of yellow chrysanthemums.

"That's heart wrenching," Augusta said. "Yellow for sorrow. And when Puccini wrote *I Crisantemi* as a eulogy, he used that flower because for Italians, chrysanthemums are linked to sad events or funerals."

She showed him the program insert. A photo of Michael framed in black with a brief bio beneath it; at the top of a page, the announcement that the members of the Summer Opera company dedicated tonight's performance to Michael Robinson, violist and beloved and esteemed member of the orchestra.

Mal skimmed it quickly. "Very appropriate. I noticed the orchestra members were pretty quiet as they were coming in. I'm sure all of them are thinking of Michael."

"Do you think they may be concerned that because an orchestra member was a victim of foul play, it could happen to them?"

"It's possible. I can't believe anyone would try anything while these two men are sitting in the middle of a performance," Mal observed. "I'll be interested to see what kind of activity there is during intermission, though."

The lights dimmed. Maestro Aaron Rubin entered the pit in a spotlight as the audience applauded heartily. He held up his hands for silence. "The members of the Cincinnati Summer Opera wish to dedicate this performance to violist Michael Robinson, who was taken from us two days ago. Michael was a beloved member of this community and he will be sorely missed."

Tentative applause soon swelled to a prolonged standing ovation for Michael, and Augusta took the handkerchief Malcolm offered. The audience returned to their seats, Maestro Rubin faced the orchestra, and the first strains to the overture of Bizet's opera *Carmen* were heard.

The "fate" theme thundered through the pavilion. *How fitting*, thought Augusta.

***

During the first act it was obvious to Augusta that Malcolm glanced intermittently into the orchestra pit. She knew his keen senses were attuned to the crowd behind them as well, and he glanced around from time to time as unobtrusively as possible. When the lights came up for the first intermission, he stood, turned around and scanned the entire audience.

"So far, so good."

"Would you like me to get you something?" Augusta stood. "Pop, maybe?"

"Thanks, club soda would be great."

She made her way to the concession stand where Milly and Garrett joined her.

"This is a terrific performance under difficult circumstances," Milly commented. "Jamie has earned his reputation as the greatest Don José in opera world these days."

"I would totally agree. Both his duets were beautiful. I can't wait to hear 'The Flower Song.' And the final duet."

"Is Mal enjoying the performance?" Garrett handed Augusta a glass of champagne. "Let me get him something."

"I'm sure he is. And thank you, Garrett. Club soda, please."

Milly stared at her. "He's working, isn't he? Otherwise he'd have a beer."

"Keep that under your hat, Mil."

"I'll bet when Mal watches the 'Gypsy Song,' though, he'll have a flashback about a Frasquita he once knew."

Augusta smiled pensively. "I wonder sometimes what might have happened back then if we'd actually met each other. I'm sure I told you that when he reminded me about coming backstage after the performance, I remembered him. Those intense blue eyes and that great smile. But of course, he was only nineteen. So I was an 'older woman.'"

Milly lifted an eyebrow. "What on earth prompted that comment?"

Augusta laughed. "Oh, nothing. Just some talk about our age difference. It's silly, forget I said it."

Milly raised her glass to her friend. "Augusta, you have never been an 'older woman.' You're the embodiment of eternal youth. You're like Merlin in the King Arthur legend … you *youthen* instead of aging."

"Thanks, Milly. I kind of needed to hear that today." They drifted back toward their seats.

Mal smiled his thanks for the drink and sipped it.

"Anything of interest, husband?"

"Actually, yes. One of the guys in the violin section was really bending Manny's ear for nearly the entire intermission. I need to find out what that was about."

"Um. What about Ari?"

"Lots of female attention. He seems to have a fan club. Is that why he reminds you of Meyer?"

"One reason, for sure. Meyer was charismatic, just as Ari seems to be. A lot of Conservatory female students really hated me once Meyer and I became a couple."

"That's right. You were an older woman." He dragged out the words. "After all, you were a junior, he was a freshman."

Augusta laughed in spite of herself. "I'm sorry I reacted the way I did earlier. I should wear the label proudly." She slipped an arm through the crook of his elbow. "Look what it got me. The absolute best."

The lights dimmed, the conductor returned to the podium, and the driving rhythm of "The Gypsy Song" filled the air. One of Augusta's favorite moments in the opera, a trio for Carmen and her friends Frasquita and Mercedes. Augusta relished it when the choreographer included them in the dance at the end of the number. She recalled she had danced at that performance when Malcolm first saw her onstage.

I wonder if Mal is thinking about seeing me on stage as Frasquita all those years ago.

As if he had read her thoughts, Mal turned toward her, covered her hand with his, and smiled in the darkness.

Just before the end of Act Two, a lighting fixture blew out above the stage, and the flash of light and loud pop drew a collective gasp from the audience. Malcolm was on his feet in an instant, then realized what had happened and dropped back into his seat.

The conductor, the orchestra, and the performers on stage didn't miss a beat, and the audience laughed nervously as they also understood what had transpired. The act concluded with a rousing choral piece as Carmen and her friends persuaded Don José to desert the army and join them as smugglers.

The relief that the sound hadn't been a gunshot combined with the effect of Bizet's spirited music created a very noisy intermission crowd. Augusta stayed with Malcolm as he watched the orchestra. Some of the instrumentalists wandered out into the crowd, others stayed in their chairs and rehearsed passages they had problems playing, others stood around and chatted.

"I need to speak to Manny. Excuse me, Gus." Mal joined Manny in the pit, and Ariel spotted Augusta sitting by herself and moved to the edge of the pit.

Ariel grinned. "That light blowing out wasn't in Bizet's score."

"Never a dull moment in live theater." They laughed together.

"You seem to be having a great time playing in the orchestra, Ari," Augusta observed. "Which do you like best, this or performing with the quartet?"

"Both. I love doing both of those things. You know, it's just such a treat to learn new music all the time. Music that speaks to me in such different ways." He grinned. "I read something recently about Rachmaninoff, something he said. About how music is enough for a lifetime, but you can never live long enough to hear all the wonderful music that's been written."

"That's exactly what he meant. I think he actually said 'music is enough for a lifetime, but a lifetime is not enough for music.' And he was certainly right about that."

Orchestra players drifted back to the pit and regained their seats, and the two final acts of *Carmen* were performed without interruption. As the opera unfolded, it became more and more apparent Carmen and Don José were star-crossed lovers, doomed to an inevitable tragic end.

***

"The violinist who was talking to Manny at length during the first intermission asked him what he plans to do about the quartet." Mal stopped at a red light and glanced at Augusta. "He suggested Manny shouldn't give it up, but should think about adding different players and find a way to keep it going. Manny says he's quite a good violinist and might work into Saul's spot."

"What about that? Did Manny say he'd consider it?"

"I'm not sure his heart's in it at the moment, but I suggested it might be a way to smoke out our killer. If he advertises that he has two openings in the quartet and schedules auditions, it would be interesting to see who shows up."

"Those cops in plain clothes who were waiting at the gate after the opera were obviously Manny's and Ari's protection details. I thought they were to be on from midnight to eight."

"Yes, I had requested they start early, so they could follow them home. It only added about an hour to their tour."

"Otherwise, you'd have felt you needed to follow one or the other, I'm sure. And would have asked Jim to do the same."

They drove in silence for a few minutes. "We haven't talked about the opera," Augusta remarked.

"Well, you know I love *Carmen*. After last year, it was a real treat to watch Jamie perform the entire role." He stretched his right arm across the back of the seat and drew Augusta close to him. "Good cast. Great cast, actually. But I kept seeing you as Frasquita. You'll always be the only Frasquita for me."

"It's a delightful role." She snuggled against him. "I enjoyed every minute of being onstage when I did *Carmen.*"

His lips brushed her forehead. "I'm told Michael Robinson's memorial service is scheduled for Saturday at Christ Episcopal Church. I need to be there, and I know you'll want to come. But I can't sit with you."

"No, that's fine. I didn't expect you could." She grew quiet.

"Penny for your thoughts, Gus."

She sighed. "Just how unpredictable life is. Even this one evening. You're on the lookout for a possible killer while we're sitting listening to some of the most beautiful music ever written, performed by a remarkable ensemble of singers and instrumentalists."

"Well, even within the opera. Extreme emotions. Love and death." He put both hands on the wheel to turn off of Madison Road onto Vista. "Love doomed from the beginning."

"Tragedy makes for good theater. And great music."

"Yes, it does. But why do we love these tragic operas? You know *Tosca* is my favorite. It's at least as emotional as *Carmen.*"

"Good question," Augusta responded. "Maybe because we know that, no matter how engrossed in them we become, when the final curtain closes, we know it wasn't real."

Malcolm commented, "And in real life, we don't know what the next act will bring."

He turned off the engine and Augusta pulled herself close to him. "Whether it will bring joy or sorrow. When you think about it—it's frightening."

She leaned back and gazed into his eyes. "And yet, every day, you face that uncertainty in ways most people can't even imagine. You're my hero, Malcolm."

Chapter 10
Le Nozze di Figaro

Sunday, June 13

Sunday mornings were Augusta's and Mal's time. After their first night together, Malcolm cooked breakfast: bacon, eggs, fruit, pastries. Over the past two years, he'd graduated to omelets, coming up with new combinations, each of which Augusta declared the best yet.

This morning, a new combination: spinach and feta cheese, seasoned to perfection in Augusta's opinion. Content, she relaxed and sipped her coffee as Mal cleared the table.

Each time Mal's phone in the alcove rang, he picked it up quickly, hoping for a break in the case. This time he wasn't disappointed. "Mitchell—Hi, Jim."

A pause and she watched as his expression changed. Mal kept a pen and pad by the phone. Augusta watched him click the pen and attempt twice to write on the pad before he stared at her and made writing motions in the air. Augusta scurried into the kitchen, grabbed a pen, returned quickly and handed it to him. While she couldn't make out the words, she could hear the excitement in Jim Edmonds' voice as she waited expectantly for Malcolm to share the news.

"Give me that address again, will you?" More scribbling, followed by, "Okay, got it. I'll get back to you after I see this guy."

"Hot damn!" He pumped a clenched fist in the air. "Have to get going. We've finally come up with what may be a lead."

"Can you tell me anything about this?" *So much for a day off.*

"Jim found a neighbor of Portnov's who knows someone Portnov was friendly with. This guy is eager to tell us what he knows." He headed up the steps to grab his jacket.

"What are your people telling those neighbors about this renewed interest in Anton Portnov's death?" Augusta followed closely. "Didn't the CPD question people last year?"

"Well, yes, but it was just perfunctory questioning. Last year they were looking for the name of next of kin." Mal slipped on his holster and shrugged into his jacket. "Now they're asking if anybody spent time with him, if they knew of any social contacts he might have had, any information they might have about where he went and what he did."

He headed for the front door, Augusta again right behind him. "So, a more thorough investigation." She smoothed his lapels and straightened his tie. "But what's your explanation about asking all these questions now, a year after the man died?"

"There's a possibility his death might be connected to a current homicide investigation."

Augusta kissed him. "Be careful out there, Detective. And—good luck."

She returned to the kitchen to handle the clean-up detail, smiling as she remembered the night they had enjoyed together.

I told him last night he's my hero. He is that, in every possible way.

She closed her eyes and breathed a prayer. "Please, Lord, keep him safe."

***

Dressed in blue jeans, an old shirt and an ancient pair of tennis shoes, Augusta went out into her garden. Donning work gloves, she knelt on an old cushion and tackled the weeds that dared show themselves. Ruthless, she stabbed the soil and ripped them up, throwing them into a bucket to join other weeds in the compost heap at the back of her property.

Augusta took pride in her garden. One of the things she appreciated about Caruso, the Golden Shepherd they'd dog-sat the previous summer, was that no matter what he did that irritated her—chief among them gnawing on her stilettos—he never bothered the garden. In fact, he stayed away from it. She smiled, thinking of the wonderful animal that had saved her life. Trevor Davidson, the young patrolman who owned Caruso, brought him by occasionally to see her, and it warmed her heart to know the dog still adored her. She had to admit that at times she missed having him around.

Finished with her weeding, she turned on the sprinkler and watched with satisfaction as it slowly moved back and forth, droplets glittering in the sun as it gently spread water over the thirsty flowers.

"Here you are." Milly's voice, making her jump slightly.

"Good Lord, I didn't expect you." Augusta self-consciously brushed her hair back from her face, blotting the perspiration on her forehead with the back of her hand. "It's warm for June."

"Not nearly as warm as it will be in July," Milly observed. "I just thought I'd drop by to ask if you knew about Michael Robinson's memorial service on Saturday." She eyed her friend. "Aren't you glad it's me? I'm sure you wouldn't want to be caught in that outfit by anyone else. The elegant Professor McKee, *en deshabillé.*"

"Yes, you're right about that," Augusta laughed. "I usually do the weeding when Mal's out. I'm not sure he's ever seen my ravishing gardening ensemble." She grew serious. "Yes, I heard about the service. Eleven a.m. at Christ Episcopal Church. Is Garrett going with you?"

"I believe so. I assume Mal will be there in an official capacity as lead investigator for the homicide."

Augusta nodded. "You assume correctly. Shall we plan to go together?" They walked to the front of Augusta's house.

"I have to be there early. Ari's playing and he asked me to be his accompanist."

"That's so nice." Augusta sighed.

"I liked Michael," Milly said. "Above all, a really good guy. He adored his family. My heart breaks for Alicia and the boys."

"Mine, too." The women embraced. "We'll make plans later in the week."

***

"Do you mind leftover lasagna?"

Augusta had pulled the dish from the refrigerator when she heard Malcolm's car pull up.

"Are you kidding? You know your lasagna is my favorite." He looked at his wife appreciatively. "Another of my favorite dresses."

A lime green and white print, with the swingy kind of skirt Augusta preferred, and a cowl neckline. "One of mine as well."

Malcolm added, "You always look fabulous."

"Well … I was in the garden digging up weeds earlier. I'm not sure you'd have said that if you'd seen my outfit," Augusta laughed.

Another night at the opera, this time for Mozart's *Le Nozze di Figaro—The Marriage of Figaro*. Mal's son Danny would join them; his fiancée Martha was making her Summer Opera debut in the role of Cherubino.

Since Mal wasn't a big Mozart fan and had never seen this opera, Augusta explained to him that Cherubino is what's called a "trouser" role—the role of an adolescent male performed by a female singer, because the composer wanted the younger, lighter sound.

"It's mostly done in operas written during earlier musical periods, though even in this century Richard Strauss included such a role in one of his operas," she said. "It works well. And Cherubino has some great music."

"Um-hmm. If you say so," Malcolm commented. "I have kind of a hard time picturing Martha playing a guy."

"Because of her curves, you mean. The costumers can handle that."

"Why don't you sit with Danny in the seats we reserved? I'll need to be in the front again."

"I'd enjoy that, thanks." They set plates, napkins, and cutlery on the alcove table. "Can you tell me about your interview with Anton's neighbor?"

Malcolm had iced tea and poured a glass of merlot for Augusta. "Nice guy. It was definitely productive."

They sat together at the table as they waited for the lasagna to heat. "Do you know a local writer named Barry Whittier?" he asked. "I believe he's also an artist."

"I know who he is. I've never met him, but I've been curious about his books. He writes mystery novels. I like his art. His style is similar to Bob Fabe's though his subject matter is quite different. Almost surreal." Augusta proudly claimed ownership of several small paintings by well-known Cincinnati artist Robert Fabe. "Why are you asking about Whittier?"

"Because John Allen, Anton's neighbor, knows him. Whittier was at John's one day when they ran into

Anton, and he introduced them. For some reason, Barry was intrigued with Anton—maybe the name? Anyway, they exchanged phone numbers and promised they'd get together. Allen saw Whittier going into Portnov's apartment a few times."

Augusta abruptly set her glass down. "Mal—do you remember when we were at the Levines' and I commented on the book Linda was reading? It was by Whittier. She also told us that Whittier seemed quite interested in the Chrysanthemum Quartet. In fact, Manny told me that as well. Whittier had been to all their concerts this season, and he talked about providing them some financial support."

"Yes, I recall that." Mal lifted an eyebrow. "I would think Whittier learned about the quartet from Anton."

"Whittier must have some information he could share with you." Augusta went into the kitchen and pulled the lasagna from the oven.

"There's an interesting wrinkle. Mr. Allen said about two weeks before Anton died, he and Whittier had a big blowup. A very nasty shouting match, and after that he never saw the two of them together." Malcolm helped himself to a generous portion of lasagna.

"Have you contacted Whittier yet?" Augusta served herself a piece about a third the size of Malcolm's.

"Couldn't reach him. He lives by himself but I was told he's out of town for a book reading. I guess he's a successful author if he's traveling for book readings?"

"That kind of depends. If he's in Florence, Kentucky, maybe not so much. If he's in Philadelphia or New York, then, yes, he's probably doing pretty well."

"Well, in any event, he's due back tomorrow. I learned that from a helpful neighbor who was watering her plants when I stopped at his house." He grinned. "A very sweet older lady."

Augusta kicked his ankle.

"No, really. I'd guess in her seventies." Malcolm took a healthy bite of lasagna. "A beer would go great with this. But I'm working tonight. Lasagna now, beer later at Meck's."

***

Augusta stopped backstage before she looked for Danny, finding a nervous Martha in costume and makeup pacing outside her dressing room, her mouth moving occasionally as she sang through her role in her head.

"You look fantastic. You're going to be brilliant." Augusta embraced her future daughter-in-law warmly. "How do you feel?"

"Excited. Nervous. More excited than nervous— most of the time." Both women laughed.

"What were you running through?"

"That pesky duet with Susanna in the second act. It's just *so fast*."

"And knowing you, you can sing it in your sleep. Relax. You're going to be fabulous."

"Oh, I hope so. Do you think I'll pass for a boy?" Martha turned around slowly as Augusta inspected her.

"Oh, yes. Are you uncomfortable in that rig?"

"Surprisingly, I'm not. The wardrobe people are just the best."

"I need to find Danny. *In bocca al lupo*, Martha." Augusta embraced her again, using the traditional Italian "good luck" expression, meaning "In the mouth of the wolf."

"*Crepi il lupo*," Martha replied— "May the wolf die."

Augusta saw Danny studying their tickets and glancing around anxiously. *He's more nervous than Martha is*, she thought. His face lit up when he spotted Augusta and he moved quickly to join her.

"How is she?"

"She's fine. She's going to be wonderful, and she'll have the time of her life. Such a fun opera."

They were seated sixth row orchestra, in the center. Mal turned and nodded when he saw them. He was again in the front row at the far right.

"I'm not sure what dad is looking for," Danny said. "I can't believe anyone who might be planning to pick off a member of the orchestra would be stupid enough to try it during a performance."

"Well, for one thing, if such a person saw him and realized who he is, that's a deterrent. I think he's keeping an eye out for anything that strikes him as unusual."

"Do you know all of these singers?" Danny studied the program.

"Many of them. Sam Varnay will be a great Count Almaviva. I love this opera."

"Augusta, is there an opera you don't love?" Danny grinned wryly.

"Not many. But this one really is a favorite. I've performed the role of Susanna. I think the best role in the opera, and the best music, belongs to Count Almaviva."

"Why is that? Martha explained the plot to me. The Count is basically a would-be philandering husband. He's after the Countess's maid Susanna, and the two women team up to trick him into looking pretty foolish, if I have that straight."

"That's the basic plot, but the Count is more than a hoodwinked spouse. He's a complex character and a dream role for a baritone. There's a dark side to his character, and you can hear it in some of his music."

The lights dimmed and the lively overture began. Danny clutched Augusta's arm when Martha first came on stage. "How'd they do that?" He hissed in Augusta's ear. "She looks so—different."

"Shh," Augusta put a finger to her lips. Later in the act, Danny grabbed Augusta's arm again as Martha performed Cherubino's first aria, "Non so più, cosa son," beautifully. The audience applauded at length and Danny relaxed.

"She's doing great." He beamed at Augusta. He was delighted with the action at the end of the act when the character Figaro, waving a huge flag, marched Cherubino off stage to join the army. Prolonged applause from the audience.

During the intermission, Augusta sat next to Malcolm and glanced into the orchestra pit. Michael Robinson's seat still wore its black drape, but the atmosphere in the pit was less somber. Manny Levine chatted comfortably with his music stand partner, but

140

Augusta noticed he glanced in Mal's direction more than once. *It's probably reassuring for him to see a cop nearby.*

Ariel was surrounded by several females, mostly Conservatory students, and obviously enjoying the attention. She knew the girls, at least by sight. Ari seemed quite taken with a pretty blonde. She looked familiar but Augusta didn't think she was a student.

Augusta rejoined Danny and watched the rest of the opera unfold, recalling her times onstage as Susanna, remembering how much she enjoyed singing this music. The stage director had his singers playing the comedy to the hilt, and there were some very entertaining moments. Martha's second aria as Cherubino went swimmingly, as did the duet with Susanna she'd expressed concern about.

In the third act, Augusta whispered to Danny, "This is my favorite moment in this opera." Sam Varnay portrayed a furious Count Almaviva in the aria "Hai già vinta la causa," and the lighting designer emphasized the dark side of the Count's character with a subtle lighting change. Sam's brilliant performance resulted in a prolonged ovation from the audience.

The opera continued through its many plot twists and turns, mistaken identity after mistaken identity, and eventual resolution, dramatic and musical.

Augusta and Danny joined in the standing ovation. "Wasn't Martha incredible? I'm taking her to Mecklenburg's to celebrate. We'd like you and Dad to join us if you can."

"Definitely. Your dad is looking forward to going to Meck's. We'll meet you there."

The audience filtered out slowly, laughing and chatting. Augusta glanced toward the orchestra pit and saw Ari having an animated conversation with the blond girl she'd noticed earlier in the evening. Something about the young woman seemed familiar, but she couldn't put her finger on it.

I wonder who she is.

Chapter 11
Another Mystery

Monday, June 14

"I have two meetings this morning. "Malcolm gulped the last of his coffee. "I'm meeting with a woman who's on the board of the real estate company that owns the apartment building where Portnov lived, and then I'm headed for the Dry Ridge Kentucky State Police Post to talk to the cop who was on scene at his accident. What's your schedule today?"

"Lessons this morning, then the rest of the day is free." Augusta picked up both cups. "I'll take care of the dishes." One foot in the kitchen, she turned back toward him. "Remember, no opera performances Monday or Tuesday nights during the season."

"Yes, I knew that. 'Dark' nights in theater jargon, correct?"

"Correct," Augusta replied with a smile. "Why don't we go out to dinner, if you're free?"

"Sure. Where?"

"How about The Cricket? We haven't been there in ages." Augusta considered the charming restaurant a favorite. A post-concert crowd often frequented the place after a Cincinnati Symphony concert.

Malcolm lifted an eyebrow. "I think the media types like that restaurant. I don't want to run into Arnold Richter."

"Well, I can't guarantee that," Augusta laughed. "You pick, then."

"No, we'll brave The Cricket. You're right, we haven't been there in a while."

Augusta followed Malcolm to the front door.

"What are your plans for the Renaissance man, Barry Whittier?" She smoothed his lapels and straightened his tie.

"Renaissance man?"

"Well, he's a writer, an artist, and who knows what else." She flicked a small piece of lint off his collar. "I think I'll stop at the bookstore in Clifton and pick up one of his books. I'm curious."

Malcolm gathered her in his arms and kissed her softly. They held each other for a moment. Hand on the doorknob, he gazed at her. *Oh, those incredible eyes.*

"You shouldn't look at me like that, Detective. I may not allow you to leave."

Malcolm laughed and kissed her again. "Hold that thought, Mrs. Mitchell."

***

Evelyn Keller, an attractive, pleasant, well-groomed woman, met Mal in her agency's office in the Carew Tower. "Thank you for seeing me, Mrs. Keller."

"I'm happy to help, Detective Mitchell." She handed him a carefully typed list. "How sad that no one has come forward yet to claim Mr. Portnov's belongings. I understand he was taken to the D.C. area for burial. The coroner's office in Florence knows we have these items, but we didn't clean out the apartment until nearly a month after the accident."

"This is interesting." Mal glanced up as he studied the list. "Some of his clothing was packed in two suitcases?"

"Yes. He had given notice he would vacate the apartment at the end of June. That may explain why we found so little in it. He may very well have already cleaned out some of his things."

Mal continued to peruse the list, resting an index finger on one line. He glanced up at Mrs. Keller. "I see a music stand listed, but I don't see his instrument ... his cello."

"No, it wasn't in the apartment. We assumed he had it with him, unfortunately. I know as a professional, his cello had considerable value."

"I'm sure it did." Mal continued reading. "No book with addresses and phone numbers? No checkbook? That seems unusual. I take it there were also no photographs or pictures."

"No, the only items on the walls were prints that were part of the apartment's décor. And of course, since the apartment is a fully furnished unit, all the dishes and linens are also included in the rental."

Mal lifted the paper toward her. "May I keep this?"

"Certainly. We prepared it for you." She paused. "Oh, we found some cash in the desk drawer. I think six hundred dollars. It's locked in our office safe."

He nodded, then leaned back for a moment. "I would imagine you found a new tenant right away."

"Yes, we did. A young woman moved in at the end of July. We cleaned and repainted prior to offering it for rental."

Before leaving the building, Mal stopped in the Carew Tower lobby to make a quick phone call to Immanuel Levine. "I hope I didn't interrupt a lesson."

"No, perfect timing. I have about a half hour break. What can I do for you?"

"Anton Portnov's cello. It wasn't found in his apartment when the real estate company cleaned it out. Do you have any idea where it could be?"

"Sadly, I thought he must have had it in his car. What a shame. It was an exceptionally nice cello, but not a Strad or an Amati, and certainly not a Goffriller."

"I've never heard that last name."

"Most people haven't. They were built around the same period as Stradivarius and Amati instruments, but great cellists think they have a superior sound. Pablo Casals plays a Goffriller. Anyway, Anton's instrument was a very good one."

"Worth a lot of money?" Mal could picture some savvy thief breaking into Anton's apartment and stealing it.

146

"Yes, it was a lovely instrument. Built by an excellent luthier in Canada. I would think worth at least forty or fifty thousand dollars. Maybe more."

"That much? Wow. Okay, thanks, Manny. I'll keep you posted."

Next stop, Kentucky State Police outpost in Dry Ridge, where State Trooper Lester Payne waited for him.

Seated comfortably with coffee in front of them on a table in the break room, Payne handed Malcolm a copy of the notes he'd made about the accident.

Mal glanced it over. The usual information: location, time of day, weather conditions, damage to the vehicle, a note that it was a one-car accident. Time the coroner's vehicle arrived to take the driver's remains away. A list of items found in the car: registration and warranty in the glove box, spare tire and jack in the trunk. Nothing more.

"There wasn't a cello in the car?" A swig of coffee.

"A what—a cello? I don't know what that is," Payne grinned.

Ol' Lester is into blue grass or country western, Mal guessed. "It's kind of like a fiddle, only bigger."

"Like some kind of fancy guitar?"

"More like a string bass—a bull fiddle—only smaller." *Wonder how Augusta would have handled talking to this guy?* Mal bit back a laugh.

"Nope. Nothin' like that. Are you thinkin' he was on his way to a gig?" Payne poured each of them a second cup of coffee.

"Good question. Which direction?"

"North. My guess—he was headed across the river."

147

Malcolm made a note on the paper, folded it and put it in his inside jacket pocket.

The men chatted for a few minutes, discussing the glory days of Kentucky's "Sin City," Newport, which still contained vestiges of organized crime.

"That guy you took down last fall? Ponti? I was on the detail that picked up some of his goons before they could cross the river. We heard about how that operation ended."

"Thanks. We sure appreciated your help." Mal finished his coffee. "I think what's left of that bunch are all in Las Vegas."

"And Ponti is in a federal prison somewhere. For a long time, we all hope."

"From your lips to God's ears." The men stood and shook hands.

Trooper Payne accompanied Mal to his car. "And the lady you rescued? How's she doin'?"

Mal grinned broadly. "She's great. I married her last month."

Payne guffawed heartily and slapped his knee. "Congratulations, Detective. Talk about a perfect ending."

***

Vengeance in Paris. The dust jacket showed an eerily-lit Eiffel Tower fading into darkness, the name "Barry Whittier" across the bottom in blood red type. Augusta shivered slightly as she glanced at the title a second time. *My word, that's some coincidence.*

After fixing herself a glass of iced tea, Augusta stretched out on the comfortable sofa in the living room, piling cushions behind her neck and head and kicking off her stilettos. She opened the book to the copyright page, curious as to when it had been published. "Copyright 1958" was somewhat reassuring, but the title still struck her as ominous. Soon she found herself engrossed in a mystery, a story of an art theft at the Louvre, an aspiring artist betrayed by a man he had considered a friend, and a beautiful model hiding a mysterious past.

Malcolm entered the living room and stood quietly, observing her. "Must be a pretty good read. Did you even hear me come in?"

Augusta glanced up at him. "Actually, it is a good read, though definitely dark. Not necessarily a great book, but it has interesting characters and so far, a plot that works."

"May I ask what you consider a great book?"

"*The Source*. James Michener's masterpiece. I just finished reading it. Maybe that's why Mr. Whittier's mystery doesn't overly impress me."

"Kind of like listening to Andy Williams after you've just heard Jamie Logan sing?"

"You might say that. Andy Williams is an outstanding pop artist, and I enjoy him. But you're right, I'd prefer to hear Jamie. I guess it's a matter of taste. I happen to love opera."

"So I've been told." Mal tossed his jacket over a chair, loosened his tie and sat at the end of the sofa. He picked up her feet and began to massage them. "What's the title of Whittier's book?"

Augusta lifted the cover in his direction and watched Mal's eyes widen. "No kidding. That's intriguing."

"Well, the publication date is 1958, seven years ago. The clerk at the bookstore said he's written four to date. This is his second. So, maybe one book every two or three years." She wiggled her toes. "Oh, that's why I married you. Nobody gives a foot rub the way you do."

"Who else is tending to your feet these days, Mrs. Mitchell?" he laughed.

"Oh, you know what I mean. You spoil me, Detective Mitchell."

Malcolm nodded toward the book. "Is it giving you any insight into the author?"

"A little. It takes place in the nineteenth century, though. I wonder if Barry studied art in Paris. I almost get that sense."

She carefully inserted a bookmark, closed the book and placed it on the coffee table. "I believe Whittier is a better artist than writer. I admire his technique. On the other hand, his paintings are like this book—a little creepy. Dark and kind of … ominous."

Augusta stood and picked up her glass. "Can I get you a beer?"

"You sure can." Mal stretched his legs out and spread his arms across the back of the sofa. "Now who's spoiling who? Or should that be 'whom'?"

"How were your meetings?" Handing him the beer bottle, she curled up next to him. "Did you learn anything?"

"The most interesting thing I learned is that Anton Portnov's cello seems to have vanished." He recounted his experiences of the morning. "I spent this afternoon doing some checking on Whittier, your 'Renaissance man.'"

"Oh?"

"Whittier is a native of Cincinnati. Comes from a family of some means. I told you I stopped by his house yesterday and he wasn't home. He lives in East Walnut Hills; a large house I would bet he inherited. Forty-four years old, never been married. I presume he's having some success with his paintings or books—the guy drives a Porsche."

"Or maybe he bought it with his inheritance. Well, from what you're telling me, he sounds like your ordinary citizen."

Malcolm frowned. "There's another side to Mr. Whittier. He has an arrest record, Gus. Four counts of reckless driving. Even more, he was charged with assaulting a man he claimed had threatened him. The charges were eventually dropped, but the guy ended up in the hospital."

He took a swig of his beer. "On my way home, I stopped at an art gallery that carries Whittier's work and met the owner. He let slide that Whittier isn't easy to deal with. He has a bad temper and a big ego."

Augusta stared at her husband. "It sounds as though Whittier is at least volatile, and I guess even dangerous under certain circumstances. Do you think he might have something to do with Anton's death?"

"At this point, I'm just telling you what I've learned."

"Here's another thing, Mal." She moved closer to the edge of the sofa and turned to face him. "Saul Kronenberg and Michael Robinson were instrumental in removing Anton from the Chrysanthemum Quartet. Just how volatile is Barry Whittier? If he and Anton were close, could he have had some kind of twisted motive about revenging Anton? Or is that just too far out to consider?"

"Anything is possible, Gus." Malcolm stretched his arms over his head and groaned. "This case is baffling. Who was Anton Portnov, anyway? If I could just get some insight into the guy." He stared at the ceiling. "He was obviously angry about being removed from the quartet, and if he were still alive that might be a motive. From what Manny said about his abuse of alcohol and drugs, it's possible his thinking might have been so convoluted he could have committed murder."

Mal rubbed the back of his neck. "But it's obvious to me Michael's killer was clearheaded. That was a carefully thought out, coldblooded act. My gut tells me there could be a connection, but I'll be damned if I have the faintest clue what it could be. And the fact that Anton's cello is missing might be a piece of the puzzle. Right now, I sure don't have many pieces, and none of them fit."

He leaned forward, elbows on knees, and sighed deeply.

Augusta stroked his back. "That missing cello. What do you think might have happened to it?"

"Good question, and I don't have an answer. The building superintendent might have helped himself to it in that month before the real estate folks had Portnov's apartment cleaned. I asked Manny about the cello and he told me it was worth at least forty or fifty grand. Maybe more."

"Or could someone have known it was there and managed to break into the apartment and steal it?"

"That was my first thought."

Augusta stood and picked up her stilettos. "What's your next move, Malcolm?"

"I'd like to set up an informal meeting with Mr. Whittier, and I'd like your help with that."

"How?"

"Let's get together for a drink. You're reading one of his books, you like his art. You've just learned he knew your friend Anton Portnov. As the *de facto* manager for the Chrysanthemum Quartet, you can tell him you hope to contact Anton's family to return some items of his that you and Manny Levine recently found when cleaning out a filing cabinet."

Augusta stared at Mal, open-mouthed. "I don't believe this. You're actually going to use my made-up story in order to see what kind of information you can get out of this man? After telling me it qualified as interfering in an—how did you put it? 'An ongoing homicide investigation.'"

"Welcome to my world, Mrs. Mitchell. We use whatever we think might work." He gave her a lopsided grin.

"Of course, he'll probably know who you are," Augusta added. "No doubt the neighbor mentioned someone had come looking for him. Shouldn't I meet with him by myself?"

"Not a good idea, Gus. He's got a violent streak—or at the very least, he's unpredictable. It needs to be both of us. Besides, he'll probably be intrigued to meet me. Whittier writes mystery novels. Mystery writers like finding out about cops. Who we are. How we do things. Whether or not he's smarter than I am."

Malcolm stood and pulled his jacket off the chair. "You can try to phone him in the morning. For now, let's put this on the back burner and get ready for dinner, shall we?" He pulled off his tie and frowned. "I need another shower. It was hot out there today."

Augusta pulled herself to him, her mouth close to his ear. "Would you like me to scrub your back?"

He wrapped an arm around her waist.

"I thought you'd never ask."

Chapter 12
Barry Whittier

Tuesday, June 15
9:30 a.m.

"Mr. Whittier? This is Augusta McKee calling. I'm a professor of voice at the Conservatory of Music and a friend of Immanuel Levine's." Augusta sat at the alcove table with pen and pad, ready to make notes.

"I know who you are, Professor McKee. How did you get my number? It's unlisted."

He sounds as if he's affecting an accent. Interesting. British? French? A little of each?

"My husband managed to obtain it. He's—"

Whittier interrupted her in mid-sentence. "A member of the Cincinnati Police Department. Yes, I know who Detective Mitchell is. And the purpose of this call is exactly what?"

Not very friendly, but maybe it's because Mal gave me his unlisted number. Augusta glanced at her husband sitting two feet away from her and wrote on her pad in large letters: JERK. She lifted the pad so Mal could see it and he stifled a laugh.

Well, let's see if I can make him a little less hostile. Ignoring his question for the moment, she continued, "First I'd like to take a moment to tell you how much I admire your art. The one piece, 'Midnight in the Garden of Evil.' Haunting. It's set in a section of Spring Grove Cemetery, isn't it?"

"As a matter of fact, that's exactly what I used for the setting."

"And I'm intrigued with your mystery novels. I'm thoroughly enjoying my read of *Vengeance in Paris* at the moment."

"Thank you."

"Oh, but that wasn't my primary purpose in speaking with you this morning. I'm calling in my capacity as manager of the Chrysanthemum Quartet. It's my understanding that you were a friend of Anton Portnov's. The founder of the quartet, Immanuel Levine, and I located some items that belonged to Anton. We'd very much like to get them to his family, but we're having difficulty locating them." Malcolm gave her a thumbs up. "I had hoped you might be able to provide that information."

A pause on the other end of the line. "I didn't realize the Chrysanthemum Quartet had a manager."

That's right, he told Manny he wanted to be a patron. Think fast, Augusta. "Manny and I only recently made it a formal arrangement. He was a little overwhelmed by some of the responsibilities."

Sounding more cordial, Whittier said, "I'm not sure I'll be of much assistance, Professor McKee. However, I can meet with you to share what I know. Anton was very … secretive about his past." Now it was Augusta's turn to give a thumbs up to Mal.

"That would be quite helpful," She used her most persuasive tone of voice. "In fact, my husband and I were just discussing that we'd like to meet you. We admire your art, and as I said, I've just begun reading one of your books. What an intriguing novel."

Whittier replied, in a more cordial tone, "Well, thank you. Yes, we could certainly get together. I have some questions for the detective if he'd be willing to let me pick his brain a little."

On her pad, Augusta scribbled hastily: JERK WANTS TO PICK YOUR BRAIN. Malcolm took the pen from her and wrote: TOLD YOU SO.

Augusta used the giggle she couldn't suppress to her advantage, "Oh, that's so funny. I'm sure he'd be fine with that. Why don't we meet for dinner? Are you free tonight?"

"As a matter of fact, I just happen to have had a cancellation. So yes, I can meet you. Where would you suggest?"

"Your choice."

"I always enjoy the Maisonette," he told her.

Slightly taken aback by his response, Augusta wrote $$$$$ on her pad.

"That would be perfect," Augusta purred. "Shall we say seven?"

"My favorite time," Whittier replied. "I'll call and make a reservation so I can request my usual table. I'll see you at seven, Augusta."

She heard the click and replaced the handset on her telephone.

"You know what he just told me? He claims to have his own table. At the Maisonette. The most expensive restaurant in Cincinnati." Augusta pursed her lips. "Well, you did tell me you thought he'd inherited his house. Maybe he also has a trust fund."

"No kidding." Malcolm studied the writing on the pad, shaking his head. "Personal table or not, I doubt Mr. Whittier is planning to treat us to this meal. Maybe we could split a Beef Wellington? We'd save a little that way."

"I'm up for that. It's my favorite item on their menu." Augusta stood and pushed her chair under the table. "Anyway, it's okay to splurge occasionally, right? Treat ourselves."

"Yes, we can take Mr. Whittier to dinner tonight at the Maisonette. Or we could book a Caribbean cruise for about the same amount of money." Mal grinned wryly. "I have to get going. Jim and I are going back to Portnov's neighborhood. There are still businesses nearby we haven't interviewed yet."

Placing his hands on Augusta's shoulders, he looked into her eyes. "And you, my darling wife. No more surprise visits to Northern Kentucky. Just because I suggested you use your fake position with the Chrysanthemum Quartet to lure Whittier to dinner doesn't mean I'm giving you license to snoop."

"It's not snooping. It's sleuthing," she reprimanded with a smile. "Not to worry, I have a full day today. Tuesdays, I teach History of Opera in the morning for two hours. Then voice students all afternoon. I may polish off that Beef Wellington all by myself."

***

After her Intro to Opera class, Augusta went into Main Hall and climbed the curved mahogany staircase in the picturesque Victorian mansion to Milly's studio on the second floor. She arrived in time to hear the opening chords of Rachmaninoff's "Vocalise" and the warm tones of a cello performing the melody.

Not wanting to break the concentration of the musicians, Augusta opened the door just enough to hear more clearly but chose not to enter the room. String instruments were her favorite, and of the strings, Augusta thought the rich sounds of a cello most emulated the human voice. Ari played cleanly and with deep expression. In his skillful hands the instrument seemed almost to breathe as it spun out Rachmaninoff's elegant melody.

What a beautiful, poignant tribute to Michael, Augusta thought as she brushed tears from her face. After the final sustained note, she quietly opened the door wider and entered. Ari sat for a moment with his head lowered, then looked up at her and smiled pensively. Milly turned her head and spotted Augusta.

"We didn't know you were here."

"I didn't come in; I just opened the door a crack so I could listen. Ari, that was truly exquisite."

He flushed and smiled again. "It's for Michael's memorial service."

"It's perfect. And what a gorgeous tone from that instrument. It's an Amati, isn't it?"

"Yes. Borrowed from a collection. What a thrill to be able to perform on this cello. I'll hate to give it up." Ari stroked the body of the instrument as he spoke, obviously feeling a strong connection.

"Manny arranged for the loan," Milly commented. "His violin is also part of that same collection."

"I didn't mean to interrupt your rehearsal. Please go on." Augusta seated herself in a chair near the piano.

"I think we're finished unless Ari wants to go through this again." Milly glanced at the young cellist, preoccupied with loosening the bow in preparation for putting it away.

"No, I thought that last run-through went well, didn't you?"

Milly closed the cover on the keyboard. "They all went well. It's so easy to work with you, Ari. It's clearly apparent where you're heading with the music."

"Professor McKee, about Michael's viola. That was also on loan from a collector, a private owner. I hope it's not sitting in an evidence locker somewhere in City Hall." Ari wiped both bow and instrument with a soft cloth to remove any rosin as he prepared to place them in the case.

"Fortunately, Detective Edmonds took personal charge of the instrument," Augusta told him. "It was returned to Mrs. Robinson on Sunday, and I understand she passed it on to Dr. Levine as soon as she could. It's safe."

Ari closed and latched the cello case. "That's good to know." He turned toward Milly. "Thanks, Professor Devereaux. It's a treat to work with you."

"Are you leaving the campus, Ari?" Augusta asked.

"Yes, after I lock this cello in Dr. Levine's studio." He gave Milly a sideways glance. "It just … I think it's better to leave it here than drag it back and forth to my apartment. Dr. Levine has given me permission to practice whenever he's not around."

"That sounds like a good idea," Augusta commented. "Well, take care of yourself."

Ari's eyes met Augusta's for a long moment before he responded, "I sure will. Thanks, Professor McKee." He turned toward Milly. "And thanks again for rehearsing with me, Professor Devereaux."

Milly watched the door close behind him before speaking. "Well, that was weird. Is something going on with that young man?"

"Oh, I think all the string players in the Summer Opera orchestra are a little jumpy these days since everyone is aware Michael Robinson was murdered."

"No doubt. Especially since there seem to be a lot of cops in the pavilion during performances. Even a detective or two." Milly put her hands on her hips. "I don't suppose you can tell me what's going on."

"You suppose correctly. You know it's an ongoing investigation, Milly."

"I figured. Why are you here, anyway? I know you didn't come up here to listen to our spur of the moment rehearsal."

"Mal and I are having dinner with Barry Whittier and I was curious if you knew him. Or knew anything much about him."

"I met him at a couple of art shows Garrett dragged me to. He's okay, I guess. Kind of a blowhard. Why the heck are you having dinner with the guy?"

Augusta ignored the question. "Mal tells me he lives in one of those wonderful old houses in East Walnut Hills. I appreciate his art, but I wouldn't buy it. And I doubt he's getting rich from book sales. Is he old money?"

"Okay, I get it. I'm not in the loop and it's a 'need to know' situation." She pushed her salt-and-pepper curls back from her forehead. "Yes, Barry comes from money. I think his great or great-great-grandfather was some kind of local transportation mogul. Streetcars and trains. Barry's no millionaire, but he certainly has plenty of cash at his disposal. He hasn't married and he's in his forties. Scuttlebutt is that marriage isn't in his future, either. Where are you going to dinner?"

"The Maisonette."

Milly raised an eyebrow. "Let Barry pick up the tab. Pocket change to him."

***

I've seen this man before. Talking with Manny's wife Linda at a Chrysanthemum Quartet concert.

Augusta smiled as Whittier moved to greet them. *And more recently. At the opera, two nights ago.*

"Please, you're here as my guests," Barry Whittier, a dapper man with a well-groomed moustache and a touch of gray at his temples, said expansively as they were seated in the elegantly appointed restaurant by not one, but two, waiters. "I appreciate the opportunity to meet Cincinnati's celebrated power couple."

One of the waiters shook out a napkin and deftly draped it across Augusta's lap. She suppressed a smile as Malcolm quickly intercepted his napkin, shook it out a second time and placed it across his lap himself.

A bottle in a champagne caddy appeared immediately. "I hope you don't mind that I took the liberty of ordering Dom Perignon," Barry said. He critically tasted the champagne, nodded his approval, and all three flutes were magically filled in a trice.

Barry lifted his glass. "To detectives who solve mysteries."

Orders were placed. Barry consumed a second glass of champagne and gazed at Malcolm. "Your wife told me I might ask you a few questions, Detective Mitchell."

"Malcolm, please. Yes, fire away. Augusta tells me the book she's enjoying has a well- developed plot."

Barry beamed at Augusta. "Thank you. Well, I try. I believe all mystery writers are fascinated by police work, as we are in awe of the crime solvers." He played with his fork. "For instance, my friend John Allen tells me the police are questioning people about Anton Portnov, almost a year to the day after the accident that took his life. Now, what on earth could that be about?"

Malcolm leaned back. "I have a feeling there's more to your question, Mr. Whittier."

"Barry, please. Well, we're all aware of the murder of Michael Robinson last Thursday night. Or was it early Friday morning?" He waved a hand. "No matter. But I found it intriguing that I had read earlier that week about another Cincinnati musician, Saul Kronenberg, who died in Paris of a heart attack on June—fourth or fifth, I believe."

"Yes, I knew about that."

"No doubt. I think you may also be aware, Detective, that both Michael Robinson and Saul Kronenberg were members of the probably now-defunct Chrysanthemum Quartet. Anton Portnov was at one time a member of that quartet."

"That's interesting," Malcolm commented. Augusta noticed the set jaw and slightly narrowed eyes. *Malcolm, in full detective mode.*

"And now here you are, and your wife has asked me if I can provide the whereabouts of Anton Portnov's family, ostensibly to return some of his belongings to them. A family no one seems to be able to locate." He leaned back, pleased with himself. "The makings of an intriguing mystery, wouldn't you agree?"

"I would definitely have to agree with that," Malcolm said, as their food arrived.

"I believe this is too heavy a topic to continue while we eat," Barry commented, very much in control of the conversation. "Augusta, which operas have you seen this summer? I'm looking for recommendations."

The elegant meal was accompanied by an equally elegant conversation about opera, singers, and art. Augusta eyed her husband warily but Malcolm appeared to relax and take part in the food with relish and in the talk with caution. Barry managed to down at least two more glasses of champagne.

"Excellent cuisine, wouldn't you agree?" Whittier asked, fork poised halfway to his mouth with a bite of his *coq au champagne*. Augusta and Malcolm, their mouths full of meltingly delicious Beef Wellington, nodded in agreement.

Dishes were whisked away and brandies were served to the men while Augusta requested cognac.

"I trust you will indulge me." Whittier produced an expensive cigar from his inside jacket pocket, and the waiter immediately materialized at his elbow, providing tools for clipping and lighting the cigar. Whittier savored his cigar as if it were as fine as the brandy the men had been served.

"Anton Portnov." Whittier dragged the name out, lingering over the syllables in *Anton*. "One of the most fascinating … and mysterious … people I've ever met. A mystery which this mystery writer could not unravel." He clipped the end of the cigar expertly.

"He intrigued me from the first. You knew him, Augusta. A handsome man. Elegant."

"I met him. I didn't spend much time with him." Augusta took a sip of her cognac. *Oh, my. This must be what liquid diamonds would taste like.*

Malcolm leaned toward Whittier. "That mystery who was Portnov. As Augusta told you, we haven't been able to locate his family. The Boone County Coroner's records indicate he was taken to the D.C. area for burial by a couple who identified themselves as his parents."

"It doesn't surprise me that you can't locate them." Barry puffed repeatedly on the cigar, a wreath of smoke encircling his head. "Whenever I asked Anton about his family, he started talking in riddles."

"How do you mean?" Malcolm asked.

"He'd drop disjointed comments. They came to the United States from Canada. He was called by a different name as a young child. Another time, they came to the United States from France. He heard them speaking in a language he didn't understand. His father worked for the CIA. His father was a medical technician. His father worked for the FBI. He might or might not have a sibling." Another puff of smoke. "That kind of thing."

Augusta took another sip of her drink. "Did he ever mention where he went to music school? If he lived in D.C. I thought he might have attended Peabody. He was a gifted musician and must have had excellent teachers. But they have never had a student named Portnov. Or Portnoy. Or any other variant we could think of."

"We?"

"The registrar's office helped me search. As I said, we would love to locate his family and send them the items we found. Nothing of any real worth, but possibly of sentimental value to a family member."

He probably knows I'm lying, but I'm going to keep up the subterfuge. I wonder how much of this conversation he'll even remember? He's had a lot to drink.

166

"That language … would that have been Russian?" Malcolm waved a hand slightly to disperse the smoke.

"You might think so. I know a little Russian, I picked it up when I lived in Paris. I tried a few phrases and only received a blank stare." Barry laid the cigar in the silver ashtray the waiter had provided. "Actually, a man who claimed to be a member of the Romanov family taught me those Russian phrases. Though there was some talk he might have been a spy."

Momentary silence followed this revelation. Augusta glanced at Mal and could sense the wheels spinning behind the lifted eyebrow and sideways glance. She managed to stifle a smile.

"When was the last time you saw Anton Portnov?" Malcolm asked Whittier.

"Two weeks before the accident that took his life." Barry's demeanor changed and he took a large gulp of his brandy. "I may as well tell you this. We parted badly."

He sighed heavily and gazed into the distance. "We had been spending time together for weeks. I believed we had become close." Whittier tensed his shoulders and glanced sideways at Malcolm. "I hope this won't shock you, Detective. I had hoped we would become even closer."

"I don't shock easily, Barry, and I don't judge."

Barry visibly relaxed and picked up the cigar again. "We'd spent many hours together, enjoying art and music. He read my books." A pause. "I gave him everything he would accept from me. He liked nice clothes. Good wine. I brought him here several times. We flew to New York a couple of times."

More puffs on the cigar. "So that night … when I suggested he move in with me, so we could …"

"Yes, I understand, Barry." Augusta lifted her tulip glass to her lips but paused. "He rejected you," she said softly. "That must have been difficult."

"I regret to say we ended up screaming at each other. I can't tell you how hurt I felt."

"And you never saw him again?" Augusta asked, gently encouraging Whittier to reveal more. "I imagine learning about his death must have been a dreadful shock."

"I read about it in the newspaper." Whittier viciously ground out his half-smoked cigar. "When I was able to function again, I went to Paris. I didn't come back for three months."

"Were you still friends at the time he ended his association with the quartet?" Malcolm folded his napkin into a small square.

"You mean when they fired him? Yes." Whittier turned toward Augusta, pressing a clenched fist hard against the table. "Why did they fire him, Augusta? Do you know? He couldn't articulate that. I don't believe he ever understood why it happened. He was a good cellist, wasn't he?"

"He was brilliant, Barry. Being part of a quartet isn't easy. It takes a certain personality, and unfortunately, Anton apparently didn't understand, or was unwilling, to adapt to being one performer among four rather than a soloist."

He stared hard at her for a moment before he sighed deeply, shoulders slumping. "It destroyed him. Does your Professor Levine know that? Anton was deeply depressed. I thought if he came to live with me, I could help him. He ran short of money. I paid his rent for May, then for June. And then he mentioned he planned to leave Cincinnati and go to California. He told me he had family there. I didn't know whether to believe him or not. That prompted me to invite him to move in with me."

Whittier rested his elbows on the table, clasped his hands and leaned his head against them. "I've done many things in my life I regret. What I said to Anton the last time I saw him I regret most."

He lifted his head and stared at them both. "I've sometimes wondered if Anton rejected me because the Chrysanthemum Quartet rejected him."

Chapter 13
I Spy

Tuesday, June 15
9:45 p.m.

"I think he told us more than he intended to, but not everything he knows." Mal turned onto Vista Circle and pulled up in their driveway.

Augusta followed him into the house, kicking off her stilettos in the living room and relaxing on the couch. Mal removed his coat, pulling his note pad from the inside pocket. He draped the jacket over the back of a chair and sank onto the sofa next to her, making notes on his pad.

"I remembered him the minute I laid eyes on him," Augusta said. "He was speaking with Linda at the final quartet concert in April. And a couple of nights ago I saw him at the opera. All that negative talk about the Chrysanthemum Quartet while he's been cozying up to the Levines. What's that all about?"

"Why the interest in the quartet now, when Anton's no longer part of it? Of course, it could be some kind of ploy." Mal shook his head.

"How much did he have to drink, do you think?" Augusta asked. "It seemed to me every time I glanced at him one of the waiters was refilling his champagne glass."

"I'd say more than he should have, but probably not as much as he seemed to." Malcolm continued scribbling furiously. "That waiter was pouring champagne in the glass when it was still almost full."

He clicked the pen and frowned at his notepad. "So, here's what I have. Let me know if I missed anything, will you?"

She nodded. "I'll try."

"Whittier has figured out that Kronenberg may have been murdered in Paris, and that his death and Michael Robinson's could be the work of the same perp. He knows we're trying to learn more about his one-time companion Anton Portnov because we think there might be a connection between him and the two more recent deaths."

"Well, he may know more about Kronenberg's death than most people because he might have been in Paris when Saul died. That's something you'll want to investigate."

"Yes, he's spent quite a bit of time in Paris over the years. Finding out if he was there the first week of June shouldn't be difficult. I also need to learn his whereabouts on the night Michael Robinson was murdered."

"You think he might have killed both men. He could be your perp."

Mal stood and began to pace, as he always did when theorizing. "He definitely had a motive. That comment he made about Portnov being so depressed by the Chrysanthemum Quartet rejecting him, he in turn rejected Whittier. Which may have led to Whittier killing off the quartet one at a time to avenge Portnov's possible suicide."

"Wait—you really think Anton might have deliberately swerved off the road and run into that tree?"

"Drugs, alcohol, and severe depression. A recipe for suicide if ever there was one." He went into the kitchen. "I'm going to get a beer. You want anything?"

"Just water. Cold water from the jug in the fridge, please." Augusta leaned back on the sofa, lifting one foot to rub it.

Malcolm grinned when he handed her the glass of water. "Looking for someone to tend those feet, Mrs. Mitchell? Too many hours in stilettos today?"

"Yes, please, Detective." She sighed when he complied. "Oh, you are the best."

"So you've said."

"Mal, what's your overall take on Barry Whittier?"

"Unstable. Impulsive. Shrewd. Probably brilliant. Could be a lethal combination."

"So, I take it right now he's your number one suspect for the two recent murders."

"He's someone we need to investigate more thoroughly."

Augusta sat up, hugging her knees, and gazed at her husband. "Some other things he said intrigued me. About Portnov maybe having a sibling."

"That was an odd comment. And I agree, he may know more about Anton Portnov than he told us. How about that off-the-wall comment about learning some Russian when he was in Paris?"

"From a member the Romanov family. Or maybe he was a spy."

"The plot thickens," Malcolm laughed.

"Seriously, though, I keep wondering why we can't find any information at all on Portnov's family in the D.C. area. The remark about Anton telling him he went by a different name when he was young. Had you considered the family might use a different name?"

"Yes, actually, Jim and I discussed that." Malcolm spread an arm out along the back of the sofa and turned toward Augusta, pointing at her with an index finger. "Here's something: 'portnov' means 'tailor' in Russian. There are plenty of Tailors in that part of the country, especially when you consider there are a number of ways that last name can be spelled."

"When we talk to Whittier again, let's see if he could tell us anything more about that mysterious sibling. I'm sure he knows more about him. Or her."

"I have a feeling Mr. Whittier will make himself scarce once he realizes he probably said way too much to us tonight."

"Do you remember what Manny Levine said? It was almost as if there were no Anton Portnov until the day he showed up in Cincinnati."

"Well, Whittier's ramblings could all be fiction. Remember, we're dealing with a man who writes mysteries. He may be trying to plant a red herring by hinting at Russian espionage."

"Don't you think it's worth looking into? I recall reading something about Russian spies appearing in this country not long after their Revolution. And more since that time, right up to the present day. Okay if I research that?"

"Sure. Have at it." Mal finished his beer and stood. "I have to agree with one thing—where better to plant a spy than in the federal government? Whittier mentioned both the CIA and the FBI. You're correct about recent cases. It hasn't been that long since Joseph McCarthy had everybody panicking about Communists lurking everywhere."

Augusta took her glass and Mal's empty beer bottle into the kitchen, and returned to find him holding her stilettos in one hand, his jacket draped over his shoulder.

"Do you remember that remark he made when we first sat down?"

She thought back over the evening. "He called us something. Oh, 'Cincinnati's power couple,'" Augusta laughed.

"No, Mrs. Mitchell. Get it right. 'Cincinnati's *celebrated* power couple.'" He put an arm around her and steered her toward the stairs. "I believe we need to investigate that, bride."

"Which part, groom? 'Celebrated' or 'power'?"

"Both." He grinned at her wickedly. "I think we can find a way to do that, don't you?"

***

Wednesday, June 16
1:15 p.m.

Wednesdays were Augusta's one day on the Cliffside Campus during the summer session, and she had a light schedule with only four voice students. She generally stayed on campus for lunch since her last lesson ended at one, and often met Dennis Halloran at the cafeteria, a spacious, airy room a short walk from the administration building.

She knew Dennis, who had been a history major as an undergrad, had a keen interest in all things Russian, including the current state of affairs in the U.S.S.R., and might be able to provide her with insights into espionage. As she was mulling over how to broach the subject, he joined her at her table, silently offered a brief prayer for his food, crossed himself, and grinned at her.

"Thanks for blessing our food, Father Halloran. I'm afraid I forgot to do that." She smiled. A moment of silence as he removed his food from the tray and she picked absentmindedly at her chicken salad.

"You seem distracted with something today, Professor McKee," he chuckled. "Would you care to share?"

It didn't surprise Augusta to notice some of the students glancing frequently in their direction. She was aware a number of the young women were smitten with the blond, hazel-eyed, movie-star-handsome young priest. *Dream on, ladies. Father Halloran is dedicated to his profession.*

"As a matter of fact, I would." Augusta sipped her iced tea. "This thing about calling up more troops to fight in Vietnam. I'm having a hard time understanding why President Johnson would make that choice. Something about saving the southern part of that country from Communism?"

Dennis sprinkled salad dressing on his lunch. "That's the stated purpose. You know about the 'Domino Theory,' of course, that the U.S.S.R and China are waiting for other Asian countries to move in that direction. If one falls to communism, the theory goes, the next could, and then the next. And before you know it, all of Southeast Asia is Communist. World domination, you know."

"I sense you also have reservations about the U.S. sending troops to Vietnam." She broke her dinner roll and spread butter on a small piece.

"Well, in some ways going to the aid of South Vietnam is logical, but I'm concerned it could come to a very bad end. South Vietnam has a corrupt government, and we'd be working with them. In the northern half of Vietnam, Ho Chi Minh wants to free his country from the domination it suffered from first the French, then the Japanese, and then the French again. It's kind of hard to sort out the bad guys from the good guys."

"Communism hoping to take over the world. I'll tell you, I'm not sure I was ever more frightened in my life than during the Cuban Missile Crisis."

"We're in a war, Augusta. The Cold War isn't just an expression. It's happening all around us, only most of the time we don't think much about it, until something happens like the Missile Crisis nearly three years ago." He took a bite of his salad. "And the combatants sometimes aren't the people you expect. In fact, sometimes it's a shock to find out who they are."

Oh, perfect. There's my opening. "You're talking about spies, aren't you? You sound very sure about this."

Dennis nodded. "Espionage has always been part of history. It's certainly not something new. Of course, during the nineteen-thirties, membership in the American Communist Party had grown considerably, because of heavy recruitment of people who were struggling in the aftermath of the 1929 Wall Street failure. It followed that the KGB enlisted some of those people as spies." Dennis took a long drink of his iced tea. "You remember Julius and Ethel Rosenberg, I'm sure. Among a number of Americans who were charged with espionage and prosecuted."

"Yes, the Rosenbergs. There were a lot of protests when they were facing execution, I recall. And didn't they have two little boys?"

Dennis nodded. "They did. But espionage in this country on behalf of the USSR isn't limited to traitorous Americans. I have a friend in the CIA. He doesn't elaborate—he can't—but he told me the Soviets have been planting spies in this country since the nineteen-twenties. They're still here, only harder to ferret out because they've become more adept at hiding themselves."

"I suppose those spies are using names like Smith and Jones, and appearing as American as apple pie."

"Without question. Undoubtedly planted in branches of the government. The CIA. The FBI. People who appear to be ordinary American citizens, serving their country. Well, they are serving their country, all right. Only they aren't serving *our* country."

"That's fascinating, Dennis." Another sip of tea. "So probably most are in the D.C. area?"

"They could be anywhere. We very likely have KGB agents right here in Ohio. Think about it. Dayton definitely, at Wright-Patterson Air Force Base, and maybe other nearby industries. Even right here in Cincinnati. They want our technology. General Electric provides engines for military jets. That's just one. There are other industries where they could learn a good deal."

"That's a lot to consider. Sobering stuff, Dennis." Augusta dabbed her mouth with her napkin.

"Don't think for a minute there isn't an ongoing effort to find and expel them. It's not easy. You could have a spy living right in your neighborhood in Hyde Park and probably never know it. That's one reason for counterespionage. You need to read some novels by John Le Carré and even Ian Fleming. I'm addicted."

"You mean James Bond is a real person?"

"Not real, but based on agents and military personnel Fleming knew when he was in British Naval Intelligence. Some of it seems outrageous. But never forget, truth can be stranger than fiction."

You don't know the half of it, thought Augusta.

179

***

Wednesday night meant another performance of *Manon Lescaut* at the Cincinnati Summer Opera. Mal picked up LaRosa's pizza for them for an early dinner as he wanted to get to the pavilion early.

"I'm trading places with Jim tonight, and I want to introduce him to the orchestra members since they're used to seeing me in the first row," he had told her before he left that morning.

Augusta had plates, a salad, and iced tea for both of them on the table when he came in the door. He greeted her with a kiss and opened the pizza box.

"Whittier was in Europe for over a month. He flew into Paris on April sixteenth. He left Paris on June third … the morning Saul Kronenberg was found dead." Jim folded his piece of pizza and took a hearty bite.

"So, he was in Paris the night Saul died."

"Most likely, but we won't be able to prove that until we know where he stayed. Paris is like a second home to him. Whittier may very well have been with friends that entire time." He grinned at her. "I talked to your French boyfriend earlier—Jean-Luc. He's checking all hotels in and near the city to see if Barry was registered during that time period. I wired him a photo, and his team will circulate it at the hotel and environs to see if anyone recognizes him."

"Well, it seems likely Barry would have been in Paris the night before—the second—if he had an early flight out."

"Yes, but again, he could have been visiting friends. I think we have motive and possibly opportunity."

Augusta cut her pizza slice into bites. "What you don't have is means. You believe Saul might have been killed by a lethal injection of digoxin. Barry is an artist and a writer, but does he have any knowledge of pharmaceuticals or access to drugs?"

"Access to drugs, probably. Knowledge of how to administer that kind of injection? Doubtful." Malcolm went into the kitchen. "You want more tea?"

"No, thank you." She paused. "A possible murder in Paris. Another in Cincinnati. How on earth are you going to investigate that?"

"I'm going to stick with Cincinnati. This is my jurisdiction. If we find he committed the crime here, the French can decide what they want to do about Saul's possible murder." He helped himself to another slice of pizza.

"Have you asked Barry where he was the night Michael was killed?"

"Not yet. Jim is doing some digging, contacting his publisher and his editor. I've talked to more art dealers and artists. Most people are non-committal, a few have said he's someone they steer clear of. I need to know more before I talk to him again. For all I know, he's already lawyered up."

He took a third slice of pizza. "What'd you find out?"

"Mainly I just confirmed what I suspected. I saw Dennis at lunch, and he has a wealth of information about the U.S.S.R. and Russian spies in the U.S."

"You want any more pizza? There are two slices left."

"Help yourself, I've had all I want." She stabbed a piece of lettuce and a cucumber slice. "Those things Whittier said about Anton Portnov's past. About his father working for the CIA or the FBI. Do you think it's at all possible his parents could be Russian spies using another name and passing themselves off as loyal American citizens? Maybe a name like Taylor or Tyler."

"I don't know that we can believe anything Whittier said, but anything's possible, Gus."

Augusta took a last sip of her tea. "I'd like to know more about the mysterious sibling Barry hinted at. I'd also like to know why Portnov suddenly decided to use his Russian name when it certainly looks as though his family is keeping it quiet."

She leaned toward him. "I think this mystery may go a lot deeper than we imagine."

Chapter 14
Rosalyn Trainor

Thursday, June 17
9:00 a.m.

The Hamilton County Public Library, one of Augusta's favorite places in Cincinnati, opened its doors promptly at nine a.m. to find Professor McKee first in line to come in. She took a moment to enjoy the beauty of the airy, spacious lobby before heading for the newspaper department.

The librarian in charge quickly provided her with what she needed: papers pertinent to the Julius and Ethel Rosenberg trial in the early nineteen fifties. The trial that ended in 1953 with the highly controversial execution of two American citizens, the parents of two young sons, convicted of committing espionage for the Soviet Union.

Dennis Halloran had mentioned Joseph McCarthy when they talked, and Augusta remembered the McCarthy era. By the time of the Rosenberg's trial the

183

American Communist Party had fallen into disfavor and in 1954 it was outlawed. The junior senator from the Midwest, McCarthy, garnered a remarkable amount of power, playing on anti-Soviet fears by accusing various respected people of being secret Communists.

McCarthy and his committee invaded libraries and swept up books they declared were written by Communists. They investigated government employees, academicians, labor union activists, and members of the film industry, resulting in the blacklisting of a surprising number of screen writers, directors, technicians, and actors.

Augusta vividly recalled watching the televised "Army-McCarthy Hearings." McCarthy went too far when he tackled the United States Army with accusations, and that, in addition to backlash from his bullying tactics in the hearings, became his downfall.

It was during that era Julius Rosenberg and later his wife were accused of stealing atomic secrets for the Soviets and were eventually put to death. Augusta found an article in a New York newspaper that implied the two boys, who were six and ten when their parents were executed, had been cared for by their grandmother before being placed in an orphanage. Eventually they were adopted.

So today, they would be twenty-two and eighteen. And they visited their parents while they were incarcerated in Sing Sing Prison, awaiting execution. Augusta shivered. *What has it done to those two innocent boys to have to live with this?*

A quick glance at the wall clock reminded her she had a lesson scheduled for ten a.m.

***

Martha Van Camp, Augusta's final lesson of the day, gathered up her music and carefully placed it in her floral-imprinted fabric briefcase. "Do you have another student right now? Or may I talk to you for a few minutes?"

"Does this have anything to do with some big decisions you have ahead of you?" Augusta asked, motioning for Martha to take a seat.

"October will be here before we know it." Martha stared at her engagement ring. "And yes, I have some choices to make."

"I think I can guess. Do you want to continue to seriously pursue a career in opera, or do you find some other way to continue to sing while you stay right here in Cincinnati with Danny?"

"Exactly." Martha gazed at Augusta, her clear blue eyes troubled. "I hate the thought of leaving him for maybe long stretches of time while I perform out of town, maybe even in Europe. I would miss him terribly. I know I'd worry about him."

"Well, then. What do you see as another option?" Augusta sat back to listen.

Martha lifted a hand, ticking off her comments on her fingers as she spoke. "I think I could probably continue to perform with the Summer Opera. The organization has a tradition of including local people in casts, even sometimes in good supporting roles. Such as Cherubino and Frasquita. I don't believe they would offer me leads if I'm not also singing professionally for other opera companies."

Another finger folded under her thumb. "I think I very well might continue to sing with the Louisville Opera Company. They really like me there." A third point. "And with the Cincinnati Symphony when a soprano soloist is needed, and maybe other nearby orchestras."

"You're speaking of occasional opportunities to perform without committing to a major career."

Martha nodded.

"I'm not sure that's going to satisfy you, Martha. Your goal has always been to try for operatic stardom. An extremely difficult goal to attain. Which would require some sacrifices. In this case, time away from Danny."

Augusta paused for a moment, gathering her thoughts. "I've always said some people sing and some are singers. Singers have a gift, a voice of natural beauty, size and range. They have the unique ability to thrill their listeners with the combination of that remarkable voice, and a deep passion for the music. I *sing*, and I have the passion, so people appreciate what I do. But I had to work hard to build my voice. You're a *singer*, Martha."

"I've been so fortunate to have your guidance. I've learned to care for my voice and appreciate that gift. But even that doesn't mean I'll have a career."

"It's true, there are no guarantees. Working toward a career in any of the arts, especially the performing arts, is a crap shoot. Luck plays a part in every successful career. Knowing the right people. Being in the right place at the right time. And again—being willing to make sacrifices. Sometimes big ones." She thought for a moment. "Have you talked to Dan about this?"

"Yes, of course. He tells me if I want it, I should go for it. He's sure we can make it work."

"It's wonderful that you have his support. He's a great guy, like his dad. Think about this. Give it a try. If you find it keeps you away from Danny too much, if you're miserable, you can step away." She put a hand on Martha's arm. "Here's something to keep in mind. You will always, I repeat always, find a way to make music. It's part of who you are."

"Thank you, Augusta. I'll talk to Danny again." She stood.

"I know whatever you decide will be right for you."

What a contrast. The Rosenberg sons and their unbelievably difficult lives, and this girl and Malcolm's son, who seem to have a happy and secure future ahead of them.

She walked to the window and gazed out onto the charming garden with its statue of Pan surrounded by flowers and bushes. *The choices people make. Didn't Julius and Ethel think about the possible consequences for their family? I suppose they were convinced what they were doing was for the greater good of everyone, including their children. But it's something I doubt I will ever understand.*

***

187

After leaving the Conservatory following her Intro to Opera class, Augusta headed out East McMillan Street toward Peebles Corner and the Alms Hotel, where the Summer Opera had their office. She had enjoyed the repeat performance of *Manon Lescaut* the previous night. Once again, the attractive blond girl and Ari were deep in conversation during intermission. After the opera she noticed they walked out together.

That concerned her, because Ari's security detail was not far behind them. Ari didn't have a car and the patrolmen had been taking him home. How would he explain that to the young woman?

Curious and somewhat alarmed, Augusta followed them, thinking wryly, *I'm tailing two cops who are tailing a cello player.*

When they reached the parking lot, she was too far away to hear the conversation, but Ari managed to say goodnight to his new friend. He helped her into her car and leaned against the door for a moment, bending down to speak to her before she pulled away. Augusta noted that her license plates were not Cincinnati plates, they were from Kentucky.

This is getting complicated. It seems to be a budding romance, and it can't blossom yet. Where have I seen this girl? I can't place her.

Augusta watched Ari head for the car where Winters and Johnson were waiting for him, and saw him driven safely away.

After what she had observed the previous night, Augusta decided she had to find out more about the girl.

Arriving at the Alms Hotel, she went to the Summer Opera office on the mezzanine off the main lobby. She spotted her friend Marianne Hofacre seated at her desk on the far side of the room.

"Hey, Augusta! We don't see much of you around here," Marianne, a pleasantly rounded woman with a youthful face and stylishly trimmed white hair, commented cheerily. "To what do we owe this visit?"

"Hi, Marianne. I'm looking for some information on one of your ushers. The thing is, I don't even remember her name." Augusta had her story ready. *Hope this works.*

"Well, that's going to be challenging. When have you seen her and can you describe her?"

"I've been at performances nearly every night the past week and I've seen her each time. That's what's so maddening. I want to speak to her but it's embarrassing that I can't remember her name. She's very attractive. About five-five or five-six, trim, shoulder-length straight blond hair. But she's not your usual ice-cream blonde. More sophisticated."

Marianne began flipping through a Rolodex on her desk. "Can you tell me anything else about her?"

"She seems to be acquainted with some of the orchestra members." Augusta sighed. "I Just can't place her. I don't think she's a student at the Conservatory. Oh, wait. I think she may live in Kentucky. Maybe I've seen her at the Lafayette Academy for the Performing Arts. I've been to a few events there. But that's near Georgetown. That would be pretty far to drive every evening to usher at the opera."

Marianne deftly removed a card from the Rolodex. "Here's your girl, and you're right, she actually lives in Covington. Rosalyn Trainor." Marianne pulled a page from a note pad and wrote down the telephone number and address. "She loves music, but she's not a musician. She moved up to Northern Kentucky last fall from Lexington. Very nice person."

"Oh, thanks so much. Well, if she was in Lexington, maybe we did attend some of the same events at the Lafayette Academy. I knew I'd seen her before." Augusta accepted the slip of paper from Marianne.

"Oh, one other thing, she mentioned that she spent a couple of years at the University of Kentucky before she came up here." Marianne replaced the card in the Rolodex. "Maybe she moved back home after she dropped out of college."

"Do you have any idea what she was studying at U.K.?"

"Yes, as a matter of fact. Pre-med. She said she hadn't realized how difficult it would be."

"Thanks again, Marianne." Augusta turned away, but stopped and returned to Marianne's desk. "I don't suppose … you wouldn't by some miracle have a photo of Rosalyn, would you? That would confirm she's the same girl. I'd feel silly calling her 'Rosalyn' if she isn't."

"How funny you should ask, because I do. Our publicity photographer took a photo of several of the ushers when we were training them, and the picture was in the *Morning Call* the week before the season began. The article was about how there are many local people who are part of Cincinnati's Summer Opera family in different capacities."

Marianne opened a drawer and removed a file folder, rifled through it and produced the article. "I'll make you a Xerox copy. Back in a sec."

Augusta glanced around the office, recalling the first time she was ever in it as a young singer, signing her first contract. She well remembered the thrill, the anticipation of performing on the Summer Opera pavilion stage.

Marianne returned with the copy she had made neatly placed in a file folder. "Here you are."

"I can't thank you enough. You've been incredibly helpful."

"Happy to do it. I hope you and Rosalyn get together."

Augusta waited until she reached home before removing the newspaper piece from the file folder. The photo of the ushers was of four smiling young women, with Rosalyn on the far right.

Why does she look so familiar? She thought. *I need to learn more about this young woman.*

A thought struck Augusta, and she went into the alcove. She searched her personal phone book for a number—Mal's Marine buddy Jed Savage, now a civil attorney in Lexington. She had met him a little over a year earlier.

The call was to his office, and his secretary put her on hold. Jed came to the phone almost immediately.

"Well, Mrs. Mitchell! Congratulations on your marriage. How's your husband doing?"

After they exchanged pleasantries, Jed asked, "What's up, Augusta?"

"Jed, I need information on a young woman who was at U.K. for a couple of years. Rosalyn Trainor. T-R-A-I-N-O-R. She must have been there from about 1962 to 1964. I'm informed she was in pre-med but dropped out of school. She's been living in Covington for the past year or so."

"What do you need to know?"

"Mainly, where she's from originally. Anything I can learn about her family." She twisted the phone cord around her hand. "I think she's from somewhere near D.C., if that's any help."

"Give me a day or two, Augusta. I'll get back to you."

Augusta appreciated that Jed didn't ask any questions. "That would be great. I'm just playing a hunch, Jed. This may be nothing. Or it might be something."

"Got it. Give Mal my best, will you?"

"I sure will. When are you coming up here to see us?"

"One of these days. I promise."

"Next month. I'll hold you to that."

They said their goodbyes and Augusta sat down, kicked off her stilettos, and spread the newspaper article on the table. She studied Rosalyn's face carefully, using a magnifying glass she kept in the kitchen, which helped the poor quality of the copy slightly.

There's something unusual about Rosalyn's beauty. It isn't American apple pie prettiness. It's distinctive.

The other three girls were facing the photographer, wearing big smiles. Rosalyn had her face turned at an angle, and she smiled pensively. *The slant of her cheekbones. The shape of her mouth. She almost looks like ...*

Augusta ran lightly up the steps and into her study, searched hastily through programs she kept on a bookshelf until she found the one she was after. She flipped through the pages as she slowly returned to the alcove.

In the souvenir program from the Ballet Russe de Monte Carlo she found a portrait of the great Russian ballerina, Alexandra Danilova. The dancer was wearing stage makeup and was posed at an angle.

But with blond hair and minus the makeup ... there is a strong resemblance. A Slavic beauty.

***

Augusta debated talking with Malcolm about what she'd found out about Rosalyn Trainor and decided against it. *What do I tell him? A young woman has taken an interest in Ari, and because I don't know her, I'm suspicious? She lives in Covington and she resembles Alexandra Danilova. I kind of doubt Malcolm would know who Danilova is.*

It concerned her that Ari had walked Rosalyn to her car, though, without his security detail. But maybe Winters and Johnson had told Malcolm about that situation and it had been handled.

On their way to the Zoo to attend the delayed opening night of *Faust*, Malcolm confirmed he'd been made aware of the situation. "I had to switch the security details on Ariel and Manny." He sounded annoyed.

"Why is that?"

"Have you noticed all the females that materialize around Ariel Rosen at intermission? And sometimes after the performance?"

"Yes, we discussed that the other night," Augusta chuckled.

"Well, he pulled a pretty stupid stunt last night. He walked one of those girls to her car. She wanted to drive him home."

"Was it one of the conservatory students?" Augusta asked innocently, knowing full well it had been Rosalyn. *Thank goodness Ari's security detail didn't notice I was behind them.*

"No, it was a young woman who lives in Covington. She's just started ushering at the opera recently." Mal frowned and ran a hand over the back of his neck. "But when Ari turned her down, he had to make up a story that he had friends waiting for him who were taking him to a private party. At least he had the presence of mind to come up with that."

"So, she saw Winters and Johnson and thought they were the friends he mentioned."

"She must have. It's a damned good thing they weren't in uniform. They've been reassigned to Immanuel Levine, and the other detail now has to get Ari out of there before anyone can approach him. Trevor Davidson and his partner, Jeff Sanders. We have to figure out how to get him from the orchestra pit to their car before anyone realizes he's left the premises."

Mal grinned ruefully. "It'd be a hell of a lot easier if he played the flute." They both laughed.

"I have a suggestion," Augusta said. "Just hustle him out without the cello. Let Manny put it in its case and take it home with him."

"I knew there was a reason I married you, Mrs. Mitchell." Mal smacked the steering wheel.

"Then the minute the curtain closes, tell Ari to get the heck out of there," Augusta continued. "There'll be a brief moment of darkness before the curtains open for bows. Have your detail waiting by the orchestra gate with their car pulled up as close as they can get it."

"That should work." He reached over and took her hand in his, giving it a gentle squeeze. "Thanks, partner."

Augusta returned the squeeze. "That may be the sweetest thing you've ever said to me."

Chapter 15
Over the River

Friday, June 18
10:50 a.m.

During the summer session at the Conservatory, Augusta held office hours from nine until eleven a.m. in her studio on Fridays. She was available to her students and any faculty members for consultations, planning, impromptu rehearsals, or even sometimes a brief catch-up chat. Just before eleven she closed and locked her door and headed for Milly's studio, to find Professor Devereaux just descending the staircase.

"Oh, good. You've finished for the day, I take it. Any plans?"

Milly lifted an eyebrow. "That usually means you want me to do something with you."

Augusta grinned. "Well, yes. How about coming with me for a brief trip to Covington?"

"What in the world is new in Covington, Kentucky? We've been there before. More than once."

"It won't take long," Augusta laughed. "I'll fill you in on the way over."

The women continued down the steps toward the entrance. "Why do I have the feeling I'm going to wish I had said no?"

Augusta headed through town toward the Roebling Bridge. "Here's the thing. I mentioned that the Summer Opera orchestra string players are kind of jumpy because of Michael Robinson's murder. Well, Saturday wasn't the only time Mal and Jim have been present at performances. They've been there every night."

"And this has what to do with us driving over to Covington?"

"I noticed one of the ushers seems to be getting very chummy with Ariel." She started across the bridge. "Oh, there's nothing wrong with that, especially since he's quite taken with her as well. I know she's not a student at the Conservatory. I just would like to be sure she's not someone he shouldn't be involved with."

"For heaven's sake, Augusta. You're not his mother. Ariel is perfectly capable of taking care of himself."

Augusta was silent for a moment. "Milly, I've learned some things about this case. I can't say much, but trust me when I say there's a good reason I'd like to check out this young woman."

"With Malcolm's blessing, of course."

"Well … no. I haven't mentioned to him that I'm making this trip."

"Oh, Lord. Stop the car and let me out."

"Relax. I'm not going to confront her or even approach her. I've learned she lives in Covington. In fact, I even have her address." She pulled a small piece of paper from the center console. "One of the Summer Opera staff members provided it to me."

"Did you tell that person it was for some Miss Marple sleuthing?"

"No, of course not. I made up a story that she bought. I'd just like to see where this young woman lives and—"

"And what? What's that going to tell you?"

Augusta had reached a traffic light and signaled to turn left. "For reasons that I can't share with you, I need to know if she's living with her family. I don't know if this address is for a single-family home or an apartment building."

Milly twisted in her seat and stared at her friend. "Do you have any clue how stupid this all sounds?"

"Yes." Augusta handed the paper to Milly. "Here, look for this street, will you? I checked a Covington map and I think I know where we're headed."

They'd arrived close to the southeastern side of the city, a pleasantly busy neighborhood. They passed a small pharmacy and a convenience store and found the address, an apartment building in the next block. Augusta eased into a parking spot a short distance past the apartment building, which was on the opposite side of the street.

"Well, that answers that question. She either lives by herself or maybe with a roommate, but not with her family."

"You're guessing. You could be right, but who knows? Maybe she lives with her parents in one of those apartments."

"No, take a closer look." Augusta twisted in her seat and pointed at the upper floors in the structure. "Look at the balconies and how they're spaced. One-bedroom apartments in the building, I'd bet money on it. I think she lives by herself." Augusta spotted the door to the front entrance as it opened.

"Oh, what a stroke of luck," she jabbed Milly in the ribs. "This is her." Rosalyn was just leaving the building, headed away from them.

"Funny, she doesn't look like a killer."

Augusta pulled forward and found a turnaround. "Wonder where she's headed."

"Augusta, I highly doubt Malcolm would approve of this. What the hell are you doing?"

"Just curious." She slowed and watched Rosalyn walk into the pharmacy in the next block. "I'll just pull up here for a few minutes."

"When she comes out, she's going to spot you." Milly leaned against the dashboard, turned and glared at Augusta. "You found out what you wanted, right? If you're both hanging around the opera these days, why don't you just talk to her?"

"Shush. All will be revealed in time."

Fifteen minutes passed, with Milly increasingly fidgety. "Can we go now?"

"Not yet. Milly, I need you to go in there and see what she's doing."

"Not on your life. Malcolm is going to be furious about this. You are going to tell him, aren't you?"

"Just walk in there and look around, see what she's doing, and then come right back out."

"No, I guess you aren't going to tell him."

"I'll tell him eventually. Please just do it."

Milly glared at Augusta but did as requested, clambering out of the car and slamming the door. Augusta watched her enter the pharmacy, musing over the expression on Rosalyn's face the previous night when she meandered down to the orchestra pit to discover that Ariel Rosen was not there. She seemed annoyed. Or perhaps dismayed, Augusta couldn't tell which. Rosalyn wandered about a bit seeking for him, finally giving up and leaving the pavilion.

Augusta laughed aloud, having a Rocky-Bullwinkle-Boris-Natasha moment, recalling the cartoon character femme fatale Russian spy saying in her smoky voice: "Ve haf ways of making you talk. Right, Boris, dahlink?"

The passenger door was yanked open, and Milly plunked herself into the seat. "She's working. She's wearing a lab coat and she's behind the pharmacy counter."

"I *knew* it." Augusta turned the key and pulled away quickly, headed for Cincinnati. "Was there anyone else in there?"

"An older guy. Probably in his seventies. He was manning the cash register in the front of the store." Milly shook the bag she was holding and removed two candy bars. "I decided I had to buy something. Want one?"

***

To Augusta's surprise, Jed Savage called her later that afternoon.

"I didn't think I'd hear from you so quickly."

"I had a meeting on the U.K. campus and stopped by the medical school. Yes, you were correct. Rosalyn Trainor was a pre-med student there for those two years, 1962 through 1964. Had a good record, too, but she didn't return for the 1964 fall session."

"That's too bad, if she was a successful student. We never have enough good doctors."

"Her records show she was from Reston, Virginia. This is interesting. Attempts to reach her at the physical address and through phone calls were unsuccessful. The phone was no longer in use, and mail was returned to the school."

"Her mail wasn't forwarded?"

"No, so she must not have left a forwarding address when she left Reston."

"That sounds as if her family may have moved." She thought for a moment. "Speaking of family, was there any information about next of kin? Who was paying her tuition?"

"She was. No information about parents. She handled everything herself. Date of birth on her records is listed as December1942, so she was nineteen when she started school. That's a little unusual, most high school graduates matriculate at eighteen."

"Where did she go to high school? There must be some record of that. Wouldn't she have had to submit a transcript?"

"Ordinarily, that would be the case. But there was a note that she was home schooled. That could explain the extra year before she applied at U.K. She was accepted on the strength of entrance exams."

A pause, and then Jed added, "One other thing—the student who was helping me in the office knew her. He said she was nice enough, but kept to herself a lot. Didn't do much socializing at all."

"Oh? That's interesting. Wonder why." A thought struck her. "If she was a private person, this is probably a long shot—but did she ever talk about her family?"

"Good question. When I get a chance, I'll phone that office and see if I can get an answer. Or you can. The young man's name is Larry Hingely. He's in that office quite a bit, I believe. You could leave a message and I'm sure he'd call you. Very helpful young guy."

He gave her the phone number of the medical school records office.

"Jed, you've been so generous to do this. I can't thank you enough."

"You can tell me at some point what this is about," he laughed. "By the way, did Mal ask you to contact me?"

"Not exactly." *And I'm not sure what he's going to say when I tell him what I've been up to today.* "Well, no. But I will pass this on to him."

"Does it have anything to do with the recent murder of that viola player?"

203

"It might. I'm not really sure yet."

They exchanged goodbyes, Augusta once again insisting Jed should come to Cincinnati soon. She tried the number he had provided but her call went to the answering machine, and she decided against leaving a message.

The clock told her she needed to think about dinner, so she busied herself with preparing a light meal. Salad plates sounded good; it was a warm evening. Cincinnati's great Findlay Market was a necessary once-a-week trip into town to keep a good supply of various kinds of salads on hand. Mixed greens, potato salad, and an especially tasty chicken salad made a pleasing plate, and Augusta was just setting the table as Mal came through the door.

He glanced at the table, shrugged out of his jacket and sat staring gloomily at the food. Augusta knew not to ask him about his day. He'd warned her early in their relationship that was a bad idea, and he would eventually share what he could with her.

She served them both iced tea, and sat down quietly beside him. He took a few bites of food before he pushed his chair back and sighed heavily. "This case is going nowhere. All we have is a person of interest who has become uncooperative. And all we have on him is that he was in Paris—or in France—when Saul Kronenberg died, and in Cincinnati when Michael was murdered. No alibi for that night, and now he's communicating through his attorney."

He drained his glass of tea and went into the kitchen to refill it. "Do you want to make a guess as to who his lawyer is?" Malcolm sat down again and gazed at Augusta.

Oh, no. "Not Garrett."

"Yes. Best criminal defense attorney in Cincinnati. Well, in all of Hamilton County."

"Oh, dear. When did this happen?" *I'm sure Milly didn't know this when she went to Covington with me. This is not good.*

"I think Garrett agreed to represent him sometime this afternoon. Whittier started bragging about hiring 'Garrett Stoddard, the best defense attorney in the Midwest' to represent him. Of course, he's keeping his trap shut about why he needs a defense attorney." Mal stirred each of his salads. "I don't blame Whittier. Garrett is who I'd want, if I thought the cops were looking at me as a suspect."

"I know you and Garrett have been on opposite sides in a criminal case before. But it's still unfortunate."

"Well, we're continuing to investigate Whittier as best we can, even if he won't talk to us. We've contacted his publisher, his art agent, people in his social circle. Neighbors. He told us he's spent a lot of time in Paris, if you remember, and I wired his photo to your old boyfriend."

"Yes, you told me you did that."

"I'm still waiting to hear something from Jean-Luc about Whittier's associates in Paris. Right now, he's the only suspect we've got."

"Maybe not." Augusta laid a hand on Malcolm's arm. "What about the young woman who has managed to create some problems for Ari's security detail? Rosalyn Trainor?"

Mal put his fork down and stared at her. "I didn't tell you her name. Where did you get that information?"

"From a friend in the Summer Opera office, who oversees the ushers." *Okay, Augusta, tell all.* "I spotted Ari walking to the parking lot with her, and it concerned me. So I ... kind of meandered down in that direction. When she got in the car, I noticed it had Kentucky plates."

"Keep talking."

"When I talked to Marianne at the opera office, I made up a story about being sure I'd met this girl somewhere but couldn't remember her name, and ... well, anyway, she gave me Rosalyn's name. And her address and phone number."

"I guess it didn't occur to you that Matt Winters and Harry Johnson got the plate number, contacted the Kentucky DMV and secured the same information."

"Oh." Augusta took a forkful of chicken salad. "No, I really didn't think about it. What did they tell you about her?"

"What Ari told them." Mal picked up his fork and dug into his food. "Her name, that she lives in Covington, and that she's been showing a lot of interest in him. She wants to get to know him better. Cello is her favorite instrument. She admires Ari, she heard him in a recital. She would love to spend some time with him. All the things a young guy likes to hear from a great-looking young woman."

"It sounds as though she's definitely a charmer. Well, I learned from Marianne that Rosalyn moved here about a year ago. She just started ushering at the opera this season. I also learned she moved here from Lexington where she'd been a pre-med student at U.K."

Malcolm sat forward, eyes narrowed, jaw set. *Full detective mode,* thought Augusta. "Now that is an interesting piece of information."

"I thought so. So, yesterday I called Jed Savage and asked if he knew anyone in the medical school at U.K. who might know more. He called me back not long before you got home."

"Go on."

"Rosalyn is almost as mysterious as Anton Portnov." She proceeded to fill him in on what she'd learned about Rosalyn's skimpy records at U.K. "They didn't have her parents' names. No way to reach her family, it looks as though they've moved. The student Jed talked to told him Rosalyn wasn't very social. She kept to herself most of the time."

"What else have you uncovered?"

"Rosalyn works in a pharmacy. In fact, it appears she works as a pharmacist." Augusta took a deep breath. "You aren't going to like this. Milly and I drove over to Covington around noon and found Rosalyn's apartment building. I followed her in my car when she left. She was on foot and she went into a small pharmacy. Not a chain, a small neighborhood shop."

"Good Lord, Gus." Mal swallowed the food he'd been chewing and frowned at her.

"I know, I know." She put up a hand. "I didn't go in. But Milly did. Rosalyn was behind the pharmacy counter, wearing a lab coat. Mal, she was a pre-med student for two years. She's working as a pharmacist. She knows about drugs, and maybe has access to them."

"I wish you hadn't involved Milly."

"It never crossed my mind Barry Whittier would retain Garrett as his attorney."

"No, of course not. Well, what's done is done. If Milly started to tell Garrett anything, I'm sure he stopped her and let her know the situation."

Augusta stood. "And there's one more thing. Do you have a copy of that photo of Portnov you've been circulating?"

"There's one upstairs. In your desk, in the drawer you gave me."

"Wait right here."

Augusta returned with the newspaper article which had a small picture of Rosalyn, the Ballet Russe program, and the photo of Anton.

She handed Mal her magnifying glass and spread the article on the table. "This is Rosalyn, the girl on the far right, with her face at an angle." She opened the program. "This is Alexandra Danilova, a famous Russian ballerina. I'm using this because I think Rosalyn looks so much like her, and it's a much better photograph."

Augusta placed the photo on the table. "And this is Anton Portnov."

Malcolm studied the three faces, then concentrated on Rosalyn and Anton.

"They could be related. The resemblance is striking."

"That's what I thought. Rosalyn Trainor could be Anton Portnov's sister."

Susan Moore Jordan

Chapter 16
The Mysterious Trainors

"I want to meet her."

Augusta sat down next to Mal and leaned toward him.

Mal frowned. "How do you plan to make that happen?"

"At the opera. She's been ushering every night. I noticed last night she and Ari go to the bar for a drink at intermission. Oh, he doesn't drink alcohol because he's in the orchestra, and I doubt she does either since she has to keep her wits about her. I'll just speak to them both, and Ari, being a polite young man who was raised right by his mother, will introduce us."

She gazed into his eyes. "I'll play matchmaker. When Ari has to go back to the orchestra pit for the second act, I'll keep talking to her. 'How nice that Ari's met someone. You must be very special. Tell me about yourself, he's kind of a protégé because he reminds me of a young cellist I knew years ago.'"

"You'd use Meyer that way?" Mal sat back and stared at her. "Good Lord, Augusta. Isn't that a little …"

"Meyer won't mind. He wouldn't want anything bad to happen to Ariel, either. Besides, in a way you're using Ari. As bait. Hoping to lure your killer into trying something."

"We've got a detail on Immanuel as well."

"Manny has all kinds of protection. I'm sure you've noticed at least two of his five strapping sons have been at every opera performance. It worries me that Ariel nearly got into Rosalyn's car two nights ago. We need to find out why he's so smitten with her."

Malcolm considered this for a moment. "Well, if anybody could pull this off, it would be you. Just be careful what you say."

Augusta put her arms around his neck and gave him a quick kiss. "Oh, good. I wouldn't have done this unless you were on board with it."

"Uh huh, right." Mal laughed as he stood and pulled on his jacket. "I need to get to Headquarters." He picked up the newspaper article. "I want to have this picture of Rosalyn enlarged and enhanced. I need to contact the airlines to learn if she was in Paris on June third and send her photo to Jean-Luc to include in the Saul Kronenberg investigation. We also need to get in touch with the Reston PD to see what they can tell us about Rosalyn's family—who they were, when they moved away, if they have any idea where they relocated."

"This is getting complicated, isn't it?"

"Depending on what we learn about the Trainors, it could get a whole lot more complicated. We may have to involve the FBI."

"Not the CIA? I thought they were the spy people."

"The CIA deals with espionage outside of the United States. They would work with the FBI if necessary. But we start with the Fibbies. Special Agent Dave Turner. I'm sure you remember him from last fall."

He bent and gave her a quick kiss. "I'll see you at the opera, partner."

Augusta cleared the table and washed the dishes, putting away the leftover salads. She gazed out into her garden, watching as the slanting rays of the lowering sun threw new shadows over the flowers and shrubs. *Should I call Milly and apologize for taking her to Covington today?*

She sighed. The idea of a young woman as a possible killer she found immensely disturbing. *Malcolm is already looking at Rosalyn as a possible suspect. But why would she do it? Kill two men I doubt she even knew? I can only guess because of Anton, maybe the same reason the other suspect, Barry Whittier, might have had—vengeance.*

Augusta glanced around her peaceful, orderly house, considering how blessed she felt with her life. A life so different from Rosalyn Trainor's—or whatever her real name might be. *What would it do to someone to live a double life as her family may have? Could it drive her to murder two men and consider killing more?*

***

"Professor McKee, this is Rosalyn Trainor. Rosalyn, meet Professor Augusta McKee, singer and voice teacher at the Conservatory and at Cliffside College." Ari took a swallow of his ginger ale as the two women smiled at each other.

"Nice to meet you, Rosalyn. I've seen you ushering this week. Are you a musician?" Augusta also had opted for ginger ale, and she noticed Rosalyn was drinking club soda with a twist of lime.

"A music lover, Professor McKee. My family is musical, and I studied piano for several years as a child. Actually, from the time I was eight until I was eighteen. I enjoyed it, but don't by any means consider myself a pianist." She spoke in an even, pleasant tone, and Augusta noted Ari moved a little closer and leaned in to hear her in the crowd. The expression on his face confirmed what she had suspected: Ariel Rosen was falling in love.

Rosalyn turned to Ari. "Playing Mozart must be so different from Puccini and Bizet. Which do you most enjoy?"

His face alight, Ari launched into a description of the challenges of each style, talking animatedly until the tones of the trumpet playing the first notes of Figaro's first act aria, "Non più andrai" reminded the crowd that the next act would start in five minutes.

Ariel downed his drink in one gulp, and Rosalyn extended her hand to take his glass. His fingers touched hers and lingered. "Thank you." He turned and hurried away abruptly. Rosalyn looked after him pensively.

"He's been rushing away after the opera the last couple of nights. I wish I knew why."

"Some musicians love to practice early. When I was a student, the pianists on my dormitory floor started at the stroke of eight. They'd have started earlier if it hadn't been against the rules," Augusta chuckled. "He may have some goal in mind. Perhaps a competition?"

Rosalyn brightened. "That could explain it. I'll ask him. He's extraordinary, isn't he?" Augusta saw no hint of guile or deceit in Rosalyn's expression.

"He's a special young man. I see him as something of a protégé." Most of the crowd around them had disbursed. "I knew a remarkable young cellist once, many years ago, who had as bright a talent as Ari. But Meyer didn't live to see his potential develop."

"Oh, that is so sad." Rosalyn glanced around. "I'd love to hear about him."

"You'll miss the second act," Augusta cautioned.

"I'd rather sit out here and learn more about Meyer," Rosalyn said, gesturing toward a bench.

She is truly lovely, Augusta thought. *Or she's one of the greatest actresses I've ever run into.*

"Meyer and I were students together at the Conservatory. He had a remarkable gift, and in many ways, he opened my eyes to what music is. Being a performer is more than being technically proficient. If we love the music we're privileged to perform, open our hearts and share what we love, we can inspire and uplift others."

"I feel that Ariel has that kind of gift." Rosalyn smiled. "Just talking to him and hearing his enthusiasm is exciting. His love for what he does."

"And you just met him recently?"

"Yes, when I started ushering. He's so easy to talk to. It makes my drive across the river fly by, knowing I'll see him when I get here."

"Have you heard Ari play? You know he's cellist for the Chrysanthemum Quartet." Augusta observed Rosalyn over the top of her glass for a reaction.

"Yes, I have. I heard their concert in Covington. It was remarkable." Rosalyn stood. "May I buy you another drink? Ginger ale, correct?"

Augusta nodded and watched as Rosalyn moved gracefully to the bar to place her order. Onstage, Martha as Cherubino began to sing "Voi, che sapete," her voice mingling with those of the animals. A roar from the lion house. Chattering from the nearby monkey compound. *Only in Cincinnati*, thought Augusta. *Part of the charm of opera at the Zoo.*

Rosalyn returned, but with two glasses of champagne. "I hope you don't mind. I don't like to drink champagne with Ari when he's being so good about sticking with ginger ale."

"Because he's performing. That's thoughtful of you. No, I'll enjoy the champagne, thank you."

They lifted their glasses toward each other and smiled companionably. *Oh, it's easy to see why Ari is so enchanted with Rosalyn.*

"You mentioned that your family is musical. In what way?"

"Mostly my mother. She was a fine pianist. I think she might have pursued a career if she hadn't had a family," Rosalyn answered easily.

What about your brother? "Anyone else?"

Rosalyn hesitated for a brief instant. "No—not really."

"You spoke of the drive across the river. Do you live in Northern Kentucky?" A sip of her champagne.

"Yes, I do. In Covington. I've only been there about a year, and I really like it. I have a job at a pharmacy within walking distance of my apartment." Rosalyn settled back comfortably.

"So, you live by yourself?"

"I do. I moved there from Lexington, where I'd been in school for a couple of years at the University of Kentucky."

"That's a great school." *How much do I dare ask her?*

Rosalyn answered Augusta's unspoken question, which surprised her. "Yes, I started in pre-med and was doing okay. But it proved to be more difficult than I had anticipated, and I decided to take some time away from college and think about what to do next. There were pharmacist assistant job listings posted on a bulletin board. I saw the one in Covington and was intrigued. I applied, and even though I had no experience, Mr. Takacs, the owner and pharmacist, invited me to come for an interview. He explained I could train while I was working."

"Takacs? That's an interesting name. Hungarian, I believe."

"It is. Mr. Takacs served in World War I, and he immigrated to the United States in the nineteen-thirties. He's such a kind gentleman. He's been very good to me. He helped me find my apartment."

"What a nice thing for him to do." *And he's enchanted with you, too, so he doesn't oversee your work too closely. Missing drugs, missing syringes, you can easily hide those from the kindly old man.* "Does he treat all his employees that way?"

"Really, there aren't any others. The pharmacist assistant who was leaving stayed for six weeks until I'd completed my initial training." Rosalyn sipped her drink. "Mrs. Takacs usually handles the front of the shop."

Augusta took another sip of her champagne, noting that Rosalyn's glass was almost empty. "You and Ari— you mentioned you only met recently."

"When I came to the Zoo for training as an usher, the orchestra was there. A special rehearsal of *Manon Lescaut*—I think it's called a '*sitzprobe*'? Where the singers are seated on stage and aren't having a staging rehearsal?"

"Yes, *sitzprobe*. It literally means 'sitting trial'— I've always found that amusing. The purpose is for the conductor to make any musical adjustments he needs to better coordinate what's happening between the orchestra and the singers."

Augusta lifted her glass and eyed Rosalyn through the golden liquid. "I'm curious—why would a busy lady such as yourself volunteer to usher at the opera? I hope you don't mind my asking."

"No, not at all. I love opera, and it was a way to see as many performances as possible without having to pay for all those tickets. And a way to meet people who enjoy music as much as I do."

"I can certainly understand that. As a music student, I ushered for the Cincinnati Symphony every weekend. For exactly that reason. Oh, please continue. I interrupted your story."

Rosalyn nodded. "Anyway, the orchestra had a break and Ariel came out of the pit and talked to us. He was so friendly, so nice to answer our questions. There were about eight of us there that day. The next night when I saw him at intermission, I was thrilled that he remembered my name."

"He certainly is a charming young man. Have you been able to spend much time with him?"

"No, we haven't found the time yet. I work almost every day, and he's been busy every night." She drained the last few drops of champagne. "We've been able to talk on the phone a few times. I hope we'll be able to get together soon."

So far, she's been almost completely honest with me, I'm sure. Except for that evasive answer about musicians in her family.

"I don't think you're originally from Kentucky, Rosalyn. Am I correct? I don't hear any hint of that typical drawl."

"No, you're right," Rosalyn laughed. "Actually, I grew up in California. My family only came east a few years ago."

"So where are they now?"

Rosalyn grew pensive. "Professor McKee, I don't see my family any more. I regret that we've become estranged. Over the past two years we've only talked on the phone three times."

Again, Rosalyn's apparent candor took Augusta by surprise. "That's distressing, I'm sure. Well, I know it can happen. I hope you'll be able to mend your differences."

"I'm not sure that will be possible. But I appreciate your concern."

She stood abruptly and reached for Augusta's glass. "Let me return these. Shall we move closer to watch the finale of the second act? I need to be on duty for this intermission."

***

"I have a hard time believing she killed two men in cold blood." Augusta poured herself a glass of wine and sat down at the table in the alcove with Malcolm, as he opened a beer. "She's the kind of girl I'd like to see Ari with. Or at least, she certainly gives that impression."

"She sidestepped a couple of important issues." Mal pressed an index finger against the table. "She avoided mentioning her brother, and she managed to not answer your question about where her family is now."

"We don't know for sure Rosalyn Trainor has a brother."

"*Au contraire*, Mrs. Mitchell." Malcolm grinned. "When we checked for the burial of Anton Portnov in the D.C. area, we came up with zilch. Checking the Virginia records for a June or July burial of a young male, last name Trainor, had much better results."

He reached behind him to the jacket draped over the back of his chair, and pulled his notebook from the inside pocket. "Anthony Trainor, age twenty-seven, interred at Reston Memorial Gardens, June 23, 1964."

Augusta took a gulp of her wine. "That sounds pretty definitive."

"Gus, I wonder if you've let Rosalyn get to you because Ari has fallen for her." Mal lifted an eyebrow at her as he rolled his bottle between his hands.

"Rosalyn just doesn't—I simply can't see her as a killer." Augusta glanced off in the distance. "Though her work at the pharmacy certainly provides her with means. And since we suspect she and Anton were brother and sister, her motive might have been similar to Barry's. But we don't know about opportunity."

Malcolm leaned toward her. "We checked airline manifests today. They showed nothing for a Rosalyn Trainor making a trip to Paris in May or earlier this month. Of course, she could have flown under an alias."

He stood and went to the large bow window, gazing out into the darkness. "On the other hand, we know that Barry Whittier was in Paris." He turned and stared at Augusta. "You say you have a hard time believing Rosalyn could kill two men in cold blood."

She nodded.

"From what I've learned of Whittier, he has all the signs of being a sociopath. He thinks only of himself, and he can be ruthless. The fact that he has money gives him a sense of power. My thought is that he was obsessed with Anton, and he's become obsessed with exacting revenge for Anton's death. There's no doubt in my mind that Whittier is capable of such an act."

He folded his arms across his chest. "None."

Chapter 17
A Funeral

Saturday, June 19
9:00 a.m.

The day dawned warm and muggy with no breeze to stir the humid air. Augusta critically surveyed the black dress spread across her bed. *The same dress I wore for Linnea's funeral over two years ago. I hate funerals. But then, who doesn't? Poor Alicia. And those two sweet boys.*

She found her black stilettos in the shoe organizer on her closet door, smiling as she recalled why it had been installed. Caruso, the Golden Shepherd she and Mal had cared for last summer and early fall, had a weakness for designer stilettos. He loved to chew her shoes. At first, she had been horrified, then secretly amused as she slowly fell in love with the smart, sweet dog who played a large part in saving her life. *I think Mal misses Caruso. I know I do,* she mused.

223

She still hadn't telephoned Milly. *I should never have insisted she go to Covington with me, but who would have known Barry Whittier would lawyer up so quickly? And with Garrett.* The phone rang, and Milly's voice came through the other end.

"Augusta, I don't know if you're aware that Barry Whittier has retained Garrett as his defense attorney."

"Mal told me last night." Augusta tucked the phone handset under her chin as she slipped out of her dressing gown. "Milly, I am so sorry I dragged you to Covington and put you in such an awkward position. Mal said he felt sure if you'd started to tell Garrett about our jaunt across the river, he would have stopped you."

"He did. Don't apologize. You didn't say a word about Whittier being a person of interest in Michael Robinson's murder. And how could you have known Whittier would contact a lawyer, or that it would be Garrett?" She paused. "You and I can't talk until this is over. That's a bummer, but it has to be that way."

"Oh, I'm well aware of that. It won't be easy. I'll miss you. Can we at least say hello when we run into each other at Michael's service?" Augusta perched on the edge of her bed as she drew a seamless stocking up each slender leg.

"I believe that's allowed," Milly replied. "Or we could at least wave at each other. I have to take off. I'm meeting Ari a few minutes early. He's playing as part of the Prelude for the service."

"I'm just dressing now. I'm sure it will be a beautiful service, but so, so sad."

"Take care of yourself, Augusta. Hopefully, we'll be able to talk soon."

Augusta found herself near tears. "Amen to that. I'll see you, Mil."

***

Christ Episcopal Church stood imposingly on Fourth Street in Cincinnati, a starkly modern church that contrasted with the two other buildings in the complex, Gothic Revival structures which housed a chapel, offices, and rooms for numerous activities, as well as the church library. The church and its large, active membership were a vital part of the life of the city in many ways, including a vibrant music program. Augusta often attended Sunday evening concerts and the annual Boar's Head and Yule Log Festival, an impressive celebration of music and drama presented the weekend after Christmas since the late nineteen-thirties.

Malcolm and Jim Edmonds were outside the church and deep in discussion when Augusta arrived. Malcolm exchanged nods with her. Augusta noted the Cincinnati music community had turned out in force. The Levine family, arriving at the same time she did, stopped to speak with her. "Are you by yourself, Augusta?" asked Linda. "Come and sit with us."

Augusta found herself flanked on either side by two of Manny's five strapping sons she had mentioned to Malcolm the previous night. The young men appeared slightly uncomfortable to be in a Christian house of worship. Augusta had met them but was still attempting to attach names to faces, and the young men grinned as they helped her out.

"I'm Aaron, Professor McKee," the young man on her right whispered. "The Number One Son. And that character on your left is Josh. He's the baby of the family."

"Thanks, Aaron. I appreciate your family inviting me to sit with you."

"I don't know about Mom and Dad, but I'm really glad you're here. I don't want to stand when I should sit and vice versa. Josh and I are kind of counting on you to show us the ropes."

Augusta smiled conspiratorially at both the Levine sons. "It's not difficult. The celebrant will generally tell you when to sit and when to stand. Just keep an eye on me if you're not sure." She glanced around the church, the vaulted ceiling high above, the intricate stained-glass windows, part of the original building which had been replaced with the starkly modern edifice, throwing patterns of light over the gathering congregation.

The organist played softly on the church's magnificent organ; a quiet piece that sounded familiar. *Maybe French? It could be a piece by Widor.* Alicia and her sons and other family members entered and were led to their seats in the front pews. Alicia, a slender, petite woman with pale blue eyes and auburn hair, looked more like the boys' sister than their mother. Michael Jr., fifteen, now the man of the family, an arm protectively around his mother's shoulders, and Jake, just thirteen, confusion and anguish etched on his young face.

Augusta's eyes filled with tears as she watched them, their faces raw with shock and grief.

Milly and Ari took their places and began the beautiful Rachmaninoff "Vocalise," the sound of the cello filling the sanctuary with aching beauty. Augusta's eyes blurred with tears as she rummaged in her purse. Immediately she became aware of an outstretched arm on each side of her, offering handkerchiefs. She took Josh's and whispered shakily, "Thank you."

When Augusta tried to return it after blotting her face, Josh waved her off. "Keep it," he whispered, his own voice none too steady. With a slight shock she realized, *It must be on their minds that this could have been Manny's funeral.*

The stately, measured language of the service from the Book of Common Prayer Augusta found soothing and comforting. She knew Alicia Robinson had selected the hymns which looked forward with hope, as did the scripture readings. The special music, John Ireland's beautiful and stirring anthem "Greater Love Hath No Man," required Augusta to bury her face in Joshua Levine's handkerchief to muffle the sobs she couldn't hold back.

The organist performed the final piece of music—an adaptation he had written of Puccini's "Crisantemi Quartet." The organ's string stops sounded hauntingly similar to that of the Chrysanthemum Quartet performing its signature composition. Not the eloquence of true strings, but more distant and veiled—conjuring the ghosts of those instruments. No one in the church moved until the last note of music reverberated gently throughout the sanctuary. The mourners filed quietly from the massive church.

Once out in the sunlight, Augusta turned to Josh as she clutched his ruined handkerchief. "I'll buy you a new handkerchief, Josh. I think I destroyed this one."

Manny's sons clustered close to their father and mother. "That's not necessary, Augusta," Linda said. "I'm glad Josh could help you out." Her eyes were moist. "Are you going to the luncheon?"

"I'll stop in for a few minutes. I want to speak to Alicia." She glanced toward Malcolm, whose keen eyes scanned the departing crowd. *Who's he looking for? Barry Whittier? Rosalyn Trainor?*

While it had been cool in the church, the noonday sun warmed the air and moisture rising from the nearby Ohio River began to generate humidity, a portent of the thunderstorms predicted for that evening.

In the Reception Hall in one of the connecting buildings, Augusta embraced Alicia and took the young woman's icy hands into her own. "There aren't any words, Alicia. I have some sense of what you're feeling right now. I lost a young man I loved many years ago and thought I would never recover."

"I'm still trying to accept what happened." Alicia smiled wistfully.

"If you ever need anything—anything at all—even just to talk—please, please call me. I mean that with all my heart."

Alicia reached for her and held her tight for a moment. "Thank you, Augusta," she whispered. "That means more than you know. And I definitely will call you."

Augusta had a glass of tea and a small plate of fruit and cheese at the sumptuous luncheon Cincinnati's music community had generously provided. She spotted Milly at a distance with other members of the Conservatory faculty and wished she could join them. Ariel must have left; he was nowhere in sight.

She continued to glance around the room and did a double take. Manny and Linda Levine stood at a distance, deep in conversation with Barry Whittier. Augusta attempted to find some way to conceal herself and avoid staring at the three of them.

Oh, I wish I were a short person right at this moment. She managed to slip behind a pair of extremely tall men who were chatting animatedly and ignored her.

Augusta stretched her neck around a broad shoulder and peered at the Levines. *If only I could read lips. I wonder what they're talking about.* The men she was using as a shield started to move away, giving her a puzzled glance, and she pulled herself up to her full height, tipped up her chin, and headed in the opposite direction, her face burning.

The last thing she noticed before turning away was Whittier and Immanuel shaking hands. *I don't like that at all*, she thought.

Before she left home, Augusta had turned on the central air conditioning and her handsome Tudor house was comfortably cool when she returned. She exchanged her dress and stilettos for a pair of capri pants, a loose sleeveless blouse, and low-heeled slip-on shoes. She selected the Brahms Requiem from her record cabinet and put it on the turntable, fixed herself another glass of iced tea, and relaxed on the sofa to listen.

The Brahms Requiem was a favorite because Augusta felt it presented death not as an end, but as a beginning. She'd heard that same expression of hope in the John Ireland piece the Christ Church choir had performed with such emotion at Michael's service.

Michael. Such an awful business. A gifted, gentle, generous man in the prime of life cut down needlessly. Meyer died as the result of a terrible illness. But someone deliberately took Michael's life. Took him from people who loved and needed him. Changed lives forever.

Augusta thought of Linnea, another young, vibrant person whose life had been snuffed out by a cruel human being who thought only of his own wants and needs. Yet if Linnea had not been murdered at Cliffside, chances were Augusta would never have met Homicide Detective Malcolm Mitchell.

As if on cue, Malcolm joined her on the sofa, pulling her close. "Tough funeral this morning."

"Yes, but the music helped. It was truly beautiful."

She sat up and turned to face him. "Mal, Whittier was there. At the funeral. Talking to the Levines."

"Yes, I saw him. And I saw that exchange as well."

"We have to warn them to stay away from him."

"I can't do that, Augusta. What would I tell them? That Barry Whittier may have murdered two of their friends, but we don't really know that for sure? That

Manny might be the next victim, but we don't have any proof of that?"

She grew quiet. "This is awful. I hate this."

Mal stroked her hair back from her face, gazing into her eyes. "I know you do. The best we can do is continue to be vigilant, keep an eye on Whittier and hope he makes a misstep so we can pick him up."

"This has been happening since the beginning of time, hasn't it? Murders. Wars. People killing each other senselessly." She pulled back and put her hands on his face. "And that has given us people like you. People who do everything they can to find the killers and see that they are punished."

She moved her hands to his shoulders. "You told me you became a cop because you wanted to help. You felt it was a calling. Do you remember what you said to me the first time I asked why you became a homicide detective?"

Malcolm started to speak, but Augusta gently pressed a finger to his lips. "No, let me see if I have it right. You said that being a homicide detective has to be one of the most satisfying occupations on God's earth. Mentally, it's challenging. It's like playing a different puzzle every day, except the outcome is very important to another human being. Bringing the killer to justice. And then you told me when you're investigating a homicide, you have the victim in your head, and you have a constant reminder of what's going to happen if you don't catch who did it. There's a chance they will kill again. And I think that's what drives you to continue the battle."

His eyes held hers for a long moment. "Yes, you got it right."

Augusta moved into his embrace again. "You know … I sometimes wonder …" Augusta murmured against Malcolm's throat. "If we'd met when we were younger … would we have had children? I think Alicia's boys will be a great comfort to her. In many ways, they'll help her survive Michael's loss. They'll help each other."

He pulled back and gazed at her warmly. "Gus, we have two sons."

"You have two sons. You and Carla."

"You have to know how much my sons love you. They think of you as another mother, not a stepmother." He smiled at her, the dazzling smile that had won her heart. "They feel a closeness to you that they couldn't experience with Carla. She never wanted me to be a cop. You understand what I do and why I do it, and you have my back. That means more than you know to all the Mitchell men."

He kissed her softly. "You may not have carried Ryan and Dan in your body, but they never doubt that you constantly hold them in your heart."

"Oh, Mal."

"Tear ducts working overtime today, I see," he chuckled and gently brushed the tears from her face.

Augusta sighed. "Have you had lunch yet? It's late, but I can make a salad plate for you."

"I can get it, but come and sit with me." He stood and pulled her to her feet. "I want to catch you up on what I've learned today."

232

Augusta realized she was hungry as well. She had only had that small plate of fruit and cheese at noon, three hours earlier. They worked together preparing plates. Mal poured himself an iced tea which told her he intended to head back to Detective Headquarters after he'd finished lunch.

"Some interesting stuff has surfaced. I spent a couple of hours with the *Morning Call* literary writer, who has read all of Barry Whittier's books. Here's something. In one book Barry used lethal injection as his killer's method."

"Well, that might just be a coincidence. Mystery writers are always looking for ways to bump off their victims," Augusta remarked.

"By a digoxin injection? The exact drug that killed Michael Robinson? We still haven't received the tox screen results on Saul Kronenberg from the Hartford coroner, but it's possible digoxin may be present."

"Well—I'll grant you, that is definitely interesting."

"The digoxin murder is in Whittier's newest book, just released in April." He thought for a moment. "And a fascinating title—*Return to Paris.*"

Augusta stared at her husband. "You've decided Whittier is the killer?"

"I think it's a strong possibility."

"But what about Rosalyn, the assistant pharmacist with access to drugs? From what she told me last night, Mr. Takacs pretty much leaves the pharmacy in her hands. And those two years of pre-med. She'd know exactly where the injection would be most effective. I've heard you say a woman is more likely than a man to choose poison as a murder weapon."

Malcolm wiped his mouth and hands with his napkin and stood. "I have to get back to Headquarters. We still have a lot to learn about Rosalyn. I'm meeting with FBI Special Agent Turner to request he investigate a family that used to live in Reston, Virginia, last name Trainor. The Reston police talked to neighbors, who have no idea why the family left so abruptly last summer, nor do they have any idea where they went. Walter and Pauline Trainor only lived at that address for about three years. They rented the house, and the owner confirmed the Trainors left with very little notice. Nobody really knew them or knew much about them, except that Walter worked for the federal government in D.C. and Pauline did something in the city as well."

"Two of those years Rosalyn was at the University of Kentucky. What about Anthony—Anton?"

"The neighbors only mentioned a daughter. I have no idea where Anton was during that time. Maybe there *are* relatives in California. Whittier said Anton had talked about going out there, and you told me Rosalyn mentioned that's where she grew up."

He leaned against the door frame. "One more thing about Rosalyn. She doesn't fit the profile of a female killer at all. Women generally kill for money or revenge—the kind of revenge you want to exact on someone who's been using you as a punching bag for years. Not to avenge a third party."

"Like Lizzie Borden and how viciously her parents were killed? I've heard speculation that it was because she'd been suffering physical mistreatment at their hands."

Mal nodded. "There's a third category, which is one I don't even like to think about. It doesn't apply to Rosalyn anyway, because so far as we know she doesn't have children."

Augusta experienced a moment of queasiness. "Oh, Mal. Thank you for not saying it." *He means mothers who kill their own children. They have to be mentally ill.*

She walked with him to the front door, an arm around his waist. Mal draped an arm lightly around her shoulders.

"Take care of yourself, my valiant warrior. Keep up the good fight."

He gave her a crooked grin. "Always." He caressed her face with gentle fingers. "I'll be back to pick you up for the opera. *Carmen* again tonight, isn't it?"

"It is. It will be a nice diversion." She put both arms around him.

"Better bring an umbrella. Thunderstorms predicted for later."

Mal's soft, lingering kiss brought to Augusta's mind the first time their lips met. That same night he had told her why he was a homicide detective.

She stood in the doorway and watched him drive away.

My detective. My hero. My dearest love.
Please, Lord, keep him safe.

Chapter 18
Storms

Saturday, June 19
3:30 p.m.

Mal stopped at Covington Police Headquarters to let them know he was in town and would be talking with a resident he thought might have pertinent information about his current case. No need for backup, he'd just be having a conversation with Rosalyn Trainor at the drugstore where she worked.

He parked just past the store and ran his fingers through his hair, pulling at it so it appeared unkempt. He also took off his coat and tie and unbuttoned his shirt, rolling his sleeves to his elbows. He pulled from his belt his small ammo case and handcuffs, removed his well-worn holster, and popped them into the glove box. *Wonder how many times I've done this? More than a thousand*, Mal thought. He re-buckled his belt, shoving the revolver into his waistband.

With his shirttail out, no one but a very experienced cop would know he was carrying. Or even know he was a cop. He was no longer well-groomed Detective Malcolm Mitchell. Fresh off the farm Barney Hayseed sauntered into the store.

Peter's Neighborhood Pharmacy stood on the corner, a small building that looked welcoming and well-maintained. Inside were shelves with toiletries, over-the-counter medications, a rack of magazines, periodicals, and paperback books including, he noticed, a couple by Barry Whittier. A pleasant-looking white-haired lady he guessed to be in her seventies greeted him as he came in.

"Let me know if you need any help," she said in a chirpy voice. Mal headed for the pharmacy counter in the back right-hand corner, pulling out his handkerchief and rubbing his eyes. Rosalyn Trainor turned to assist him.

"How can I help you?" Friendly and polite. A nice smile.

"I was just down to Lexington, and driving back to Cincinnati I had to pull over because my eyes started to sting so bad." He pointed to his reddened eyes. "I think maybe it's the humidity. Guess I've got me some kind of allergy. This is the worst it's ever been." He blew his nose vigorously. "Maybe I should see my doctor. But it'd be great if you have something I could buy that'd give me some relief."

"Of course." Rosalyn came from behind the counter and walked with him to a shelf marked "Sinus and Allergy" and pointed out several different medications. "Your eyes are really red. That must be uncomfortable." She picked up a bottle. "These eye drops are probably the best medication you can get without a prescription, and they should definitely help."

Mal accepted the bottle and pretended to read it carefully. "You think this would be the best one?"

"It's what I would use. But you really should see your doctor."

"Thanks." He stared at her. "Say … I don't like to be forward or anything, but haven't I seen you at the Cincinnati Summer Opera? I think maybe you were an usher? Sorry, I hope you don't mind my asking. Were you at that Mozart opera the other night?"

"As a matter of fact, I did usher that night. Did you enjoy it?"

"I sure did. It was terrific. Matter of fact, I know one of the singers in the cast. That's pretty cool."

"Are you an opera lover?"

"I'm not sure I'd go that far. I like some operas. *Carmen* and *Tosca* are my favorites."

"Those are two I especially enjoy as well."

"You know what else I like? Hearing the orchestra. They're just great." Mal continued to clutch the bottle but didn't pull out his wallet.

"Yes, they certainly are."

His voice dropped to almost a whisper. "Did you notice that chair in the orchestra pit? The one with black cloth on it?"

"The chair for the violist who died, you mean. Michael Robinson." Rosalyn seemed a little less friendly. *This discussion has taken a turn she doesn't care for.*

"Yeah, that's the guy. You know, I think he was a member of a string quartet. I heard them play a concert last fall. They were pretty good."

"Yes, I've heard about them," Rosalyn commented warily.

"You know something else? Another member of that quartet died a couple of weeks ago. Did you read about that in the paper?"

"No, I don't recall that. How unfortunate."

You're lying, sweetheart.

"Yeah. In Paris, of all places. I mean Paris, France. Not *our* Paris." He guffawed heartily and Rosalyn relaxed.

"Yes, that's what I thought you meant. Have you ever been there? Paris, Kentucky?"

He laughed again, slapping his knee. "Now that's pretty funny. Yep. Sure have. Never been to Paris, France, though."

"It's a beautiful city," Rosalyn said warmly. "You must go sometime. Everyone should see Paris at least once."

"When was the last time you were there?" Mal fumbled with his wallet, watching her out of the corner of his eye.

"Oh, not long ago, actually. Earlier this spring."

Mal handed her money and the bottle. "Say, thanks a lot for your help. I sure hope these will do the trick."

Rosalyn went behind the counter to ring up his purchase. "They should, but remember, if they don't, be sure to get in touch with your doctor. He can give you a prescription that will be more effective."

240

"Nice talkin' to ya. See you at the opera, maybe?"

***

The storm had struck Saturday night during the third act of *Carmen*, just as Don José and Escamillo began their onstage fight, enhancing the drama. It struck hard, with driving rain and strong winds. The Zoo employees assigned to lower the tarpaulins on the sides of the pavilion fought with them for several minutes, leaving some members of the audience drenched before the tarps were secured.

This distracted some sections of the audience, who responded with sounds of dismay mixed with muffled laughter. The action on stage didn't stop, and the worst of the storm soon receded. The cast and orchestra were protected by the pavilion ceiling and were far enough from the sides to not be affected by the rain. Augusta had been sitting with Mal near the orchestra gate and only felt the strong wind for a few moments.

She watched as Ariel left the orchestra pit immediately after the curtain closed. As she heard the unmarked police car pull away Augusta had thought, *I'm sure he's not happy about this. I didn't see Rosalyn tonight. I would guess Ari has been on the phone with her, though. I wonder how he explained his recent hasty exits.*

Sunday morning dawned clear and cool, with the promise of an unusually nice day ahead. Mal left the house early; he wanted to telephone Jean-Luc to find out what he had learned about Whittier's Paris connections.

241

"I have an appointment with Dave Turner later," he told Augusta. "He expects to know something one way or another about the Trainors by then. We'll probably grab lunch but I should be home by late afternoon."

Rosalyn not being at the opera the night before was unusual, and the first time she hadn't been there since June 12. There seemed to be a full complement of ushers, and Augusta assumed she had the night off. *Doing what, I wonder. Well, she must have made some friends in Covington after living there for over a year. Maybe a girls' night.* Still, it seemed a little odd not to see her talking with Ariel.

Maybe there's a perfectly logical explanation for her family's unusual behavior. On the other hand, there was Anthony Trainor, a brother who suddenly appeared in Cincinnati using the name Anton Portnov, parents who crept out of Reston in the dead of night to claim his body and left no forwarding address. *Nothing logical about any of that.*

A phone call from Alicia Robinson broke Augusta's train of thought. "Augusta, I'd like to ask a favor of you."

"Of course. Anything, I told you that."

"It's just … well, what I really need is a favor from Detective Mitchell." A sharp breath on the other end of the line. "I've been going through Michael's clothing. The items he had on the night he died."

Oh, dear God. She shouldn't have to do that alone. "Can I come and help?"

"No, Linda Levine is here with me, but thank you for offering. There was a lapel pin in Michael's tux jacket, and it doesn't seem to be here. I wondered if your husband could tell me if the police kept it for any reason."

"I'll certainly ask him, but I can't imagine why they would have done that. Can you describe it?"

"Seeing Ari play reminded me about it. It's very small, about a half inch in diameter. A gold chrysanthemum. Manny had them made for the quartet, and he gave each of them a pin the night of their debut recital. They are so proud of them. Michael always wore his when he played. Ari had his on yesterday, and that's what made me think of it."

"I'll ask Malcolm the first chance I get. I would think the police must have it." *Or it was in the car, or maybe came off his tux jacket when Dennis and Sam pulled him out? And could be buried in dirt outside Mecklenburg's Bier Garten.* "I'm sure it's somewhere safe."

"Thanks so much." Alicia's voice shook as she added, "I try not to keep thinking if I'd only been there that night, he'd still be alive."

"Alicia, please don't do that. Are you sure you wouldn't like me to come out there?"

"I'll be okay. Linda's making breakfast for the boys, and I have neighbors coming later. I would love to see you, though. Maybe one day later this week? Hopefully, with Michael's pin."

Augusta wiped the tears from her face as she replaced the handset. *Whoever murdered Michael and Saul, that person has to pay. This killer destroyed good people's lives.*

243

She took her second cup of coffee out into the garden and wiped down a bench so she could enjoy the pleasant, cool air. A dog barking off in the distance brought Caruso to mind. One thing about him—despite plenty of other mischief, he had never dug in the garden, which had surprised her. She envisioned the animal's sweet face, eyes fixed on her when she sat at her piano to play and sing. And when Augusta sang, Caruso joined in, especially on high notes. She laughed when she recalled sometimes deliberately singing high note after high note just to egg him on. *I really do miss the beast. And I know Mal does.*

"I figured I'd find you here."

Augusta, startled, glanced up to see Milly standing in her garden.

"You can't be here."

"As a matter of fact, I can. Garrett resigned as Whittier's attorney last night. That coffee smells good. Is there any left?" Without waiting for a reply, she went behind the house to go into the kitchen through the back door, reappearing moments later, coffee in hand.

"Of course, he couldn't tell me why," she said, settling comfortably on the bench beside Augusta. "But I have some ideas. Whittier can be a pompous ass."

"He is certainly that. I get the feeling he's sure he can outsmart anybody. From what I've learned about him, I would imagine he's impossible to work with."

"Well, that would make him a difficult client to defend. I take it that Whittier remains a person of interest in Michael Robinson's murder, so he'll be looking for another lawyer."

"He certainly won't find one as talented as Garrett." Augusta said.

"I won't ask you this, but I've been wondering if Malcolm thinks Whittier is the murderer. But if he had proof of that, he'd have arrested Whittier."

"You know one of the first things Mal ever said to me when he was working on Linnea's case? 'It's one thing to know something. It's quite another thing to prove it.'"

"Yes, especially beyond a reasonable doubt." Milly took a gulp of coffee. "We should probably talk about something else."

The women were quiet for a few minutes, and Milly said, "Were you at the opera last night? How bad was the storm at the Zoo?"

"Bad. Some people in the audience were drenched."

"Been there, done that," laughed Milly. "You didn't go out after, did you?"

"We came straight home. Mal didn't get much sleep, though. He wants to get Michael's killer behind bars." Augusta sipped her coffee.

"We weren't going to talk about that."

"Right. Okay, new subject. Just before you showed up, I was thinking about Caruso."

"I get the distinct feeling both of you miss having him around," Milly remarked. "Do you ever see him?"

"We do. Trevor stops by occasionally and brings Caruso to visit. I'd swear he's happy to see us. Lots of tail wagging and dog kisses." She finished her coffee. "The house seems too quiet when they leave."

"Just go ahead and do it. You know you want to get a puppy."

"They're a lot of work," Augusta chuckled. "But you're right, I've thought about it more than once." She glanced at her watch.

"Do you have an appointment or something? That's the second time you've done that since I got here."

"Well … no. But Mal's making an important phone call. I'm eager to hear what he learns."

"This is awkward." Milly stood. "I can't keep tiptoeing around the thing you and I are both thinking about. Don't answer this. But do you honestly think Rosalyn killed Michael Robinson?"

"I don't like to think so. And don't consider that an answer to your question."

"Far from it. And on that cheerful note, I'm going to get out of here."

The two women went inside and Milly rinsed her coffee cup in the kitchen sink. "I hope Malcolm makes an arrest soon so we can all put this behind us."

"You and me both."

They headed for the front door where Milly embraced her friend. "Let me know when you're going puppy shopping. I'd like to be there."

Augusta laughed. "You're pretty sure about this."

"It's going to happen." Milly sauntered to her car and waved goodbye.

Augusta shook her head. *What on earth am I thinking? Puppies require a ton of effort. And time. Still … Mrs. Bluefield loves dogs, and she was great with*

Caruso. And I know she's available to come twice a week if I need her. Mal would be thrilled.

She went into the living room, relaxing on to the sofa as she picked up Barry Whittier's novel, intrigued by the latest development. The beautiful, mysterious model was a Russian spy, and she and the victim had been romantically involved.

Engrossed in the book, Augusta jumped when the phone rang.

"I just have a couple of minutes before I meet with Dave Turner," Malcolm said. "But your Frenchman had some interesting information about Whittier and his associates in Paris."

"Well, don't leave me hanging." Augusta replaced the bookmark and closed Whittier's book.

"Jean-Luc has done some follow up. Nothing so far on Rosalyn in Paris, but he did learn Barry Whittier very likely was spotted at the Sorbonne while Saul Kronenberg was there. A couple of people recognized his photo, and they said he was talking to Kronenberg. They also recalled it was June second, the final day of the seminar."

Augusta felt a chill run up her spine. "Mal—he could have been in Kronenberg's room in our hotel. We'd just checked in that evening."

"We had no idea Saul was a guest in that hotel. Don't even go there, Augusta."

"I'll try not to."

"Jean-Luc also learned that along with rubbing elbows with a Romanov, Barry has contacts in the black market from his many trips to Paris. That would definitely be one way he could procure any items he would need for both murders."

Mal frowned. "I'd sure like to be able to search Whittier's house. But no way do we have enough for a warrant. If we had the tox screen results on Saul that might give us more leverage, but right now we've got nothing but speculation."

"I'm not sure you'd find anything even if you did search his house. He's a mystery writer, and it's unlikely he's going to have evidence just lying around for the police to find."

"No doubt you're right, but I'd still like to get in there. Even smart people make mistakes."

"Mal, did you know that Garrett has resigned as Whittier's attorney? Milly stopped by and told me. Don't worry, we didn't discuss the case, even though he's no longer involved."

"I just found out this morning. Bad luck for Whittier. Garrett is a great criminal defense attorney. He's going to be hard to replace." He paused. "Hang on a sec."

Augusta heard Malcolm greet Special Agent Turner.

"Have to go. My appointment just arrived. I'll see you this afternoon."

Augusta moved restlessly through her house, stopping in the alcove to gaze out into the garden. *What a lovely wedding and reception we had here. How happy everyone was. Not a care in the world.*

Life can change so quickly, she mused. Her husband was now deeply embroiled in one of the most difficult cases he'd ever been handed.

Mal's meeting with Dave Turner could shed more light on Rosalyn Trainor and her family.

And then we might finally get to the bottom of this.

Chapter 19
The Portnovs

Sunday, June 20
5:30 p.m.

After setting the table, Augusta moved into the kitchen, trying to decide what to prepare for dinner. Mal breezed in, a bag from Skyline Chili in hand.

"I brought food," he announced.

"So you did, and just in time. Yum. I haven't had Skyline recently. Three-way?"

"Three-way for you. Five-way for me."

"What do you want to drink?" Augusta opened the refrigerator door.

"Do we have any Dr. Pepper?" He carefully transferred the chili to their plates, putting the bags with oyster crackers next to them.

"Whoa. This must be a celebration. You never drink Dr. Pepper."

"Well, when you hear what I learned today, you'll understand." Mal liberally sprinkled crackers over his spaghetti with chili, cheese, onions, and beans and picked up his knife and fork.

"From Special Agent Turner?" Augusta took a bite of her Skyline three-way: spaghetti, chili, and cheese. *Oh, I love this stuff.*

Mal studied his notebook, taking several large bites of his chili before answering. "Vasily and Petrova Portnov. Married in 1930. Both joined the NKVD. Moved to Toronto, Canada, in 1933. They were assigned the names of Walter and Pauline Trainor from deceased residents of the U.S. and were relocated to San Diego, California, in 1935 and established themselves as an average American couple. Both children born in La Jolla, California, Anthony in 1937 and Rosalyn in 1942. Americanized versions of Anton and Roksana."

"Hold on a minute. What's the NKVD?"

"The foreign intelligence and state security service that preceded the KGB, which came into being in 1954. At which time the Trainors were moved into that service. Until 1954, Vasily—Walter—worked at several different occupations, learning helpful skills. When General Dynamics was established in the early 1950s, he applied there and was hired. Not until then did his real work begin. Actually, not until General Atomic became an offshoot of General Dynamics."

"In San Diego, correct?"

"Yes. And guess what General Atomic does. Designs nuclear reactors."

"When did the Trainors come to the east coast?"

252

"In 1961. Not long before Rosalyn enrolled at the University of Kentucky." He drained half the bottle of pop.

"Do you know why?"

"Well, ostensibly because General Atomic has offices in Reston. But soon Vasily moved into the U.S. federal government. Into the State Department."

"Dave Turner gave you a lot of information on these people. Tell me this. Anthony Trainor was a gifted musician. What did you find out about that?"

Mal went into the kitchen and returned with a second Dr. Pepper.

"He attended school in Canada. McGill University in Montreal."

"That's a fantastic school. So, he graduated when—and what did he do after that?"

"He completed his graduate degree in 1959. That fall he joined the Montreal Symphony where he was a member until December 1963.When Dave contacted the Montreal Symphony people, they had no idea where he had gone." Mal dug into his remaining chili.

"Dear Lord. Anthony Trainor disappeared from Montreal just before Anton Portnov surfaced in Cincinnati in January of 1964. What on earth happened?"

"Dave wasn't sure, but he and the CIA agent he spoke with made a guess that Anton learned about his parents just prior to leaving Canada. His personality seems to have gone through a complete change at that time. Can you imagine the shock? You think you're a nice kid from San Diego, California, with a nice mom and dad named Walter and Pauline … and then you somehow learn they are spies for the country you've been taught by your culture to hate and fear. Those kids had been lied to their whole lives—by their own parents."

"But why would Anton take his Russian name? I don't understand that at all."

"Nobody does. Here's the thing. The FBI has been aware of the Portnovs for several years. Rather than arresting them, they've kept them under surveillance—along with some other Russian agents operating in this country."

"Everything Dennis told me about Russian espionage in the U.S. is true, obviously."

Mal nodded. "We know that when the Portnovs left Reston after Anton died, they headed for Canada, fairly sure their cover had been blown. Maybe by their son."

"Why Canada?"

"The Russian embassy in Toronto. Most of the spies in this country are processed there, just as the Portnovs were. It's a safe way for them to get back to the Motherland."

"They just left Rosalyn here to fend for herself? Had she been in touch with Anton? Or rather, had he been to see her at U.K.?"

"Yes, we learned he had been to see her several times. So, I believe she must know about her parents."

"What about that story about family in California?"

"No family, but they did have close friends in La Jolla, which is where they lived. Have you ever been there?"

She shook her head no.

"It's pretty close to paradise. One of the most beautiful spots in the U.S. The information their La Jolla friends provided indicated that Anthony and Rosalyn were very close."

Malcolm leaned his elbows on the table. "When he died, that must have been devastating for her. Her parents were getting ready to go back to Russia—which is where they are now—and her brother, depressed and lonely, the only family she had left, died in an auto accident. Like Whittier, she might have believed it was suicide."

"And like Whittier, she might have held the Chrysanthemum Quartet responsible for his death, because they had kicked him out," Augusta mused. "In her state of mind, avenging Anton by eliminating the other members of the quartet could have seemed … justified."

"One more thing: I went by the pharmacy where she works yesterday and we had a nice chat about what medication I could buy that would help me with my horrible allergies." He grinned. "She let slip that she was in Paris recently."

Augusta thought about this for a moment. "I feel sorry for her. She's not in her right mind. You must know that."

"Gus, she may have killed two men—and could be planning to do away with two more. Including your buddy Ariel."

"Mal, she's disturbed. Deeply troubled. She may need psychiatric help more than jail time. Is there anything that can be done for her?"

"I happen to agree with you that she needs help. Here's the thing—we don't have proof that she killed anyone at this point." He folded his arms across his chest. "*If* we arrest her, I have to believe she's far too smart to keep anything incriminating in her apartment. Why would she need to?"

"She's going to need a lawyer."

"That's entirely possible."

"I'll call Garrett. Now that he's no longer working for Whittier, he could represent Rosalyn."

"I can't tell you not to do that."

Which means I should make the call. Augusta put down her fork, her appetite gone.

"Rosalyn could take just the items she needed from the pharmacy," Mal continued. "She probably ushered that night and could have parked on a side street and watched the entrance at Mecklenburg's until she saw Michael leave. Somehow, she got into Michael's car— maybe in the back seat—surprised him and stabbed him with the syringe. Exited the car and tossed the syringe and the vial into a trash can or a dumpster anywhere."

"She's not a big woman. Why couldn't he have fought her off?"

"Excellent question. She may be a lot stronger than she appears. And maybe Michael did fight back. You remember there was blood on his neck, so it wasn't clean. It took two tries for the injection. She might have even had a rag or cotton soaked with chloroform and knocked him out first."

He cocked an index finger at her. "You know firsthand how fast that stuff works. And again, she could have just pitched everything after she was far enough away from the restaurant. We can't know exactly what happened in that car, but there was blood on Dennis' hand and on Michael's collar. The cops searched the dumpster outside the restaurant and even the sewers nearby and didn't come up with anything."

As Augusta was attempting to wrap her mind around this barrage of information, the phone rang. Malcolm picked it up, identified himself and listened carefully.

"Thanks for letting me know. I'll get in touch with his security detail and we'll begin an immediate search. If you hear anything, call back. Augusta will be here."

He hung up and turned to Augusta. "That was Manny Levine. Ariel was supposed to be at his house at five-thirty for dinner, and they planned to go to the opera pavilion together afterward."

Augusta checked her watch. "He's forty-five minutes late." A feeling of dread began to creep through her body.

"Yes, he is."

"Malcolm ... is there any chance Rosalyn recognized you when you were in the pharmacy yesterday?" She stood. "You've been pretty visible every night at performances." With shaking hands, she stacked their dishes in preparation for carrying them into the kitchen.

"I didn't think she had. I was acting a role, and I thought I did a pretty good job. But it's possible."

Augusta went into the kitchen and placed the dishes into the sink, dropping a plate in the process. It hit the bottom of the sink noisily, but didn't break. She took deep breaths to steady herself and returned to the alcove with a sponge in hand.

"It might be why she didn't show up last night." Augusta wiped the table vigorously. "She may have been alerted to the fact you suspect her of killing Michael." It annoyed her to hear her voice shaking as she spoke.

Mal put his hands on hers to steady her. "Easy, Gus. Why would she think that? We haven't released the information as to how Michael died."

"It's been in the news that foul play is suspected. And if the police have in fact discovered that lethal injection is the cause, and if they've made the connection between the Chrysanthemum Quartet and Anton's death and his sister who works in a pharmacy, and if she recognized you yesterday.... It's a whole bunch of *ifs*, I know, but maybe Rosalyn does think you're looking at her as a suspect, at least in Michael's murder."

Mal stood, grabbed his jacket and headed for the door. "Stay here. I'm going to Headquarters. Call me if you hear from Manny."

He paused. "Or from Ariel. He might be with Rosalyn, though I hope not. But if they are together, she just made a big mistake."

"What are you thinking?"

"That she may have decided to get out of Dodge. And she's persuaded or threatened Ariel to go with her as a hostage or an accomplice."

He headed for the front door, Augusta at his heels.

She caught his elbow. "I'm sure she's scared. She can't be thinking straight."

Mal stopped and stared at her. "You're defending her? She's not thinking at all, which means she's dangerous. This could have a very bad end, Augusta."

"Now you're really scaring me, Mal."

"Just stick by the phone. When I get to Headquarters and get a search organized, I'll call to check if you've heard anything. I also think I need to send a detail out here. In fact, I'll send Danny and his partner Jesse Wilkins."

He opened the door and turned to her. "Sit tight, Gus."

"You think she—they—might really show up here?"

"Well, she knows you're sympathetic with her and fond of Ari." He bent his head and gave her a quick kiss. "Danny should be here in fifteen minutes or so."

"If Rosalyn and Ariel come here, what should I do?"

"I don't think they will. I think it's more likely one of them might call you. On the other hand, they could be long gone. But if they show … keep them talking. I know you can do that. I've seen you do it. If Danny spots a car when he gets here, he'll contact me immediately. And we'll go from there."

"If she calls or shows up, what should I say to her?"

259

"That we know she's frightened, that we understand she's been going through an awful ordeal. That we just need to talk to her, to give her a chance to answer some questions we have. Remember, we have no evidence that she's harmed anyone at this point. But it sure looks bad if she's running."

He strode quickly to his car, turning to give her one last word.

"Here's the good thing … one way or another, this could be over tonight."

Chapter 20
The Cello

Sunday, June 20
8:15 p.m.

Eight-fifteen. Curtain time, thought Augusta, *and no Ariel.*

She wandered into the living room, coffee in hand. Danny and his partner Jesse had arrived quickly, even sooner than Malcolm anticipated. Augusta brewed a pot of coffee, and the young patrolmen discussed their responsibilities with her briefly. At the moment, Danny was checking dispatches on their patrol car radio and Jesse was making a quick tour of the area on foot.

Augusta had called Garrett as soon as Malcolm left the house, explaining the entire situation to him, and he agreed to represent Rosalyn. Despite Malcolm's comments, despite the fact that Rosalyn may have somehow abducted Ari, Augusta still felt protective toward her.

She sat on the piano bench and softly played through the opening of Debussy's "Clair de lune," a piece she had learned when she was in junior high school. A piece every intermediate piano student was assigned. What had Rosalyn said? *Her mother was a talented pianist. And Anthony was a gifted cellist. Her five years older brother, who showed promise probably from an early age.*

Yes, Rosalyn grew up in one of the most beautiful cities in southern California, but what kind of childhood did she have? The FBI had learned Anthony and Rosalyn were very close. And then just as she was entering her teens, Anthony went to Montreal for college, far from La Jolla. Jed Savage told Augusta he learned Rosalyn wasn't very social, that she kept to herself a lot.

Yet the girl I talked with was delightful. Poised and engaging. Could that have been an act? Her public face, yet underneath that is uncertainty and who knows what else. Is it possible she learned about her parents before Anthony did? And perhaps tried to shield him from the truth?

That would explain a lot. If she knew her parents were Russian spies, she'd be very guarded at college. Why did she go to the University of Kentucky, when they were living in the D.C. area, which has numerous fine schools?

Danny came into the house. "Just had a call from Headquarters," he said. "The Covington police checked Rosalyn Trainor's residence. Her car isn't there, but when the super let them into the apartment, it didn't look as if she planned to be gone for any period of time. They checked her closets and they looked pretty full. Her luggage was there. It sure didn't appear she'd taken off."

"Thanks, Danny. Do you know if anyone has checked Ariel Rosen's residence? Or if any of his neighbors know anything about his whereabouts?"

"A detail went to his apartment building. The same time we were sent here. I'm sure Dad has found something out by now. He may call you on your home phone, Augusta. I know you're concerned about Ari."

A light tap at the door, and Jesse joined them. *Another poster boy patrolman for the CPD, Augusta thought.* Both these handsome young men wore the uniform with pride and were dedicated law enforcement officers. Augusta thought Jesse resembled Sidney Poitier, an actor she especially admired. Jesse, a former Marine, had played football with Danny at West High. The strong friendship that had begun then had become even stronger since Jesse had joined the force, and he was to serve as a groomsman for Danny's and Martha's wedding in October.

"All quiet on Vista Place," he grinned. "And the nearby stretch of Madison Road as well."

"Can you both sit down for a minute and have some coffee?"

The young men glanced at each other. "Five minutes," Danny said. "Thank you." He smiled at her. "How did you know we'd like coffee?"

All of them laughed as they moved into the alcove, where Augusta had the coffee and cups waiting. "Cream or sugar, or should I even bother asking?" She commented.

"Black," they said in unison. More laughter.

Malcolm and FBI Special Agent Dave Turner strode into the house, and Danny and Jesse jumped to attention. Mal waved a hand. "As you were."

Dave Turner, at six feet four, was one of the few people who made Augusta feel small. His sharp eyes and craggy features belied his good nature.

"Agent Turner," Augusta said. "Thank you for your help. I'll get more cups."

Danny and Jesse quickly drained their coffee cups and turned to leave as Augusta reappeared from the kitchen.

"No, stay," Malcolm told them. "You might as well hear this. Augusta, Dave and I were at Ariel's apartment building and talked to a few of the residents who know him. They said he left around one o'clock. He was picked up by a young blond woman in a blue coupe—a '62 Chevy."

Malcolm pulled out the chair next to his and indicated Augusta should sit down. "Here's the part you'll find fascinating. He told a couple of his neighbors he was very excited, because a friend had a gift for him. They were driving to Lexington to pick up a cello."

Augusta felt her heart beat faster. "Anton's ... Anthony's cello. Rosalyn had it. He must have taken it to her for some reason. Well, that's one mystery solved."

Mal nodded. "My guess is he did that the day he died. He was headed north on the interstate when he wrecked his car. Remember, Whittier told us he had talked about driving to California? He probably told Rosalyn the same thing, and asked her to take care of the instrument for him until he made some decisions about what he was going to do next."

"But why didn't she bring it to Covington with her? Where has she been keeping it?" Augusta poured herself another half cup of coffee.

"It's possible she thought she might not be in Covington for long. And since she'd be in an apartment, she might have thought it safer to keep it in Lexington, in a good storage facility, where it would be securely locked up," Dave Turner remarked. "I understand it's worth quite a bit of money."

"It is, but I would think its emotional value to Rosalyn is much more than that. It's all that's left of her older brother, whom she apparently adored. What an awful shock to her when he was killed so abruptly." Augusta's voice shook slightly as she fought back tears. *What a horrible ordeal this young woman has been living.*

"It's possible that's why she became so friendly with Ariel. She wanted to find someone worthy of having Anton's cello. Passing the torch, in a way," Mal said.

"There's an APB out on her car," Dave told them. "If she took Ariel down there to give him her brother's cello, chances are she wanted to hear him play it. I have no idea where they might have gone. But it's been—" he checked his watch. "—close to eight hours since they left Cincinnati. Since I believe she planned to bring Ariel back here—where the hell have they been, and what have they been doing?"

Silence all around. Jesse cleared his throat. "Detective Mitchell, were they romantically involved?

No marriage license and no blood test required in Kentucky."

Augusta answered Jesse's question. "Ariel was quite smitten with Rosalyn. She seemed to like him, but maybe it was because of his musical ability. It doesn't make a lot of sense they'd suddenly decide to get married, but nothing about this situation makes any sense. And I know anything is possible. It's good to know, though, that he must have gone with her willingly."

"Regardless of whether they're married, it's certainly possible they might have decided to spend some time together," Mal said. "From what I've seen of Ari, it's hard to believe he'd miss a performance and not contact anybody. That concerns me."

The sudden ringing of Malcolm's private phone caused Augusta to jump. He picked it up quickly, identified himself, and listened briefly. "I think that means we have enough for a warrant for Whittier's house, Jim. Now we know both Saul Kronenberg and Michael Robinson had digoxin in their system, which contributed to their deaths. Whittier was seen in Paris in Kronenberg's vicinity on June second, the night before Kronenberg was found dead in his hotel room. No alibi for June tenth, the night Michael was found in his car. You're looking for the drug, maybe in bottles, and syringes. Possibly chloroform as well. Whittier could have used it to subdue Robinson before giving him the digoxin."

Augusta realized she was holding her breath, and glanced around at the other people in the room. They seemed to be doing the same thing. *Hearing it laid out like that* ...

Mal had been listening to his partner. "We'll start with Whittier. We'll need the cooperation of the Covington Police Department to get a warrant for Trainor's apartment."

I hate hearing them lumped together like that. Augusta pressed her lips together. *But she's as much a suspect as he is.*

Dave Turner and Malcolm stood, preparing to leave. "Patrolmen Mitchell, Wilkins, remain here for the present. There's still a possibility Mrs. Mitchell may hear from Rosalyn or Ariel."

"Yes, sir," they responded, speaking over each other.

Augusta glanced at the window, watching twilight turn to night. *June 20. It's nearly Midsummer's Eve. One of my favorite days of the year.*

The jarring sound of the telephone split the air, causing Augusta to jump again—and this time her heart went into her throat. It was her house phone.

Ariel on the other end. "Augusta, this is Ariel Rosen." *He sounds strange. Not like himself.*

Malcolm yanked his pad and pen from his jacket pocket and leaned close to the phone to hear the conversation. Once again, the people in the alcove seemed to have stopped breathing.

"Where are you, Ari? We've been worried about you." Augusta turned the handset slightly so Mal could hear more clearly.

Mal pointed an index finger at Danny, who understood immediately. Jesse followed as Danny unplugged Mal's private phone and quickly took it into the living room, plugged it into a wall jack, and called Bell Telephone, trying for a trace on the call.

KEEP HIM TALKING, Mal scribbled on his pad, lifting it for Augusta to read.

"You aren't hurt, are you? Or ill?"

"No, I'm—all right." A pause. "I'm with Rosalyn." *Something isn't right. Ari sounds as if he's holding on by a thread. He sounds stiff. Almost as if he's clenching his jaw.*

"Well, that's a relief. Is she okay?"

"I think so." Another pause. "We drove down to Lexington."

"I know Rosalyn used to live there. Her car didn't break down, did it? It's just not like you to miss an opera performance, Ari."

"No. I know that. The thing is …" Augusta heard a sharp intake of breath, Rosalyn's voice behind him.

"Professor McKee?" Rosalyn's voice coming through her handset, a little shrill, a little shaky. "First of all, I want you to know I would never hurt Ariel."

"I know that, Rosalyn. You care about him."

"Second of all, I'm sure you've learned a lot about me recently. About me and my family."

"Why would you think that?"

"I realized the man who came into the pharmacy yesterday was Detective Mitchell. I didn't recognize him at first, but after he left, I figured out why he looked so familiar. I'm sure he's been doing a lot of investigating."

Augusta stared at Malcolm. TELL HER YES, he wrote on the pad.

"Yes, that's true."

"He thinks I murdered Michael Robinson. I didn't kill anybody, Professor McKee. I swear it."

"Tell me where you are, Rosalyn."

"I want Ariel to be safe." A sound like a sob. "He has my brother's cello. I told him everything."

"You must trust him, then."

"I just want this to be over." Augusta could hear the stress in Rosalyn's voice as it increased in pitch, and she started talking faster, tripping over her words. "I want to meet you in downtown Cincinnati. Close to the bridge. I need you to know what happened. I don't like feeling you think ill of me."

"Tell me where you are, Rosalyn."

"No police. Just you. You can take Ariel with you after we talk."

Mal wrote FOUNTAIN SQUARE. DESCRIBE CAR.

"Why don't we meet at Fountain Square? Tell me what your car looks like, and I'll come to you. You won't even have to get out of the car."

Mal gave her a thumbs up.

"I rented a van in Lexington. It's blue."

Augusta grabbed Mal's pad and pen. WHY RENT A VAN?

"Are you in Cincinnati right now? You could come here. To my house."

"No, we're in Covington. I can be at Fountain Square in … in less than fifteen minutes." Rosalyn now

269

sounded near hysteria. *"No police.* If I see police, we'll drive away. I don't want to do that, but I will. We will."

Mal showed Augusta his response to her question: VAN BETTER FOR THE CELLO. SHE HAS 2-DOOR COUPE.

"I understand. No police. Rosalyn, I don't think ill of you. I know you've been overwhelmed with what's happened to you recently. I want to help you." Augusta kept her voice low and calm.

She glared at her husband in response to his frown. *Well, I do want to help her.*

Rosalyn let out a sob. "Thank you for saying that. Ariel has been driving."

Mal grimaced. ARI'S DRIVING. SHE MAY HAVE A GUN, he wrote.

Augusta felt her eyes widen and heard blood pound in her ears.

"You say he's safe, though."

"Yes. I would never hurt him. I'm hanging up now."

The click and sudden silence were jarring.

Danny and Jesse returned to the alcove, Danny shaking his head. "Not enough time." He replaced Malcolm's phone.

"Wilkins, Mitchell, head for the Roebling Bridge," Mal instructed them. "That's where she'll come across. It's the route she normally uses." Danny and Jesse ran from the house, and Augusta heard their car pull away quickly.

He picked up his phone and called Police Communications. "This is Detective Mitchell. Put out an immediate broadcast, including Northern Kentucky…

'Wanted for possible abduction'… a blue rental van possibly with Kentucky license plates. May be in Covington and en route to Fountain Square in Cincinnati. Occupants are one male and one female, white. The female is early twenties, five-six, one twenty, blond hair and may have a weapon. The male is early twenties, five-eleven, one sixty-five, curly dark hair, and glasses."

He added, "Then dispatch District One cars to the north end of the four bridges."

Dave Turner headed for the door as Malcolm took Augusta's elbow. "You're coming with us."

She nodded. *I guess I shouldn't ask if I can run upstairs and grab my purse.*

Chapter 21
At the Bridge

Sunday, June 20
9:45 p.m.

Augusta slid into the back seat, her heart pounding. After slamming her door shut, Dave Turner sprinted to the passenger side and jumped in just as Malcolm pulled away from the curb.

"How do you like these things?" Dave lifted a dark gray, rectangular object, about the size of a brick, with a slender extension sticking out at one end.

"Jury's still out. They have their uses. I have it set on Channel 1 and so is Jim Edmonds' walkie-talkie. Contact him, will you, and update him on our situation?"

Oh, it's part of the new technology the CPD recently acquired, Augusta thought. *I read about this in the newspapers just a few months ago.*

Dave had used one before, obviously, because he studied the item, turned a knob, toggled a switch and soon became engrossed in a conversation with Mal's partner. Augusta listened as he briefly described the events of the past few minutes, ending by saying, "Over."

Jim's voice, loud and distorted, filled the car. "En route to Whittier residence, search warrant in hand. ETA eight minutes. Over."

The car radio crackled to life. "All units, blue rental van, Kentucky plates, seen on approach ramp to Roebling Bridge."

Augusta said abruptly, "Malcolm, I need Garrett to be there. I spoke with him right after you left."

Mal glanced back at her and nodded. "Dave, get Jim back and tell him to call Garrett Stoddard as soon as he gets to Whittier's to let him know what's going on, and that we need Stoddard to come to the Roebling Bridge," Malcolm instructed.

Augusta took deep breaths, attempting to stay calm. *What had Rosalyn said? "I just want this to be over." You and me both.*

Dave transmitted the request to Jim, again ending with "Over." He turned toward Mal. "What about Stoddard? How is he involved in this?"

"It's my understanding he's been engaged to serve as Rosalyn's defense counsel. I have a feeling Ari is under duress, no matter how much he may be in love. There may be some form of coercion going on. The girl has some legal trouble ahead of her, regardless."

They had reached downtown Cincinnati and were headed for the John Roebling Bridge, and Malcolm said over his shoulder, "Hold on to your hat, Gus. You aren't going to like this." He gave Dave Turner a wry grin. "You might, though. Big Law doesn't get a chance to play policeman very often."

Dave glanced back at Augusta, and she was sure he refrained from responding to Mal's remark because she was in the car. She was well aware local police and FBI agents sometimes clashed, though Mal and Dave had a good working relationship.

Red lights began to flash and the siren kicked in, causing Augusta to want to cover her ears and eyes. *How can he drive with all that racket and distraction? I had no idea the siren would be so—LOUD.*

Conversation inside the car had effectively ended. A sudden squeal of brakes, and Augusta watched in horrified fascination as Mal skillfully maneuvered the patrol car around a civilian's auto frozen in the middle of Vine Street, barely avoiding a collision.

"Hell and damnation, friend. That's the wrong way to react." Malcolm yelled as he smacked the steering wheel.

Augusta saw the blank expression on the driver's face and had to agree with her husband. *Move to the right, stop your car, don't impede the police. Why don't people just automatically do that? He may have his radio turned way up. But surely he saw the lights.*

They reached the bridge, stopped abruptly and Mal and Dave jumped out. Malcolm jerked open the passenger door for Augusta.

"You want me to come with you?"

He spoke to both of them. "I have no idea what we're walking into. This is one disturbed young woman, and she may have a gun. If I motion you to hit the deck, do not hesitate. Get on the ground immediately."

Augusta clenched her jaw to keep her teeth from chattering. She gazed at Mal and nodded without speaking.

Patrol cars blocked each end of the bridge, all with their lights flashing. The humid Cincinnati air threw off reflections, giving the scene a surreal, hellish atmosphere. Augusta still heard sirens from a couple of the Kentucky units. *Rosalyn has to be terrified*, she thought. As they hurried onto the bridge the van came into sight—pulled across both lanes of traffic at an angle.

Mal stopped short and stared. "Well, I'm blessed. I never expected this."

Rosalyn had ducked under the beams and was on the outside walkway to their left, half sitting on the railing, one knee against it, as if she intended to roll backwards into the Ohio River. She clung to the railing with her right hand, and in her left, she held a revolver which she moved back and forth.

Ariel stood in front of her, and Danny and Jesse were close by. Neither had drawn their guns. They appeared to be attempting to reason with Rosalyn.

The strange lights, the sense of being high up, the fear, Ariel speaking—it's my dream, thought Augusta. She staggered back a step and felt Dave Turner put a hand on her shoulder to steady her.

The officers in the Kentucky patrol cars that were closest to the scene had exited their vehicles. Some had their guns drawn, but they all looked confused as to what to do next.

Augusta saw Mal assess the situation in an instant. "Stay here."

He sprinted quickly toward the Kentucky contingent on the bridge. "Only fire on my order," he yelled. They stared at him, and he roared, "And cut those damned lights and sirens!"

Sirens and lights were cut on the south side of the bridge. The CPD cars on the north side cut their lights as well. Other than Danny and Jesse, the CPD patrolmen formed a perimeter near their cars as they waited for further orders.

Augusta started to move closer, but Dave caught her elbow and held it in a firm grip.

"She's terrified. I just want her to know I'm here. She isn't going to shoot anybody."

"Maybe not intentionally. But she's got to get rid of the gun. The way she's waving it around, it could go off accidentally."

With the lights and sirens no longer a factor, the atmosphere became less surreal. Mal strode toward Rosalyn, stopping while still on the roadbed of the bridge. He looked back at the Kentucky patrolmen with their guns trained on Rosalyn. "I'm going to talk with her."

Mal took a step closer to Rosalyn, lifting his hands. "I want to hear what you have to say, Rosalyn. I'm going to put my gun down here—" he bent and placed it on the pavement— "and I'd like to come closer."

"I have to talk to Professor McKee." Rosalyn's voice rose shrilly. Traffic sounds from Cincinnati seemed faint and far off this high above the water.

"She's here with me," Malcolm said calmly. "First I need you to put down the gun."

"I can't. You'll stop me from doing what I need to do. I just want to explain. I didn't kill anybody, Detective Mitchell."

Her gun waved wildly around in a half circle, and Augusta tensed. *Dave's right. It could just go off without her meaning for it to. Good Lord, Rosalyn. Please put it down.*

She called out, "Rosalyn, I'm right here. But you have to put down the gun before we can talk. You're scaring everybody."

Mal frowned as he glanced back at Augusta, but Rosalyn stopped waving the gun and stared at it, as if she hadn't even realized it was in her hand.

"The only person I want to shoot is myself."

"Why would you want to do that? There are people here who care about you." Augusta called to her.

Ariel spoke up. "I love you, Rosalyn. Hand me the gun."

Dave murmured, "Jesus. Stupid-assed kid."

"He's in love with her." Augusta told him.

Mal motioned to Ariel to step aside. "Rosalyn, come down off the railing and put the gun on the sidewalk. Then you can talk to Professor McKee."

"I just want this to be over," Rosalyn sobbed. She stared again at the gun, and with a sudden, swift movement pitched it over her head and off the bridge. There was a long moment of silence as they all waited to hear the faint "plop" as the revolver hit the river.

Mal called to the Kentucky patrolmen, "Stand down. New situation. Possible jumper."

He stepped between the cross beams and onto the walk, and Rosalyn stood, holding onto the railing with both hands behind her.

"You know you don't really want to jump off this bridge," Mal said. "And I'll tell you why."

Matter-of-factly, he enumerated points for her. "First, you'll be sorry the minute your feet leave the railing and you start to fall. Next, when you hit the bottom, the river's not very deep, and you'll think you can just bounce up and we'll save you."

He took two steps closer to her. "But that can't happen, because when you hit the bottom, there's mud and silt, and you'll get stuck. Then you won't be able to breathe. Then you'll *have* to take a breath, only you'll breathe in Ohio River muddy, dirty water."

Another step. "You'll choke on it as you keep trying to breathe, until your lungs are filled with it. That will be your last memory of life on earth."

Malcolm extended his arms as he took two more steps toward Rosalyn, and she fell into them, sobbing.

Augusta's knees nearly buckled. She felt a strong arm around her waist and turned to see Garrett standing beside her. "That has to be one of the finest displays of police work I've ever seen in my life. Protect and serve."

Ariel began to weep, and Malcolm allowed him to embrace Rosalyn. The Kentucky cars slowly backed up, turned around, and moved to the end of the bridge, waiting for orders to leave the scene.

Danny and Jesse stepped forward to arrest Rosalyn, and Mal put up a hand to stop them.

"No, give them a minute."

The walkie-talkie in Dave's hand emitted a signal, and he responded, this time using the earpiece so the transmission was heard only by him. Mal motioned to them to come closer.

"Jim says Whittier is raising holy hell, insisting they get out. No luck with their search, but one thing struck Jim as odd."

"What was that?" Mal asked.

"A four-foot pedestal in Whittier's art studio. Only thing on it was a small crystal dish with two gold cufflinks."

Augusta had a sudden flash of memory. *I totally forgot to tell Mal about Michael's missing pin.* "Ask Jim to check again. Those may not be cufflinks. They could be lapel pins."

Jim relayed the information as Malcolm and Augusta stood by.

"What's going on, Gus?" Malcolm asked.

"Lapel pins. Manny Levine had four made up by a jeweler for the quartet members. Alicia called this morning to tell me Michael always wore his in his tux jacket, but it wasn't with the items the police returned a couple of days ago. She asked if you could check on it."

Dave turned to them. "How'd you know? He says they *are* lapel pins. Gold, about a half inch in diameter. Some kind of flower."

"Chrysanthemums," Augusta and Malcolm said in unison. Augusta felt almost giddy with relief.

Mal added, "And two pins—Saul's and Michael's. That's it. Confirmation that Whittier murdered Saul as well. Tell Jim to arrest the S.O.B."

Dave grinned as he relayed the message. "He says with great pleasure. Over and out."

Mal motioned to Garrett to join him, and gently extricated Rosalyn from Ariel's arms. "Garrett Stoddard, defense attorney, meet Rosalyn Trainor, your new client, and her young man, Ariel Rosen."

"I can't go to prison," Rosalyn gasped out. "I didn't do anything."

"Well, that's not quite true, Rosalyn," Malcolm said, "But you won't spend tonight in a jail cell. You've been exonerated. The man who murdered Saul Kronenberg and Michael Robinson was just placed under arrest. But you did break the law, right here on this bridge. Threatening people—including police officers—with a loaded gun."

Ariel said immediately, "The gun wasn't loaded."

"No, Ari, it was. Don't lie for me. I know what I did was wrong." She gave Mal a shaky smile. "I'm sorry, Detective Mitchell."

She glanced from Mal to Augusta. "Professor McKee, Detective Mitchell, I'm so relieved you know I didn't murder anybody. And really, I know why you thought I could have." Her eyes continued to dart from one of them to the other as the words tumbled out. "I know you've been told my whole history. But I do want you to know this—I would never have harmed Ariel."

Rosalyn clasped her hands together. "Anthony's cello was a mission I had to fulfill. The last time I saw him, he said if anything happened to him, I had to find the right person to give it to." Her eyes met Ariel's. "I knew it had to be Ari."

Ari gazed at her, his eyes again filling with tears.

"We'll keep the cello safe, Rosalyn. Mr. Stoddard will explain to you what happens next," Mal told her. "You'll have to be arraigned. We'll take you to General Hospital where there are people who can help you."

Garrett moved with Rosalyn and Ariel toward the end of the bridge as they talked, explaining what would happen, promising he would be with her at every step.

Mal gazed at his wife, a smile tugging at his lips. "Detective McKee-Mitchell strikes again. Good work, Gus."

"Not that great. I almost forgot about Michael's missing pin. May I go with Rosalyn? She wants to talk to me."

Mal thought it over. "Yes, you can do that. Poor girl needs a friend."

He turned to Danny and Jesse, who stood by awaiting orders. "Wilkins, Mitchell, excellent work." Mal said. "I need one of you to take the van to the impound yard and secure it. Bring me the keys, I'll be at Headquarters." Danny nodded and strode to the van. "Jesse, I need you to transport Ariel Rosen in your patrol car to City Hall. I have to take his statement. Wait there until I show up."

"What happens to Rosalyn now?" Augusta asked. "Does Garrett take her to City Jail?"

"No, I'll drive her to General Hospital. Under these circumstances, it has to be a police officer who transports her. Garrett will meet us there." He turned to Dave. "I need to request your cooperation as a law enforcement officer to ride with us. Augusta, you sit in front with me."

Augusta took Rosalyn's hand. "Detective Mitchell has given me permission to go with you, Rosalyn. You can tell me the rest of this story while we drive."

Mal motioned to Ari. "You're to go with Patrolman Wilkins, who will transport you to Detective Headquarters at City Hall. I need a full statement about what happened today."

Ari gazed longingly at Rosalyn. "I can't stay with her?"

"Not right now. You'll see her again soon," Mal told him.

Ariel nodded and followed Jesse off the bridge.

Rosalyn began to weep again, and Augusta put an arm around her as they walked to the car. "Can you even begin to imagine what it would be like to learn your entire life was a lie?" Rosalyn gulped out. More sobs. "And the people who had lied to you were your parents?"

"No, I honestly can't," Augusta said. She watched as the other patrol cars on the north end of the bridge pulled away, reopening both lanes to traffic. Soon the beautiful, historic John Roebling Suspension Bridge— the magnificent structure that preceded his Brooklyn Bridge—began to hum with traffic, fulfilling its intended purpose.

Before getting into the car Augusta glanced around her, drinking in the city she loved. *New York, you may claim eight million stories in your "Naked City," but I'll bet Cincinnati isn't far behind. What a story this one is.*

And parts of it won't ever be told, in order to "protect the innocent."

Lord. I've become such a fan of TV cop shows.

Chapter 22
The Rest of the Story

June 22, 1965
10:00 a.m.

Malcolm and Jim Edmonds took seats near the front of the courtroom, waiting for Barry Whittier to appear for his arraignment. They were both confident he would be held without bail. The timing of Whittier's trip to Paris, the discovery of the lapel pins, his lack of an alibi for the night Michael Robinson was murdered, plus Jean-Luc's continuing investigation into Whittier's criminal contacts in Paris, were enough for him to be remanded into custody.

Flanked by three attorneys from a high-powered firm in New York City, Whittier strutted into the room, an expression of defiance and superiority on his face. Jim elbowed Malcolm and shook his head. "Never quits, does he?" He muttered under his breath.

This was a high-profile case, one District Attorney Ray Shannon opted to handle himself rather than passing it on to an assistant. He glanced around the courtroom and nodded to Malcolm and Jim, acknowledging their invaluable part in bringing Whittier to justice. The charge of first-degree, premeditated murder was acknowledged. Whittier pleaded "not guilty" and the judge asked the DA about bail.

"The defendant is a man of means with close ties to a criminal element in Paris, France, your honor. We feel he is a flight risk and request he be remanded," Shannon stated.

Whittier sneered as one of his attorneys replied, "My client is an author and artist and respected member of this community. Mr. Whittier's health is compromised and he is currently under a doctor's care. He won't receive the medical attention he requires if he is in jail," the attorney argued.

"Our office will guarantee Mr. Whittier's doctor can have access to him whenever necessary, provided a guard is present. He'll be kept away from the general population."

The judge slammed his gavel and pronounced, "Sounds reasonable to me. The defendant is remanded."

Mal and Jim watched the hurried conference with Whittier and his lawyers and saw him taken away.

Shannon strolled over to them as they stood to leave. "I'm going to push for a timely trial, but we're playing with some big city boys here and that might not happen. I have to thank you both for exemplary police work on this case. There's no way he's going to walk, not with everything we have."

He grinned at them. "He's a piece of work, isn't he? The guy talks in riddles. He even hinted at a possible insanity defense. Any idea what he has in mind?"

"Sure do," Malcolm responded. "The dreadful string quartet members drove him to kill. Unrequited love, revenge—a plot worthy of a mystery novel."

***

"Why, Detective Mitchell. It seems like you just left." Augusta sat at the table in the alcove, papers spread around her, pen in hand.

Malcolm bent and kissed her. "My boss gave me the rest of the day off. Officially, it's 'accrued' time. Time off the books because I didn't put in for overtime on a couple of hundred occasions. Do I smell coffee?" He went into the kitchen.

"You do, indeed. Your boss? Chief Schrotel?"

"No, my immediate boss, Lieutenant Kramer. Chief of Detectives, the remarkable man who gives me a ton of leeway."

"Because he knows how good you are."

Malcolm returned, removed his jacket and relaxed into a chair.

Augusta leaned forward and rested a hand on his. "So? What happened at the hearing?"

"What we expected. Whittier was remanded and hauled off to jail. It may be some time before the case comes to trial." He indicated the papers strewn across the table. "Writing a book? What, did coming into contact with Whittier inspire you?"

Augusta smiled. "You know, I might do that someday. No, I'm trying to make some sense out of what we just experienced. All the spy stuff is still making my head spin. I never dreamed that kind of thing happened."

"Well, it's not something you run into every day." He gestured toward her stack of papers. "Looks like you've been a busy girl, bride. I know you've been to see Rosalyn several times."

"Yes, and she's told me quite a lot." She bit the end of her pen as she gazed at her husband. "You could help me with this. Can you share with me what Rosalyn told you when you took her statement?"

"Sure. You've heard most of it already, stuff Dave Turner told us."

He took a gulp of coffee. "You know her family history, and you know what happened to Anton. You guessed this part, Gus. Rosalyn was the first of the Portnov children to find out who her parents were. She was sixteen and was supposed to be at a slumber party that had to be canceled. Her parents, not knowing she was upstairs in her room, came into the house with two KGB agents and had a loud argument. After they left, Rosalyn went downstairs and they told her everything, and begged her not to tell Anthony."

"And she agreed?"

"Yes, providing they refused to do what they'd been ordered to do—kill someone. She learned later that this man died just before they left for Reston. Of course, they denied killing him."

"Of course. She told me that Anthony found out on his own about their parents, though. A friend in the Montreal Symphony started talking one time about Russian spies being planted in the U.S. after being processed through Toronto. It made Anthony start thinking about some odd things that had happened when he was very young, maybe four or five. And at other times while he and Rosalyn were growing up. What his friend told him made him wonder about his parents."

Malcolm leaned his elbows on the table and gazed at her. "What those kids went through." He shook his head.

"But for all those earlier years, life seemed pretty 'normal.' The family took vacations to places such as the Grand Canyon. They drove up to Vancouver and visited Victoria. Other trips as well. Anthony wasn't considered a prodigy, but certainly had unusual ability. He took some cello lessons with the first cellist for the Los Angeles Philharmonic. But he also played tennis, though he never played team sports. Rosalyn was very much a typical American teenager. Cheerleader. National Honor Society. Worked on the school newspaper. She said she occasionally had a chance to ride, and really loved it."

"Motorcycles?" Mal grinned.

"No, horses," Augusta laughed. "And that's one reason she decided to attend the University of Kentucky. She hoped she'd find a way to do something she loved that might help ease the stress she dealt with constantly." She sat back. "I'll quit interrupting. Continue, please."

"One question I had: what was she doing in Paris just before Saul Kronenberg died? Her mother sent her a

289

ticket, under another name and a phony passport—which we suspected might have been the case. They met in Paris. They were together for only a couple of days. She said her mother explained why they had to leave the U.S. so abruptly. The KGB pulled them out after they learned Anthony had started using his Russian name. Since Rosalyn was on her own and was by this time over twenty-one, and the Portnovs claimed she had no knowledge of their background, Rosalyn wasn't included. So, when they were in Paris, her mom apologized and begged Roksana to come home to Russia with her."

"And she refused. She did tell me about that. She blamed her parents for Anthony's death, not the quartet. She blamed them for everything bad that's happened to her."

"Understandable. Rosalyn knew Saul Kronenberg was in Paris at the seminar, but while she knew who he was—part of the Chrysanthemum Quartet—she had never met him. She had heard the quartet play at least twice. But she flew home on June first. The day before he was killed."

"The quartet. Anthony—calling himself Anton by then—was excited to be part of it. Rosalyn said he spoke highly of all the members," Augusta said. "When they let him go, this already damaged young man was devastated. I don't know if you are aware of this: Anthony had talked to Rosalyn about Ariel, a young student cellist he admired. He felt no animosity toward Ari when he replaced him in the quartet; he told her he thought Ari had a great future."

"Actually, a big reason for Rosalyn's interest in Ariel was because she wanted to give the cello to him," Mal commented. "She told us she had planned to do it later in the summer. When she thought she might be arrested for Michael Robinson's murder, that pushed her to change her plans. She needed to give it to him right away. It was exactly what she told us that night on the bridge—a mission for her beloved brother."

"We know she was tipped off that she might be a suspect in Michael's murder when you visited her at the pharmacy."

"Want more coffee?" Mal brought the coffeepot into the alcove without waiting for an answer. "There were several contributing factors. While she was in Paris, her mother warned her she was probably under surveillance by the FBI. Even though she wasn't at Mecklenburg's when Michael was found in his car, some of the other ushers were, and they told her about Sam and Dennis attempting to resuscitate him. That's why they all thought he'd had a heart attack."

He poured himself another cup of coffee. "As a former med student, she knew there were certain drugs that in the correct dosage could mimic heart attack symptoms. And when she realized I knew she worked in a pharmacy and I mentioned the Chrysanthemum Quartet, she put two and two together and believed she could be a suspect in the murder. Especially if the FBI had told me about Anton. She knew that we would realize she had a connection to the Chrysanthemum Quartet and a possible motive—to avenge Anton's death."

He gazed out of the window for a moment. "There's more. She realized if someone was out to kill off the quartet, Ariel might be the next target. That's why she was so frantic to get him back to you and to safety. She knew if Ariel was with you, he would also be with me, and he'd be protected."

He put a hand over Augusta's. "Here's the part I have a tough time with. That this vibrant young woman had made up her mind to take her own life. Completely overwhelmed by the circumstances she'd been living with for nearly three years. Or even longer, actually—since she was sixteen and learned about her parents. Finally, totally unable to deal."

Augusta laced her fingers through Malcolm's. "Rosalyn and I have talked about that. Ariel is in love with her. She doesn't think she deserves him. Yet she's done nothing wrong. She is completely the victim here, even if she was waving a gun around."

"The gun," Mal commented. "She bought it when she got back from Paris. The Takacs helped her with that purchase. I don't know where they got it, but she told them she was worried about her safety. Remember where they came from—Hungary. They didn't ask any questions. She always carried it in her purse."

"Well, now it's at the bottom of the Ohio River. You don't need to pursue that with the Takacs, do you?"

"They don't live in my jurisdiction, so, no."

"Did she tell you what happened that day that made her use it?"

"Ariel did, when he gave me his statement. He said after they picked up the cello, they went to a nice motel just outside of Georgetown. He played for her for a long time. He'd never seen her so happy. It seemed so natural to make love after that."

"It was the first time for both of them," Augusta said softly.

Mal's eyes widened. "He didn't tell me that. He just said 'we wanted to be together.' I knew what he meant. Then they fell asleep, and when they finally woke up it was well after six. Ariel knew he might be too late to play the performance, but he wanted to try. Rosalyn wanted to spend the night at the motel. Ari insisted they leave. That's when the gun came out. She kept apologizing, saying 'I never wanted to do this.' She made him drive the van. And she asked him to stop and place the call to you. Remember, when I first talked to Ariel and Manny, I gave each of them my card and wrote my private number on it—and your house phone."

"Dear Ari. He knew she wasn't in her right mind." She sighed. "She's still being diagnosed at General Hospital, but I'm told it's apparent she's suffering from some kind of extreme stress disorder and will need extended treatment."

"What else has she said to you?"

Augusta shuffled through her papers. "Quite a bit. When she applied to U.K., she insisted she handle it herself. Her parents gave her cash, and she set up a bank account in Lexington to pay for her tuition. Jed told me there was no record of a high school transcript, that she claimed to have been home schooled and was accepted on the basis of an extremely demanding entrance exam. Rosalyn wanted to try to leave her past behind. She didn't want to think of those happy high school days. Happy until halfway through her junior year, when she realized her entire life was a lie."

She picked up a sheet of paper. "Here's more she's told me about Anthony. While she was at U.K., he came to see her a few times. The last time he told her he'd found out about their parents. He asked her if she knew, and she told him when she'd learned about them. At first, it made him angry that she hadn't told him, but then he understood. When he left Montreal and moved to Cincinnati, he came to see her three times. On the second visit, he told her about Ariel. But he seemed strange. Very agitated, restless, nervous, also laughing a lot. Now she wonders if he'd been doing cocaine." She glanced at Mal. "Remember, Manny Levine was sure Anton was doing drugs … that was the last straw for the group."

He nodded, and she continued, "The last time she saw him was the day he died. He seemed clear-headed, but was extremely sad. He told her he couldn't stay in Cincinnati, and planned to drive to La Jolla to see if being back there might give him some peace. He brought her his cello to keep for him, saying he didn't want to risk damaging it in a cross-country trip. He also told her if anything happened to him, to find someone who would love it as he had. Who would play beautiful music on it, beautifully. After she learned of his death, this made Rosalyn wonder if the accident that took his life was actually a suicide."

Malcolm again glanced out the window. "That, we will never know. Unbelievable, what those people did to their children."

"Anthony was traumatized when he learned about his parents. He told Rosalyn he didn't know who he was anymore—Anthony Trainor was a lie. That's why he used his Russian name and tried to see if he could create a new life for himself. But he didn't like the person Anton Portnov became. He didn't want to be that person, and he couldn't be Anthony Trainor."

"What a thing to have to deal with."

"On the other hand, Rosalyn tried to become a new Rosalyn Trainor. She liked being close to Cincinnati, because Anthony had found some happiness there, however brief. Then she began to love the city for itself. She made some friends—which wasn't easy for her, because she had difficulty trusting anyone. She and her friends sometimes went into Cincinnati to shop and to attend concerts. Meeting Ariel was a highlight of her life. She found herself immediately attracted to him."

"And then Michael Robinson was murdered, and her house of cards collapsed."

"You could put it that way." Augusta rubbed her forehead. "What a world we live in. So many ways for people to go down the wrong path. To become bad guys who make life difficult if not impossible for the rest of us, people who are just trying to lead decent lives."

"What will happen to them, do you think? Our star-crossed lovers?" He gazed at her wistfully.

"Only time will tell. But I think Ariel is strong and steadfast, and loves Rosalyn very much. Maybe enough to wait until she is well enough to return that love."

Mal leaned close to his wife, resting his forehead against hers, clasping both her hands. "Do you know how glad I am that I have you in my life?"

She kissed him softly. "I know how much it means that I have you in my life. So yes, I think I do."

Chapter 23
A New Tale

Saturday, July 10, 1965
2:30 p.m.

"Garrett told me Rosalyn's hearing went well." Milly and Augusta were setting up a table in the garden for a late lunch. Garrett and Malcolm planned to be there by three, both had a few loose ends to tie up with paperwork after Rosalyn's hearing before a Kenton County, Kentucky, judge.

"Yes, and the best part is that Rosalyn's outlook has improved quite a bit. She was nervous but handled herself well."

The previous day, Rosalyn Trainor, charged with several misdemeanors, pleaded guilty to the charges on the advice of her legal counsel, Cincinnati Defense Attorney Garrett Stoddard. Speaking in Miss Trainor's behalf were Detective Malcolm Mitchell of the CPD, Special Agent David Turner of the FBI, Dr. Elaine

Mackey, a psychiatrist on the staff of Cincinnati's General Hospital, and as a personal friend, Professor Augusta McKee.

The judge listened carefully to all of them, and then spoke directly to the defendant. "Young lady, you have an impressive number of officials speaking in your behalf here today. You understand you broke the law."

"Yes, your honor. I know what I did was wrong, and I regret my actions more than I can say. I'm so grateful no one was harmed. I also know that I will need continued treatment to deal with my emotional and mental issues."

"Under the circumstances, Miss Trainor, I sentence you to one year incarceration in the county jail."

Rosalyn turned abruptly to stare at Garrett, who put a warm hand on her shoulder. "Wait, there's more coming," He murmured.

The judge continued, "I also hereby suspend the one year, and place you on five years' probation, with the condition that you see your psychiatrist on a regular basis and that she reports on your progress, as well as any other stipulations your probation officer may establish. You and your psychiatrist may appear before this court in the future if it is her opinion you are recovered and your probation can be terminated."

He looked over his glasses at Rosalyn. "Do you understand, Miss Trainor?"

"Yes, your honor. Thank you."

A whack of the gavel. "Court is adjourned."

Rosalyn's entourage followed her out into the sunlight, where there were hugs and smiles of relief all around. Ari had been in the courtroom as well, and he and Rosalyn embraced for a long moment.

Augusta set the last plate on the table as she added, "You heard that Ari was there. He's become a big part of Rosalyn's life. He may be instrumental in helping her heal—if she can heal." She turned to Milly. "I really like Dr. Mackey. You know, she also spends time at a private psychiatric clinic near Dayton, and we've talked about more advanced treatments they've been using there. Especially with women patients."

"What, exactly?"

"Well, with mood disorders there's been a history of trying to shock a patient 'out of it' –both literally, with electric shock treatments, and using techniques such as shaming. Pretty harsh, if you ask me, especially for someone as fragile as Rosalyn."

"I agree." Milly poured herself an iced tea and relaxed into a lawn chair. "So, what exactly does this forward-thinking clinic do?"

"I don't know exactly, but more positive treatment. Maybe some physical and occupational therapy. Encouraging the patient to talk, to explore her issues. Along the lines of psychoanalysis. Talking seems to help Rosalyn, even when it's me she's talking to. Or Ari. He's been to the hospital every day."

"It's probably expensive. Rosalyn doesn't have any money, does she?"

"No. But I do."

Milly knew about Augusta's generous trust fund, which she seldom touched. "You'd do that for her?"

"You know what, Milly? I would have paid for any treatment Meyer needed when he was ill, but the treatments weren't there. Rosalyn's illness is as severe as his, and I can do this for them. I'm fond of Rosalyn and Ariel."

Milly gazed at her friend. "You have a good heart, Augusta."

The women smiled at each other warmly and completed their task.

"What's the latest on Whittier?" Milly asked.

"You know Mal attended his hearing. Of course, he requested bail, but it was denied. He was deemed a flight risk. Last week Jean-Luc called Mal and told him to take a close look at Whittier's luggage from his most recent trip to Paris. The Paris police had conducted a routine sweep of black marketeers from Marseilles and turned up a guy who claimed to have sold digoxin to an American he identified as Barry Whitter from his photo. Well, Whittier had a stash of suitcases, so the CPD took them all to HQ and as Jean-Luc suggested, ripped the lining in every one of them."

"And they found something."

"You bet they did. Enough drug paraphernalia to kill at least two more people. It made my blood run cold, since Whittier had been cozying up to the Levines. Manny would have been his next victim. And then Ariel. With the evidence they now have, there's a strong case against Whittier. It'll be interesting to see what his pricey defense team comes up with, because I can't see him pleading guilty."

"Jean-Luc has been a huge help to Malcolm on this case."

Augusta laughed. "He certainly has. Mal told me he may even show up and testify at the trial. He suggested if that happened, we should invite him to stay with us while he's here."

"Well." Milly was speechless.

"I told him no way." Augusta laughed again. "Jean-Luc belongs in 1930s Paris. Talk about worlds colliding. Anyway, it's unlikely that will happen."

Augusta helped Milly bring the food outside. "Here's some good news, though. Ariel has convinced Manny to resurrect the Chrysanthemum Quartet. They put up an audition notice last week, and eighteen string players have contacted them."

"That *is* great news. Rising from the ashes. Always a good story."

Malcolm joined them, beer in hand. "Nice day for a picnic."

"A pretty elegant picnic, Detective," Milly responded. "I'll have you know we're lunching on quiche Lorraine this afternoon. With *salade* and brioche rolls."

"Shades of Paris." Mal lifted an eyebrow. "Yes, that definitely sounds elegant."

Garrett appeared from around the front of the house. "Are you ready to receive the guest of honor?" he asked.

Milly nodded. "Absolutely. Please invite him to join us."

Garrett headed to the front of the house as Malcolm glanced at the table. "What's this? I only see four place servings here. Guest of honor?"

Augusta put her arms around his waist. "I think you'll like him. It's my surprise for your birthday. I know it's early, but it just worked out this way."

Garrett reappeared, carrier in hand. He put it on the ground, and Malcolm sat down beside it to gather up the adorable puppy that emerged, body wiggling in excitement.

Mal laughed and hugged the puppy as it frantically licked his face. "Who's this? Augusta, what on earth have you done?"

He looks like a little boy on Christmas morning, Augusta thought, smiling at her husband. *I knew this was a good idea.* "We've both missed Caruso. I thought we needed some noise and confusion in the house."

"He's a Golden Shepherd, isn't he? Just like Caruso." Mal continued to stroke the tiny animal, who snuggled into his arms.

"He's more than that, Mal," Milly commented. "Caruso sired the litter."

"No kidding. Incredible."

Augusta bent down and petted her new troublemaker. "He is adorable, isn't he?"

"For now. Gus, are you sure about this?" Malcolm laughed heartily as the puppy tried to climb up his neck.

"Positive. He needs a name, though. That's up to you. I know it could be something operatic, but I hardly think Scarpia is suitable for this sweet animal. Even though he's your favorite character."

"Yes, but Scarpia is evil. This dog is going to be the best dog that ever lived." Mal set the puppy on the ground and stood, the little creature running around his ankles.

"We don't eat until Son of Caruso has his own name," Milly pronounced. She glanced at Augusta. "Why not name him after his new mommy?"

"I can't name him Gus," Mal answered. "That would be too confusing."

"No," Garrett offered, "But you could name him Gussie. With Augusta's approval, of course."

Augusta shook her head. "That's just not the right name. Maybe Enrico, since we can't name him Caruso?"

"You could call him Rico. Or Ricky," Milly offered.

Mal gazed at the puppy. "Maybe. That might work. Or ..." he snapped his fingers. "How about another great tenor? The guy we heard in Vienna, Gus. Fritz Wunderlich. You said you thought he might be the next Caruso."

He picked up the puppy and scrutinized its face. "What do you think, fella? You look like a Fritz to me."

The puppy wiggled and squirmed, and managed to lunge forward to lick Malcolm's face.

Laughter all around. "I think he likes it, Malcolm." Augusta scratched the pup behind his ears.

Mal bent down and placed his new friend on the ground. He took four steps, turned and said, "Come, Fritz."

Fritz yipped and trotted up to Mal, his entire body wagging.

Acknowledgments

When *The Case of the Purloined Professor* ended with Augusta and Malcolm making wedding and honeymoon plans, I knew I'd challenged myself to begin this book with the wedding. While I enjoyed writing it, I felt I couldn't let too many chapters go by without jumping into the mystery … and my thought was to have two murders take place early in the book, members of a string quartet. The first discovered in the hotel in Paris where the happy couple were honeymooning … the second back in Cincinnati. Then came the idea for a mystery within a mystery: another member of the quartet who would have been the prime suspect if he hadn't died a year earlier.

1965 was during the height of the Cold War and the beginning of the Vietnam "conflict." A frightening event in my lifetime, the Cuban Missile Crisis, came to mind, along with thoughts of American spies we were made aware of not long after the end of World War II … among them Alger Hiss (though the jury is still out on him), Whittaker Chambers, and especially Julius and Ethel Rosenberg.

While it was Vladimir Putin's KGB that established the spy program called "The Illegals" during the 1990s—training Russian nationals to pose as average Americans, giving them false identities, and planting them throughout the United States—Russian spies were placed under deep cover in the U.S. all during the Cold War, and even earlier. And as was the case with children of "The Illegals," Rosalyn and Anthony Trainor had no inkling of their heritage until they were young adults.

First and foremost, I must thank my good friend and more-than-editor Ashleigh Evans, who definitely was my partner in crime for this story, beginning with her suggestion for the name of the quartet and the title of the book. As soon as I heard Puccini's music I immediately agreed. She was immensely helpful in the scenes that took place in Europe, having been to all those places Augusta and Mal visit during their honeymoon. Ashleigh helped me work through the twists and turns in the plot and solve the knotty problems that kept arising.

As in every book in this series, Det. Lt. Stephen Kramer (ret.), CPD, provided insight into the police procedural matters. I can never thank him enough for his invaluable assistance and patience in helping make those scenes work as well as they do. He is my consultant for police procedural issues, but he has also become a friend. It was my great good fortune to connect with him through the Greater Cincinnati Police Historical Society and Museum a few years ago.

My appreciation for string quartets goes back to my student years at the College-Conservatory of Music at Cincinnati, and the fine performances of the LaSalle String Quartet in that era. Thanks to violinist Chris Souza for confirming what I believe makes string quartet music so magical, and to cellist Charles Calvert for introducing me to the equal magic of Matteo Goffriller, a Venetian luthier whose cellos are apparently considered the finest in the world.

Thanks to my generous and excellent readers. First, Michaele Benedict, a fellow author, who has been supportive and encouraging from the beginning of my career as a writer. It's interesting that Ashleigh, Mikie, and I all attended Oak Ridge High School within a few years of each other, and amazing that we've reconnected all these decades later. I highly value Mikie's opinion and consider her read a second content edit. She sees the manuscript before it's passed on to any of my other readers.

Eric Mark, another writer and journalist, has also been an important part of this journey, and it pleased me that he pronounced this book his favorite of the "Detective Gus" series. Thanks as well to Ken Van Camp, Marti Lantz, Audrey Henry, and Nathaniel Taylor for their insightful and valuable feedback. All of these people gave me suggestions which I know strengthened the story.

Thanks also to my Lady Writer fellow authors and local friends, who read portions of the book and offered helpful suggestions: Belinda Gordon, Catherine Schratt, Evelyn Infante, Kelly Jensen, Mary Anne Moore, and Sahar Abdulaziz.

At the end of Chapter 9, when Augusta and Malcolm are discussing opera being a world of make-believe, he comments: "And in real life, we don't know what the next act will bring." When I wrote that, I had no idea that within a few weeks, life in this country, and indeed, in this world, would be turned upside down by the onset of a viral pandemic. Life as we knew it ceased to exist, at least for a time. It was intriguing to learn that after the last such global health disaster, the 1918-19 viral influenza that killed millions, there seems to have been a "collective amnesia" about that pandemic, at least in this country. Of course, it took place at exactly the same time we were embroiled in the first World War which took precedence over all. We can only hope we learn valuable lessons this time around.

It was also intriguing to learn that there were no major literary works about the pandemic at that time. It will be interesting to see how writers and other artists handle this one. While we are in the midst of the turmoil hardly seems the time to write about it, because so much is still unknown as I write this, in early May of 2020. Time will tell.

In the meantime, back in the mid-twentieth century, Augusta and Mal, now happily married and "partners for life," could very well have further adventures!

Susan Moore Jordan
The Pocono Mountains, Pennsylvania
May, 2020

Videography

I Crisantemi by Giacomo Puccini
    Enso String Quartet

"Er, der Herrlichste von allen" from
    Frauenliebe und-leben by Robert Schumann
    Elly Ameling, *soprano*
    Dalton Baldwin, *piano*

"Yours Is My Heart Alone"
    from *The Land of Smiles* by Franz Lehar
    Anna Moffo, *soprano*
    Sergio Franchi, *tenor*
    ("Anna Moffo –The Complete RCA Recital
    Albums")

"Gypsy Song" from *Carmen* by Georges Bizet
    Elīna Garanĉa, *mezzo-soprano*
    Elisabeth Caballero, *soprano*
    Sandra Piques Eddy, *mezzo-soprano*
    Metropolitan Opera, 2010

"Non so più, cosa son" from *Le Nozze di Figaro*
    by W. A. Mozart
    Frederica von Stade, *mezzo-soprano*
    Paris Opera 1980

"Hai già vinta la causa" from *Le Nozze di Figaro*
    by W.A. Mozart
    Simon Keenlyside, *baritone*
    Vienna State Opera, 2001

Après un rêve by Gabriel Fauré
  Yo-yo Ma, *cello*
  Patricia Zander, *piano*

"Greater Love Hath No Man"
  by John Ireland
  King's College Choir

I Crisantemi by Giacomo Puccini
  transcribed for organ
  Stefano Tarchi

After a lifetime as a musician—performer, teacher, musical theater director—Susan Moore Jordan wrote and published her first novel in 2013 at the age of seventy-five, and she hasn't stopped since.

In her first four novels, the author drew from her life experiences as a voice teacher and stage director, and those historical novels were inspired by real people she encountered.

"Companion" novels, *Memories of Jake* and *Man with No Yesterdays* were released in 2017. A departure from her earlier historical novels, these two books detail the struggles of two brothers, Andrew and Jake Cameron, whose lives were irrevocably changed by their service in the Vietnam War. *Memories of Jake* was the recipient of an honorable mention Red Ribbon Award from the 2017 Wishing Shelf Book

Awards. *Man With No Yesterdays* was a Finalist in the 2019 Wishing Shelf Book Awards.

Recently, Jordan has embarked on a "cozy mystery" series, "The Augusta McKee Mysteries." Book one, *The Case of the Slain Soprano*, was released in April, 2018 and *The Case of the Disappearing Director* followed in October, 2018. Additional books in the series are *The Case of the Toxic Tenor, The Case of the Purloined Professor,* and now *The Case of the Chrysanthemum Murders. The Case of the Slain Soprano* was a finalist in the 2018 Wishing Shelf Book Awards and a semi-finalist for the 2020 Kindle Book Awards. *The Case of the Disappearing Director* was a finalist in the 2019 Wishing Shelf Book Awards.

All of Jordan's books are "music-centric" (in the words of one reviewer), and readers comment on the strength of the element of music included in her work. Jordan sees writing as another way to share the music she loves, which she considers "the most powerful force in the universe."

Articles by Susan Moore Jordan have appeared in *Musical America* and *The Guardian*, and on August 2, 2019, she appeared on Hour Three of "The Today Show" as a Super Senior.

***

If you enjoyed
The Case of the Chrysanthemum Murders,
please consider leaving a reader review on
Amazon. Reviews are a standing ovation! They
are also valuable to indie authors and greatly
appreciated.
More information and links to all my books
can be found on my website,
www.susanmoorejordan.com